LOSING HIS COOL

LINDA FAUSNET

For anybody who ever had a dream.

My books contain steamy sex, bad words, and human beings of all sorts, include gay people. If you're not a fan of those things, you may want to stop reading now. If you're cool with that stuff, come take my hand and join me on this journey…

Published by Wannabe Pride 2017

Editing by Linda Hill

Cover Design by Chuck DeKett

FIRST EDITION.

Library of Congress Control Number: 2017918900

ISBN: 978-1-944043-19-3

❀ Created with Vellum

CHAPTER 1

*I*t was bizarre being friends with a billionaire, but I was getting used to it.

I knocked on Johnny Creel's penthouse door, and he answered with a grin. "Hey, Susie!"

"Hey yourself," I said with a smile. I slung my arm around his neck and squeezed him. Johnny's grin widened as he returned my warm embrace.

"Rosemary's on her way," he said after he let go of me. Rosemary was the love of Johnny's life, and my best friend.

"Cool," I said as we headed toward the living room. All Johnny's furniture was sleek black leather, and the lamps and ceiling light fixtures were made of the finest crystal. The living room was huge—it had enough seating for more than twenty people. A seventy-five-inch television was mounted on the wall. Johnny's pad was the best place to hang for all our friend gatherings. Too bad he and Rosemary were leaving for New York soon.

My heart squeezed in my chest whenever I thought about it. I was thrilled that Johnny was taking Rosemary to New York so she could pursue her dream of performing on

Broadway, but I would miss her terribly. She was my dearest friend, and the only one who truly understood me. Performing on Broadway was my dream, too. Rosemary and I had been in lots of shows together over the years, and we'd spent hours fantasizing about being on the stage in New York.

"Mindy's got your Prosecco chilling," Johnny said.

"Nice!" Mindy was Johnny's housekeeper. She was a sweetheart, but it felt weird to have somebody wait on me. I doubted I would ever get used to it.

"Hey, hey everybody," I said to my buddies Ryan and Tim who were sitting on opposite ends of a comfy leather couch. I took a seat between the two guys, and my friend Erica sat across from us.

I LIFTED my arms and pulled Tim and Ryan in for a hug.

"How we doin', fellas?"

"Good. Tired, though. Long week," Ryan said as he rested his head on my shoulder. The guys were used to my hugginess and never minded me hanging on them. It was all platonic, of course. Tim was single at the moment, but I had a boyfriend and so did Ryan. Actually, Ryan had a fiancé and would be married as soon as Jack came back from his latest tour with the U.S. Marines.

Mindy emerged from the kitchen with a smile and glass of Prosecco for me.

"Here you go, Susie," she said. I let go of Tim and Ryan to grab my drink.

"Ah, you are the best, Mindy. Thanks so much," I said, feeling guilty about not getting up to get the drink myself. Johnny always reassured me that it was okay to let Mindy do her job, and that she was well-compensated. I still felt weird, but at least I'd finally gotten her to stop calling me Ms. Peters.

Johnny accepted a fresh beer from Mindy with a smile and a nod of thanks. After taking a healthy sip from the glass, he turned to me. "So, how's Carl?"

"Overwhelmed as always," I said with a sigh. My boyfriend, a medical student at Georgetown University, was crazy busy all the time. All he ever did was study, and it was tough on our relationship. We'd been dating for more than a year, but we rarely saw each other anymore. Fortunately, I had a wonderful network of friends to keep me from being lonely. "How are the plans for New York coming?"

"Great! We found this amazing apartment in Chelsea, in a place called London Terrace Towers. Once we get all settled, I can bring you all up to see it."

I smiled. "Bring you up" likely meant that Johnny would arrange for all of us to travel in style to New York City. He'd probably rent a stretch limo to take us all from Washington D.C. to visit him and Rosemary.

"I can't believe Rosemary hasn't heard back from NYU," I said, feeling a knot of anxiety form in my stomach. It had always been Rosemary's dream to go to college, to get her theater degree. She didn't like the idea of having her wealthy boyfriend pay for everything in her life, but having Johnny's rich family offer to pay for her education was too much for her to resist. Her only caveat was that the Creels did not interfere with the admission process. Rosemary was determined to apply to NYU on her own and hopefully get in on her own merit. I admired Rosemary's courage, but I just hoped to God she got into the school.

"I know," Johnny said, looking as I worried as I felt. "She's going crazy with all the waiting."

"Have you figured out what you're gonna do in New York yet, John-boy?" I asked. Last I'd heard, Johnny still had no clue what he wanted to do when he got there. He and Rosemary were going to New York whether she got into school or not. If she didn't make it into NYU, she planned to get a part-time job and focus on landing some auditions. She said she couldn't bear the idea of Johnny's family handing her free rent and food. She wanted to at least contribute some money. Johnny certainly didn't have to work, but he needed something to do with his time.

"Yes, actually," Johnny said. "I have an idea that I'm really excited about, but I haven't talked it over with Rosemary yet. If she's on board with it, you all will be the next ones to know about it."

I heard Johnny's front door open, and a few seconds later, Rosemary walked into the room. She looked upset.

"What's the matter?" Johnny asked with concern.

"I heard back from NYU," she said quietly.

My heart sank. *She didn't make it.*

"Oh, Rosemary," Johnny said tenderly, rushing toward her.

"No, it's not—I mean, I just got the email. I can't look," Rosemary said, her eyes filled with fear. "You do it. Please."

Rosemary thrust her phone at him.

Johnny hesitantly took the phone from her. From the agonized expression on his face, I knew he had kept his promise and hadn't interfered in helping her get into the school. He clearly had no idea what the email would say, and it would be unbearable for him to be the one to break her heart if the news wasn't good.

I jumped up from the couch and so did Erica, Tim, and Ryan. Rosemary smiled gratefully at us as we gathered around her to show our support. Ryan, who was particularly dear to her, put his hand on her back.

Rosemary drew in a deep breath and nodded at Johnny.

"Rosemary, whatever happens, remember that I love you,

and I am so incredibly proud of you," Johnny said in a voice filled with emotion. Rosemary nodded, holding her breath.

Johnny swallowed and pressed the button to wake up the phone. He clicked on the email from NYU, then his face split into a huge grin. He looked up at Rosemary and said, "You did it, Princess."

Rosemary let out her breath and we all burst into applause. She grabbed the phone from Johnny and read over the email to make sure. Then she opened her arms and Johnny ran into them, squeezing her tight and lifting her off the ground.

"Congratulations, Rosemary. You deserve this so much." Johnny held her tight and rubbed her back. When he finally let go, he chuckled softly to see tears dripping down her face. She always teared up when she was especially emotional, and it was wonderful to see her tears of joy. Johnny gently wiped the droplets from her eyes, then stepped back so the rest of us could descend upon her.

"You did it, sweetie!" Ryan exclaimed, grabbing Rosemary and pulling her into a hug. He squeezed her as tightly as Johnny had, and she laughed happily. She spun around to greet me next.

We locked eyes, and I said, "Rosemary, oh my God!"

"I know!" she said, laughing. We hugged each other, Rosemary crying, both of us laughing.

Except for Johnny, everyone gathered here in his penthouse were theater types. We all performed in local community shows, but only Rosemary and I were truly serious about our craft. I'd been lucky that my parents could afford to send me to college, so I had both a theater and a teaching degree. Now it was Rosemary's turn, and my heart was ready to explode with happiness for her.

"Mindy?" Johnny called out. "You can bring it in, now."

Mindy emerged a moment later carrying a tray with a

bottle of champagne and a bunch of empty glasses. She seemed prepared, like she'd overheard the celebration going on in the living room. She set down the tray, then expertly opened the champagne and started pouring. She left the glasses there, then walked over to Rosemary.

"Congratulations, Rosemary," Mindy said, opening her arms. Rosemary hugged her warmly.

"Thank you so much," Rosemary said.

Mindy handed out the glasses of champagne, starting with Rosemary and Johnny and then to the rest of us.

"You too, Mindy," Johnny said with a grin.

Mindy poured herself a glass.

"To Rosemary Sutton, NYU theater student and the next big star to hit the great white way," Johnny said with enthusiasm.

"Hear, hear!" we all shouted as we drank a toast to our friend.

I waited patiently as Rosemary took turns chatting with our friends. Finally, she settled in a chair next to me with her drink.

"I'm so excited for you, Rosemary. I can't even tell you how happy I am. Can you imagine studying theater in New York?" I gushed.

We squealed like a couple of schoolgirls, making Johnny laugh.

"I know," Rosemary said, drawing in a deep breath. She looked ecstatic and incredibly relieved. It had been a long, painful admission process, and the waiting had been awful.

"I don't know what I'm gonna do without you," I said.

"I'm gonna miss you like crazy. You could always move to New York, too. I'm sure you could find a job there. And, you know, Johnny can always ..."

"I know," I told her. Johnny could pay for me to move to New York so I could go on auditions and try to make it to

Broadway. We'd been through that scenario a bunch of times, and as tempting as it was, I couldn't accept his generous offer. It wouldn't feel right. Besides, my life was here. "And it's so sweet of him. But I have a job I really like, and of course, there's Carl. He's still got two years left of med school here in D.C., so it's not like he could just up and move to New York."

"I understand," Rosemary said sadly. "It just would have been so wonderful."

"Yeah, it really would be," I said as physical pain stabbed my heart. Being in New York with Rosemary, supporting each other through tough auditions and the triumph and heartbreak of being a performer, would have been incredible. I was in my mid-twenties, and I wouldn't be young forever. It was a long shot to make it to Broadway, and the older I got, the less likely it was that it would ever happen. I did want to go to New York someday, to at least give it a try, but it never seemed to be the right time.

"I can't believe I got into NYU," Rosemary said with a dreamy smile. Then she looked thoughtful for a moment.

"What's the matter?" I asked her.

"Sometimes I can't help but think …" Rosemary took a sip of her champagne, then set down the glass and looked at me. "Do you think they let me in because of the video?"

She was referring to the infamous video of Johnny's grand gesture of apology, in his effort to win her back after a terrible fight. He was already a celebrity at the time—the notorious playboy son of famed bank attorney Walter Creel. Johnny also used to be a big jerk. He'd been a womanizer, a big spender, and he also used to be Rosemary's boss. Johnny had treated her badly when she worked as his executive assistant, but then he'd learned some harsh lessons about life when he suddenly lost his fortune. Walter Creel had been accused of some white-collar crime, and while he was under investigation, his assets were completely frozen. For the first time in his life, Johnny had had no money and no prospects. Rosemary graciously helped him get back on his feet, and that's when they fell in love. He supported her theater dreams and loved that she was a performer, but when his dad's name was cleared and Johnny was rich again, he'd fallen back into his old, spoiled ways. Rosemary overheard him trash-talking musical theater to all his friends behind her back, and it broke her heart. Johnny knew he had been an idiot for trying to fit back in with his asshole friends, so he made a public apology to Rosemary by serenading her with a showtune in the middle of a crowded restaurant.

"Of course not, Rosemary. You got in on your talent. End of story," I told her firmly.

The video had been a viral sensation, and the odds were that NYU had gotten wind of it. It was big news everywhere, but particularly in the theater community. Johnny had sung "Rosemary," a showtune from the musical *How to Succeed in Business Without Really Trying.* He sounded pretty good, but he was nothing compared to Rosemary. She was *incredible.* Rosemary had fired back at him with an impromptu medley of showtunes, telling him exactly how she felt. She started with an angry song called "Forget About the Boy," which contained lots of lyrics about him being a double-crosser and pulling the rug out from under her. She sang snippets of a few different songs, giving a full-out performance and making him sweat a bit, before ending with a song about love and forgiveness. Someone had captured the video on a cell phone, complete with all the emotion and drama.

"Even if the admissions people did see the video, it really showcased your talent. Maybe that did help you get in, but not because you're famous. It's still because you're an incredible singer," I said.

"Maybe," Rosemary said thoughtfully. She gazed over at

Johnny who was talking with Ryan and Timothy. "I love him so much, but sometimes it's tough to be only known as Johnny Creel's girlfriend. I worry that NYU is hoping they'll get a big donation from the Creels if they let me in."

"I understand. But seriously, that video showed how great a singer you are and that you can hold your own, even up against the Creel bigwigs. You showed you are nobody's fool, baby."

Rosemary smiled with pride. "Yes, I suppose that's true."

Johnny truly was a changed man. Losing all his money and falling in love with a poor girl made him realize what was really important in life. It had nearly destroyed him when Rosemary broke up with him, and I knew he would never take her for granted again.

"Now all you guys need to do is figure out what Johnny's gonna do to keep himself out of trouble in New York," I said in a loud voice, making sure Johnny heard me. He looked over at me and grinned. A wave of affection swept over me. Johnny was like the goofy brother I never had. I realized how much I was going to miss him, too.

"Oh, I got some ideas," Johnny said.

"Is that so? Well, that's news to me," Rosemary said with a smile. Johnny wasn't exactly what you could call ambitious. For most of his life, he'd been able to afford to sit around and do nothing, so that's what he did.

"I'll tell you about it later. Tonight is your special night," Johnny said. "I figured I would discuss my idea with you first and then tell everybody, if you approve."

"Honey, if it's something you want to do, of course I'll approve," Rosemary said, green eyes sparkling. "Tell me, tell me, tell me!"

Johnny chuckled. He came over and sat down in the chair next to her, then leaned over and gently ran his fingers through her long red hair. Though I was pretty happy with my bright blue eyes, I would kill to have that red hair of hers. Mine was such a boring brown.

"Okay, so here's what I'm thinkin', and you can tell me if you think it's crazy," Johnny said, gazing at Rosemary tenderly. "I thought it would be cool if I started an arts and theater kind of foundation for underprivileged kids. It would have after-school programs like theater, voice lessons, acting, dancing, and maybe arts and crafts kinds of stuff. All free for the kids, of course. We could build it in some poor neighborhood in Brooklyn or somewhere, and then we could have the kids bussed in from other poor neighborhoods."

I smiled as I watched Johnny explain his idea. He spoke quickly and with great excitement, like a little kid. It was *adorable.*

"And just think, Rosemary," Johnny said, his gentle gray eyes lighting up. "The place would have a big auditorium where you could rehearse your monologues for classes and for auditions and stuff. Your own private stage when the kids aren't using it. My dad would totally be on board, because it would be a huge tax write-off and it would make him look good. And it's like I could really help these kids make their dreams come true, and finally do something useful with my life."

We all looked at Rosemary for her reaction, and none of us was surprised by what we saw. She covered her mouth with her hand as fresh tears spilled from her eyes. When she finally composed herself enough to speak, she whispered, "Oh Johnny, that's so beautiful."

Oh, yes. Johnny Creel was a changed man all right. The foundation idea was such a wonderful way to help others less fortunate than him, and it was a lovely testament to his love for Rosemary.

Carl would never do anything like that for me in a million years.

Rosemary threw her arms around Johnny and hugged him tight. When she finally let him go, he looked into her eyes. "And Princess, I want to name the foundation after you. The Rosemary Sutton Foundation."

Her eyes opened wide and she looked downright panicked. "Johnny, you can't do that. Oh, it's so sweet, and I love you for it, but you just can't. I don't want anybody to think I'm trying to curry any favors on my auditions. If you use my name, Broadway producers might hear about it and when I go to an audition, they'll think I'm some spoiled rich girlfriend of a billionaire. They'll think I'm trying to buy a role, or they'll think—"

Johnny chuckled softly. "It's okay, Rosemary. I understand. We'll call it something else. The Creel Foundation, maybe. I'm sure that will make my dad happy anyway. It doesn't matter what we call it. I just want you to know that you are the inspiration for it. Because of your kindness and generosity. The way you helped me when I needed it most, and the way you inspire me every day by reaching for your dreams and never giving up."

Rosemary smiled through her happy tears. She was too choked up with emotion to speak, so she wrapped her arms around Johnny and they held each other for a moment.

"Okay, my turn," Ryan said firmly but with a grin. Standing in front of the couch, he offered Rosemary his hand. She smiled and allowed him to pull her into a standing position. Hugging her tightly, he said, "Sweetie, I'm gonna miss you so much."

I got up from the couch, prepared to wait my turn to embrace Rosemary again. Ryan grinned at me, then pulled me in for a group hug. Ryan and I hugged her tight as we all tried not to cry.

"You're gonna make it, baby. I just know it," I told Rosemary.

11

I glanced up to see Johnny looking at me thoughtfully.

"What?" I asked him.

"You really should be moving to New York, too," Johnny said with a look of gentle concern on his face.

I let out a sigh. The idea of leaving everything behind and heading to New York was far more tempting than I wanted to admit to myself.

"I wish I could, Johnny. Really." Thoughts of Carl, my job, and all my other responsibilities swirled in my head.

"Hey," Johnny said, reaching for my hand and then squeezing it in both of his. He looked me straight in the eye and said, "I'll tell you what I told Rosemary not so long ago. Just promise me you'll think about it."

I smiled gratefully and nodded.

"Okay, Johnny. I promise."

CHAPTER 2

Two Years Later

In the years that had passed since Rosemary and Johnny moved to New York, not a single day had gone by that I hadn't thought about running off and joining them.

Two years later and I was no closer to my dreams than I was when they left.

I was still stuck in the same rut, still teaching at Western High School in Washington D.C., and still dating Carl. I had thought his time in medical school was bad, but that was nothing compared to his medical residency. He was working insane hours, and it was hard for him to find time to see me. It would only be a few more years of residency, but sometimes I wondered if things would get better once he was a full-fledged, practicing doctor. He would still be busy then, and I worried what that meant for our future.

Snapped out of my thoughts by the sound of the bell, I stood up behind my desk. "Okay, guys, don't forget the test on Monday on prepositional phrases. Also, your literary analysis paper is due at the end of next week," I said to my English class. The students groaned, and I felt like joining them. Even I felt that studying grammar and analyzing works of literature took the fun out of them. It would be so much better if we could just read books like *The Catcher in the Rye,* or even better, simply perform the works of Shakespeare rather than analyzing them to death.

A flutter of excitement rippled through me as I packed up my tote bag and grabbed my purse, preparing to go to theater practice. It was the same thing every day. I did my best to slog through the school day so I could get to the only part I truly enjoyed; moderating the after-school drama program. Our year-end theater production was next week, and we were doing *Bye, Bye, Birdie.* I had such a talented group of kids this year, and I was so proud of all of them.

I rushed to the auditorium so I could have a few moments to myself. The first thing I did was step onto the stage, close my eyes, and draw in a deep breath.

How I loved the smell of the theater. It was funny the way theaters tended to smell the same, wherever I was. This high school, my old college, the community theater where I performed—they all had the scent of paint and wood and *magic.* I closed my eyes and imagined I was in the middle of a Broadway stage instead of some dingy gymnasium.

I opened my eyes and started dancing to the music in my head. I performed the song and dance routine "America" from *West Side Story,* which was one of my favorites. I'd been in the show years ago in college, and I still remembered all the steps. The door to the auditorium opened, and some of the kids started streaming in, but I ignored them. They were used to coming in and seeing me in full performance mode. I couldn't help myself, and they knew it.

I sang and danced the entire routine, feeling all my stress and boredom from the day slipping away. The stage was where I came alive. My heart pumped and my adrenaline surged as I performed the high energy routine. It was like

14

therapy for my soul. I finished my dance with a big flourish, and my kids applauded and whistled.

"Wahoo, go Ms. Susie!"

"You're killin' it, Ms. S!"

I laughed and took a gracious bow, panting and happy to be onstage.

I clapped my hands. "Okay! Show next week, so we don't have a minute to lose. We need to run through the whole shebang at least once, so let's get a move on."

My heart swelled with pride as I watched my kids run through the show. They were so talented and entertaining, and *Bye Bye Birdie* was such a fun show to do with kids this age. It was about a heartthrob singer named Conrad who gets drafted into the armed forces, causing a frenzy among his adoring fans. It was based on what happened when Elvis Presley got drafted during the height of his popularity.

The drama students this year were terrific. They'd worked really hard, so they needed minimal direction from me at this point. Too bad none of the kids were interested in performing as a career. There was nothing I loved more than mentoring a kid with theater dreams like mine. Sometimes I felt like a fraud, though. Who was I to tell anybody how to make it in show business? I wasn't even a full-time drama teacher, let alone a successful performer.

I grinned from ear to ear as I watched my prized pupil, Antoine Jackson, sing one of Conrad Birdie's showstopping tunes, "If You're Really Sincere." I adored Antoine. He was a gentle soul with dark skin and dark brown eyes. I watched proudly as he strutted across the stage, giving a full-out performance that rivaled Elvis himself. No matter how many times I'd seen it in rehearsal, it always made me laugh to watch him perform as his "fans" screamed in adoration around him. Antoine was incredible, but I knew he didn't have the heart of an artist. He was more technically minded, and would probably go into the computer science field or something. He was rather shy, but I recognized his talent immediately and implored him to audition for me. Being in the show seemed to draw him out of his shell, and even though he might never do another show, I hoped he would look back on this experience as something really cool he did once back in high school.

I drew in a deep breath, letting the peace and happiness of being in the theater surround me. I felt like I spent most of my life biding my time so I could get here, where I wanted to be. Where I belonged.

And Johnny has an entire school devoted to teaching theater. In New York.

The idea of spending my days teaching and auditioning in New York City seemed impossible. I spent hours daydreaming about it, the same way people fantasize about what they would do if they won the lottery. The urge to run off to the Big Apple was growing stronger every day, but I loved my high school kids, and I loved Carl. I couldn't just up and leave.

Could I?

The deadline for renewing my teacher contract for the next school year was in two weeks. I did enjoy teaching, but it was always painful for me to start back every September, after spending the summer doing nothing but theater-related stuff. It was only May, and I was already dreading the beginning of the next school year.

But what would Carl say if I told him I wanted to go to New York? We had talked about getting married after his medical residency in two years.

My mind suddenly started whirring with possibilities. What if I went to New York for two years while Carl finished his residency at the hospital?

My breath caught in my throat. The mere thought of

going to New York made me want to cry with joy. I wanted this. Dear God, I wanted this so much. Theater was in my blood, and I knew I would live a life full of regrets if I didn't at least give myself a good, honest shot at making it onto Broadway.

I stood there watching my precious kids perform the show's finale, my heart filled with renewed hope and a sense of purpose.

Oh my God, I think I'm really gonna do this thing.

CHAPTER 3

I told Carl I needed to see him as soon as possible. In my heart I knew what I wanted to do, but moving to New York would affect his life, too. It was only fair that I discussed it with him first.

As usual, Carl was working constantly, so the only way I could see him was to meet him in the hospital's cafeteria. I sat at the table and nervously scanned the room for him. I had gotten us a couple of burgers and fries already, since I knew he was pressed for time.

My heart lurched with sympathy when I saw Carl approach. He looked utterly exhausted as he headed toward me. He collapsed into the chair across from me, flipping his light brown hair out of his face.

"Are you okay?" I asked, taking his hand in mine.

"Yeah, I'll survive. Only two more years, right?" he said with a weak smile.

People always complain about how much money doctors make, but they certainly paid their dues first. Between the years of medical school and the hell that was a physician's residency, they deserved to be rewarded.

"What's up?" Carl asked. "Everything okay?"

"Oh, yeah. I'm fine. There's just something important I wanted to tell you. It's nothing bad..." I took a deep breath. I wished we had more time to ease into this discussion, like over a leisurely dinner or something. That wasn't possible, so I knew I had to get right down to it. "Carl, I've decided not to renew my contract with the school this year. I want to go to New York."

Carl looked stunned for a moment, then said, "What? What are you talking about?"

"I'm not getting any younger, Carl. If I'm going to realistically pursue a career on Broadway, I can't waste any more time."

Carl grabbed his cheeseburger and starting eating. He did not look pleased.

"I know it's going to be an adjustment for both of us, but the truth is we don't see much of each other as it is. You've got a couple more years on your residency, so it's kind of perfect, in a way. I can take two years to go to New York and give it my best shot. Then, when you're done your residency, I can come back if things don't work out."

I wasn't sure what would happen if things did work out, but what a wonderful problem that would be to have. My stomach fluttered with joy at the thought. And even if I didn't make it, the thought of living in New York for two years and focusing entirely on theater made me want to jump up and scream with excitement.

"You cannot be serious," Carl said, a grim look on his face.

"Of course I am. I've always been serious about performing. You know that," I said, trying to swallow my disappointment at his initial reaction.

"Susie, this is crazy. You can't just up and go to New York," he said.

I stared at him a moment. Deep down, I had known he

wouldn't be supportive. He never had been. Sure, he came to all my shows, but his eyes tended to glaze over whenever I talked about theater. Carl was good about asking how my day was and all that, but he never seemed to grasp the notion that I didn't want to talk about teaching high school. That was only my day job; theater was my whole life.

"Why can't you support me for once? I've been supportive of everything you're doing with your life. It's not easy being the girlfriend of a med student. You're never around. I hate it, but I'm supportive because I know how important it is to you."

"Yeah, exactly," Carl said irritably. "What I'm doing is important."

"And what I'm doing isn't?"

Carl snorted. "Really, Suze? You're gonna compare musical theater to being a doctor and saving lives?"

I drew in a deep breath to steady myself. It wasn't enough, so I took a sip of my Diet Coke in an effort to calm down before I said anything I would regret. I was proud of Carl for wanting to be a doctor, and I certainly admired the hard work and effort he was putting into it. But he could be so *insufferable* about it sometimes. It was hard to explain that theater meant as much to me as being a doctor meant to him. This wasn't the first time he'd made the issue into a contest that I simply couldn't win. Saving lives *was* more important than entertaining people. Fine. I conceded that. But why wasn't there room for both in this world?

My heart was heavy. I wished I had the words to express how much it hurt that he didn't have my back. "After all this time, how do you still not get how important this is to me?"

Carl sighed wearily. I understood he was too tired to have this conversation now, and yet it was painful that he couldn't be bothered to comfort me. I felt like nothing but an annoying inconvenience to his oh-so-important life.

An image of Johnny flashed through my mind. He not only supported Rosemary's dreams, but he was so proud of her. He watched her, enraptured, every time she sang. Sure, being as rich as he was made it easy to support her financially. When she allowed it, anyway. But it was more than that. He understood how much she wanted this. Johnny knew this wasn't some silly hobby of hers. It was part of who she was. Just like it was a part of who I was.

A sudden realization hit me, one that I should have figured out long ago. Being a theater performer was the very essence of who I was, and Carl thought it was silly and stupid. Which meant he thought *I* was silly and stupid. He thought of me as some vapid, selfish theater diva, while he was a noble hero off saving lives.

"I'm sorry, Susie," Carl said. He didn't sound sorry for hurting my feelings. It was like he was saying, *Sorry, I don't get it.* He didn't get it, and he never would.

We ate in silence for a few minutes. My heart physically hurt in my chest. I realized that if I moved to New York, it would most likely be the end of Carl and me. We had been together for three years. Was I really ready to throw all of that away?

I thought of Johnny again. Even when he was flat broke, he had encouraged Rosemary to go to New York to pursue her dreams. He had told her that he'd miss her like crazy, but he would understand if leaving was what she needed to do in order to be happy. Johnny was prepared to wait for her. He'd have been utterly lost without Rosemary, but he loved her enough to let her go.

"Do you have any idea what the odds are of you making it to Broadway? Like, a billion to one," Carl said suddenly.

That was probably the cruelest thing anyone had ever said to me. The physical pain in my chest was so sharp that Carl might as well have punched me in the heart.

21

I closed my eyes, determined not to let loose the tears of pain and anger that were welling in my eyes.

Of course I knew the odds. Every artist knows the terrible odds of making it. We think about it a thousand times a day, but something deep inside us keeps us going each day, in spite of the odds. We face rejection, heartache, loneliness, and despair, but we face the storm head on anyway. Yes, doctors were brave. But so were the actors, singers, writers, poets, and dreamers who put their hearts and souls on the line every day. We were all brave. *It's not a goddamned contest, you heartless bastard.*

Despite my best efforts, my tears spilled openly down my cheeks. Carl looked alarmed at my expression. Of course he was surprised at my reaction. He had no idea how badly he'd hurt me because he had no understanding of who I really was.

My hands were shaking with anger. I was angry at Carl but even more furious at myself. I had always considered myself a strong, independent woman, but it was time to face the harsh fact that *I had put off my dreams for two solid years for a man.* A man who was in no way, shape, or form worthy of me.

Poor, heroic, put-upon Carl sighed. "I guess it's okay if you want to do this thing—"

"Oh, honey," I said with a bitter laugh, standing up, then slamming my chair into the table for good measure. "I don't need your permission to do 'this thing.' I'm doing it. Without you."

Carl looked up at me, wide-eyed. I gazed deeply into his eyes, trying to take a moment to mourn the life that I thought I'd have with him. I had been his girlfriend for three years. We'd planned to get married. It was all falling apart now, and I felt like I should have been devastated. I was shocked to find that I only felt one thing.

Relief.

Relief that I no longer had to perform the tentative balancing act that was trying to keep Carl happy. I'd been doing it for so long, it was hard to imagine not having that burden. No more carefully worded explanations that I couldn't go somewhere because I had rehearsal, no more steeling myself for his underwhelmed reaction when I got a part I really wanted, all the while knowing he wouldn't care.

"Susie, come on now. Can't we talk about this?" Carl said. He stood, holding his hands out plaintively. He looked at me like I was nuts. He had no idea where all this was coming from because he never listened to anything I said.

"I've tried talking to you about it, Carl. You either don't hear me, or you just don't care. Either way, I'm done trying to make you understand."

I stared into his eyes, finally feeling a sense of loss for what might have been. I still loved him, but I knew he wasn't the right guy for me. He was acting like a total asshole, but he wasn't a terrible person. He was just a snob.

"I know you don't mean to, but you're always belittling my dreams. Telling me that what I want in life isn't important. Going to New York is something I need to do, and it breaks my heart that you refuse to support me. I'm much better off being on my own than being with someone who holds me back."

Carl rolled his eyes and sighed, clearly dismissing me once again as an overly dramatic diva. I realized I'd need to spell it out for him.

"You can come over and get your stuff from my place when you have time. You can keep or toss out whatever I have at your apartment. I'll need to downsize anyway."

"You can't just up and leave!" Carl said, sounding more angry than hurt.

"I can, actually. I'm going to New York. I'm sorry, Carl." I turned to leave, then thought better of it. I turned back and said defiantly, "No. I'm *not* sorry."

My mind was made up. I knew I was doing the right thing, not only by going to New York, but by breaking up with Carl. I would call him later so we could talk rationally. After three years together, I owed him that much. I wanted to end this on good terms, and I wished him love and happiness for the future. He deserved no less.

And neither did I.

CHAPTER 4

"Johnny, great to see you, my good man," I said, greeting my old friend with a firm handshake. "You're looking good."

Johnny grinned. "I got to, man. I know I gotta step up my fashion game when David Groff is in the hiz-zouse."

I chuckled. "That's for sure."

New York was clearly treating Johnny well. He seemed happy and relaxed, and he did look good clad in a black Burberry Cambridge shirt and Brioni trousers. We hadn't seen each other since he moved from Washington, D.C., two years ago. I called him last week to let him know I would be in town on business, so he recommended we meet up at a steakhouse near his apartment in Chelsea.

"You're not looking so bad yourself," he said, checking out my Kiton dark blue shadow suit. Made in Italy, this baby was 100% cashmere. I always dressed to the nines, but I wore only my finest attire while schmoozing my way through New York. This particular suit seemed to make my dark brown hair and brown eyes look even darker, giving off a serious businessman vibe. Johnny gestured to a seat at the table. "Ordered you a scotch."

"Perfect," I said, as I sat across from my friend. I surveyed the restaurant. Sweeney's Steakhouse featured dark rosewood tables and a long, sleek bar stocked with an extensive array of microbrews. There was also a variety of dead animals nailed to the opposite wall. It was like a rich guy's man cave. I loved it.

My scotch arrived, and after a quick review of the menu, we put in our orders.

"So, David, what brings you to the Big Apple?" Johnny asked before taking a healthy chug of his microbrew.

"Taking a tour of the garment industry, among other things."

Johnny chuckled. "Why am I not surprised?"

I nodded, then sipped my scotch before continuing. "Had some meetings with some investors, too."

"Really? Now what would David Groff need investors for?" Johnny asked, looking curious and a tad worried. He knew I came from an exorbitantly wealthy family, just like he did. He'd found out the hard way that it could all be taken away in the blink of an eye. Fortunately, it didn't last long. Still, I didn't think Johnny would ever forget what it was like to be broke.

"Don't worry. My family's still rich. It's nothing like what you went through."

"Well, that's a relief. Then what are you doing in New York looking for investors? You're still working in real estate for your dad, right?"

"At the moment, yes. But I'm leaving soon to start my own business. Here in New York."

Johnny's gray eyes opened wide. "You're kidding! That's great. What kind of business are you starting?"

I grinned. "Can't you guess?"

"Gonna go out on a limb here and say it's something to do with clothes."

"Precisely. I want to start my own men's fashion line." I felt uneasy saying that out loud. Starting my own line of formal men's clothing was something I had thought about for years, but I'd never verbalized the thought to anyone other than my father. That conversation hadn't gone too well. David Groff Sr. had said it was a ludicrous idea, that most businesses fail, and I should stay where I was and keep working for him. Even so, he gave me a large amount of money to invest, so I could hardly complain.

"Wow, that's great. That's really great. Cheers to you, my good man," Johnny said, clinking my scotch glass with his mug of beer.

"It's time I did something with my life," I told him.

"You've done pretty well for yourself so far, I'd say."

"No, my father's done pretty well for himself. I've been riding his coattails most of my life."

"So, what's wrong with that?" Johnny asked with a smirk. He'd done the same thing his whole life and was fairly unabashed about it.

"Nothing, I suppose. I'm just ready to get out of my father's shadow. Make something of myself on my own."

"But ... aren't you using your dad's money for startup? I'm sure he's willing to give you a ton."

I nodded grimly. "Yes. I admit that I am using his funding for a lot of it, but like I said, I'm also trying to get some outside investors. The plan is to eventually have a viable clothing business that I can run without Daddy's money."

"You got more ambition than I ever did. I'll give you that. Every dime of The Creel Foundation for the Arts that I'm running comes from dear old Dad."

I was about to ask Johnny how things were going with the foundation when our food arrived. My mouth watered at the sight and the sound of my medium-rare New York strip steak, still sizzling on the small skillet in front of me. I cut into it to make sure it was done to my satisfaction.

"This looks incredible," I said.

"Ah, I love this place. Haven't had a bad meal yet," Johnny said, then nodded at the server to let him know we had everything we needed.

I took a bite of the delectable steak and found myself becoming more enthusiastic about moving to New York by the moment. There was so much to love about the city. The food was just the beginning. I was thrilled at the idea of putting down stakes in one of the fashion capitals of the world.

"So how are things going with the foundation?" I asked Johnny.

"Great. It's going great. It's incredible being able to give all those kids something safe and fun to do after school." Johnny paused, contemplating for a moment. "They've got nothing, those little guys. Really makes you think. And Rosemary's great with them. She loves teaching them when she's not in class."

"How does she like NYU?"

Johnny's face lit up. "Loves it. She fuckin' *loves* it, man. Works her ass off, that's for sure. But she's having the time of her life there. She's learning so much, and then she comes to the foundation and rehearses and stuff. Brings her college friends, and they get to use the stage and all. God, I love that I can do that for her. Give her this huge theater space where she can pursue her dreams."

It was clear that Johnny was head over heels in love with Rosemary. He truly had become a different person with her. Rosemary was such a sweetheart, but she didn't take any shit from him. Johnny really admired that about her, and so did I. She was the first woman who had refused to kiss his ass simply because he was rich, and she was the first woman to love him for who he really was.

"So, she's adjusted to being the girlfriend of a billionaire?" I asked.

"Yeah, I guess she has. It was tough for her to take my dad's money for school, but I know she doesn't regret it. She earned her way into NYU all on her own, and she's working hard and making the most of it. She loves our apartment here in Chelsea, which is good." Johnny wrinkled his nose. "She still takes the subway, though, which makes me nuts. I know she doesn't want everything handed to her, and she wants to feel like she's earning her big break, but I still worry about her safety."

"I can understand that," I said. The thought of a sweet girl like Rosemary riding around on the NYC subway late at night made me nervous, too. I couldn't help but admire her, though. I had a limo driver take me everywhere I needed to go. I would probably end up getting lost in some god-forsaken neighborhood in the Bronx if I tried to navigate the subway. Besides, the mere thought of public transportation made me shudder. It seemed so *dirty*.

"Has she been on many auditions?" I asked.

"Yeah, actually. She's had quite a few. She's even done a few shows, you know, off- Broadway, which is pretty cool." Johnny's eyes twinkled with pride when he spoke about Rosemary's success. "She even managed to get into Actors' Equity—the actors' union. That's been a big help in getting her more auditions. Even so, she still has to wait in crazy long lines for auditions. Out in the freezing cold or the sticky humid heat. She never takes any special treatment, though, and she doesn't let anything stop her."

"Impressive," I said, and I meant it. Rosemary worked incredibly hard, and if there was any justice in this world, she would get her big break someday.

"Rosemary's got incredible ambition. I don't get it," Johnny said, laughing heartily. "I just don't have that kind of drive."

"Sounds like you've done some great work with the foundation. That can't have been easy," I offered as I dug into my baked potato.

"Oh, you'd be surprised. You know how it is. My dad gave me a shit-ton of money, and I've got great people working at the place. I do come to work most days, but on days when I just don't feel like coming into work, well, then I don't." Johnny shrugged.

"Spoiled bastard," I said with a chuckle.

"You know it," Johnny said proudly, toasting me with his beer.

I tipped my nearly empty scotch glass at Johnny, then made the same gesture at the server. He nodded and rushed off to get me a fresh glass.

It occurred to me that I was somewhat of a mix between Rosemary and Johnny. I had enough money that I could sit around and do nothing if that's what I wanted, but that idea bored me. For the first time in my life, I was ready and willing to work incredibly hard, like Rosemary, in order to make a name for myself. Even though I literally shared my father's name, I wanted my name to stand on its own for once. It was time to create my own legacy.

"So where can a rich, single, impeccably dressed man get laid in New York?" I asked bluntly, making Johnny nearly choke on his drink.

When he recovered, Johnny responded, "Pretty much anywhere he likes, I would imagine."

I nodded, glancing over at the bar. Slim pickings right now, but it was 1pm on a weekday. I had several go-to ladies back in D.C. who were always willing to put out sexually, as long as I put out financially, but I looked forward to getting some new action in NYC. My cock tightened in my pants just thinking about it. I was looking forward to some new bedroom adventures. Maybe I'd ask my limo driver, Stewart, to start scoping out some places to take me tonight where I could pick up a lady. I had a huge bed at the St. Regis hotel, and I was looking forward to putting it to good use.

"So, when are ya moving?" Johnny asked.

"Next month."

"Nice. How long are you in town for this trip?"

"Until Monday."

"Perfect. You should come by and see The Creel Foundation while you're here, if you've got the time."

"Absolutely. I'd love to see it."

"How 'bout tomorrow? Rosemary's got a friend coming in from out of town, and we were gonna give her a tour tomorrow afternoon. Around three or so. Would that work for you?"

"It would actually," I said, as I nodded at the server who finally brought me another scotch. "Got a couple of meetings in the morning, and that's it."

"Perfect." Johnny grinned at me. "It'll be great to have you living in town, man. Can't wait to see what trouble we can get into."

"I'll drink to that," I said, raising my glass.

CHAPTER 5

$\mathcal{M}$y limo driver dropped me off right in front of The Creel Foundation for the Arts, which was unfortunately located in the middle of a dreadful neighborhood in Brooklyn. Why couldn't Johnny have bought a place in Manhattan proper? Walter Creel could certainly afford it, and Johnny was having the poor kids brought in from poor neighborhoods anyway.

Stewart opened the limo door, and I stepped out onto the street. I surveyed the drab-looking building that took up an entire city block, hoping the inside was more attractive than the exterior.

It has to be. Couldn't be much worse.

I inwardly chastised myself for being so judgmental. This was my friend's special project, and it was for underprivileged kids, for God's sake.

I opened the front door, and a pretty, young receptionist smiled warmly at me.

"Hello," she said.

"Good afternoon. I'm David Groff. I'm here to see Johnny Creel."

"Oh, yes. Mr. Groff. He's expecting you. Just one moment."

She picked up the phone and pressed an extension. "Johnny? Mr. Groff is here to see you."

Johnny? He let his employees call him Johnny? I didn't have staff yet, but when I did, they would call me Mr. Groff.

Moments later, Johnny bounded into the room wearing jeans and a T-shirt. Granted, they were *designer* jeans. 7 For All Mankind brand to be exact, and his T-shirt was Michael Kors. Still, he didn't exactly look like the President and CEO of a prominent foundation.

"Hey, hey. Lookin' good," Johnny said, admiring my Brioni pin-dot striped navy suit. "You know you're just hanging out with Rosemary and her friend, and not the Queen of England, right?"

I shrugged and said, "I had business meetings all morning."

It was true, but I doubted I would have dressed any differently if I had been hanging out at my hotel all morning.

"Come on, I'll start showing you around a bit. Rosemary's friend should be here in a few," Johnny said. As he turned to leave, he saluted the receptionist and said, "Thanks, Ellie."

As Johnny led me through the building, I was pleased to note the inside was, indeed, much nicer than the outside. The hallways were brightly lit, and there were kids' drawings hanging on the walls. Overall, it had a relatively cheery vibe. I could see how this place would be a respite for poor children to visit and explore their creativity. As we continued walking down the hall, we heard a woman singing. Her voice was beautiful; powerful and strong. Johnny's expression softened and he smiled.

"Is that Rosemary?" I asked.

Johnny nodded. "Yeah. She's prepping for another audition."

He opened the door to the auditorium and we walked in. The place was impressive to be sure. It was a huge theater space with maybe two thousand seats or more. Rosemary stood in the middle of the stage, belting out "Anything Goes." I recognized the song, but only because it was in the movie *Indiana Jones and the Temple of Doom.* She waved at us without missing a note. Johnny walked down the middle of the aisle as he watched her, grinning proudly. We both applauded wildly when she finished her song.

Rosemary laughed, then took a gracious bow and walked down the steps from the stage. We went over to greet her. She slipped her arm around Johnny and kissed him, gazing fondly at him for a moment. Her pretty, green eyes were filled with love and affection. I hadn't thought any woman, never mind one as talented and gorgeous as Rosemary Sutton, would ever look at my goofy buddy like she looked at him.

Rosemary knew I wasn't the touchy-feely type, so she offered me a sweet smile instead of a hug.

"It's so good to see you again, David," she said.

"You too, Rosemary. This is quite a place you have here."

She drew in a breath and let out a happy sigh. "Oh, it's a dream, isn't it?"

"You looked beautiful up there, Rosemary. You're a natural onstage."

"Thanks." She smiled again, the joy reaching all the way up to her eyes. The best compliment you could give Rosemary was to tell her she was talented. It was obvious that performing meant the world to her.

The door to the auditorium opened, and Johnny's receptionist ushered in a woman who was about Rosemary's age. Mid-twenties, I would say. At least five years my junior.

Rosemary and the other woman locked eyes from across

the room, then girlish squealing ensued. The woman, who had long brown hair, light blue eyes, and a killer body, rushed over to us. She threw her arms around Rosemary, and they hugged happily.

"So glad you finally made it. I've been waiting forever for you to come see this place," Rosemary said.

"I know. Can't believe it's taken me this long." Rosemary's friend turned to Johnny and threw her arms around him.

"Great to see you, Susie-girl," Johnny said, embracing her warmly.

Susie let go of Johnny, then gently punched him on the shoulder. "Thanks for the Rolls you sent to pick me up. Overkill much?"

"Nothing but the best for you, darling. How's your hotel?"

"It's just beautiful," Susie said, her pretty, blue eyes sparkling. "Thanks so much, Johnny."

"Anytime. Anytime at all," Johnny said. "David, this is Rosemary's friend, Susannah Peters."

"It's a pleasure to meet you, Susannah. David Groff," I said, offering my hand.

"Nice to meet you," she said, shaking my hand warmly. "You can call me Susie."

I immediately decided that I wouldn't. I didn't like the name Susie for her. She was a beautiful woman, and the name Susannah fit her so much better.

Susannah took a step back, looking me up and down. "Wow, you look terrific; like you just stepped out of GQ." She drew in a deep breath. "And that's great cologne. You even smell like the pages. Very nice."

"Yes well, you smell very nice too, Susannah," I said with a smirk.

"This is incredible fabric," she said, eying my suit. She rubbed her hand down the arm of my jacket, which took me by surprise. I flinched a bit, and she took her hand off my arm. Her eyes opened wide, and she said, "Sorry."

Susannah seemed confused at my reaction, and I couldn't blame her. I certainly didn't mind being touched by a beautiful lady; I just hadn't been expecting it. I wasn't used to being touched, except in the bedroom. Growing up, my parents never hugged me, nor any of my younger siblings. It simply wasn't done.

I raised an eyebrow and said, "No harm done."

She eyed me curiously and nodded. Then she turned around to take a good look at the auditorium. Her expression softened, and she had the same dreamy-eyed look that Rosemary had a moment ago. I realized she must be a performer, too.

"Rosemary, oh my God," Susannah said as she scanned the auditorium and stage.

"I know," Rosemary said. "Can you believe this place? Come on. Come see the stage."

Susannah nodded happily. The two women were so excited, I almost expected to see them hold hands and skip toward the stage. Johnny watched proudly as the two friends explored the place.

"This is like her playground," he said with a smile.

"I can see that." I watched, amused, as the two grown women ran around on the stage.

"I'm so happy I could do this for her," Johnny said. "She wants this so much, you know? To make it on Broadway. And I want to give her everything. I'll never forget what it was like when I had no money. I would have given anything to help fulfill her dreams, but I couldn't do anything for her. I'm just so goddamned grateful to have a rich family that can send her to school and give her all of this. Now, if only I could get Susie to move up to New York. She's in D.C. now, but she wants this every bit as much as Rosemary does."

Johnny was right. I could see it in Susannah's eyes. I found myself wanting to take a closer look at her, so I started walking toward the stage.

"This is *amazing*," Susannah said in a deliberately loud voice as she stood in the center of the stage. "Projecting," I believe it was called in theater-speak. Her voice reached all the way around the auditorium.

"You gotta try it out," Rosemary said, smiling next to her onstage. Susannah looked out into the auditorium, clearly tempted at the idea.

"Really?"

"Of course. Go for it," Rosemary told her.

"Okay, I gotta think about what to sing," Susannah said. She performed a few vocal warm-ups, and even that sounded good. Then she laughed and said to Rosemary, "I've got the perfect song."

Susannah whispered to Rosemary, who burst into laughter. "That's perfect. Do it, do it!" Rosemary stepped down from the stage so Susannah could have the spotlight.

Johnny and I took seats in the front row and gave her our full attention. Susannah was clearly at home on the stage; she displayed a commanding presence, even before she sang a single note. She took a deep breath, looked straight at Johnny, and proceeded to belt out a truly hilarious song about a guy named Johnny who could only sing one note. Johnny threw his head back and laughed, and even I couldn't help but smirk.

I couldn't take my eyes off Susannah as she strutted around the stage, singing about poor Johnny One Note. The song was obviously directed at my buddy, but I wished she was singing the song to me.

That thought took me utterly by surprise. It was a bit unsettling. Women never had this kind of effect on me. I was always the one who was cool and in control. Women came to *me.*

The song was a perfect choice, and not only because of the lyrics. It gave Susannah a chance to really show off her voice, especially during the parts where she got to belt out the actual one note that the Johnny in the song could sing. She had a tremendously powerful voice. She wrapped up her song with a dramatic flourish, and Johnny whistled and applauded. I clapped for her, too, and found I had to resist the urge to jump up and give her a standing ovation.

What the hell was wrong with me? I was not the jump-excitedly-out-of-my-seat type. I was wearing a five-thousand-dollar suit, for God's sake.

Susannah laughed and then took a gracious bow. I stared at her. I couldn't remember the last time I met a woman with such passion, such enthusiasm. This girl was a firecracker. I wondered what she'd be like in bed. My cock grew rigid thinking about it, and I was suddenly horny as hell. I had just gotten laid last night. Quite well, actually. The woman I picked up at the cocktail bar at my hotel had been incredibly flexible, and we'd had one hell of a night together. And yet, after watching Susannah strut sexily across the stage, I felt like I was in the middle of a sex drought.

I leaned over to Johnny and asked, "She's not *available*, is she?"

Johnny let out a sigh. He glanced up at Susannah on the stage and looked back at me. He took his time answering. "Technically, yes. She's single at the moment. But she just broke up with a guy she's been seeing for years and years. A doctor. Believe me, she's better off without him, but still, it's tough. They were supposed to get married."

"Wow," I said, still eying Susannah as she chatted happily with Rosemary on the stage.

"I mean, she's the one who broke it off. I think she's kind of over men at the moment, so it's probably not the best time to hit on her. Besides," Johnny said with a grin, "Rosemary would kill me if I let you turn one of her best friends into one of your conquests."

"Fair enough," I said, keeping my tone breezy and cool. Inside, I felt crushed. I wanted nothing more than to take Susannah back to my hotel where we could spend the rest of the day, and night, getting to know each other. All I could think of was seeing this incredibly exciting woman on her back, legs open, crying out my name in pleasure. I bit my lip to keep from moaning out loud.

I knew Johnny was right, though. I'd never want to hurt Rosemary. Or Susannah for that matter. She was likely in a vulnerable state due to her recent breakup. Besides, a vivacious, force-of-nature woman like her would probably want a passionate love affair when she was ready to date again. I never dated women seriously, but I never led them on, either. I always made sure my lady friends knew the score. Any girl who wound up in my bed knew it was just for fun. No commitments, no attachments.

Johnny and I stood up as Rosemary and Susannah walked down the steps from the stage.

"That was quite a showstopper, Susannah. Well done," I told her.

I wished I could have found a more eloquent phrase than *well done*. *Well done* best described a goddamned *steak*. Susannah's performance was more along the lines of *terrific, incredible, rousing*. That last word said it best.

"Thanks," Susannah said, blue eyes shining. She was practically glowing; electrified after performing. Obviously this was what she was born to do. "And that song is totally not true, by the way. Johnny is actually a terrific singer."

"Yes, that's what Rosemary says, too. I always assumed she was a tad biased," I said.

"No, he really is good. He used to sing *karaoke* all the time back in D.C.," Susannah told me, and I felt a little thrill when she looked me in the eye. After seeing her fantastic performance, I felt like a movie star was giving me personal attention.

I turned to Johnny, and then gestured up at the stage. "Well, get on up there, hot shot. Show us how it's done."

Johnny laughed. "No, no. I work behind the scenes. People like these two are the stars." He looked at Rosemary and Susannah with a grin.

Susannah drew in a deep breath, taking in the auditorium and the stage. "I just can't get over this place."

"Oh, you haven't even seen the best part yet. It's free now, right Johnny?" Rosemary asked.

He nodded. "Oh yeah. I made sure nobody was using it so Susie could have free rein."

"Yay," Rosemary said, clapping her hands excitedly. "Come on, follow me." She was speaking to Susannah, but Johnny and I followed her, too. I wondered what the next stop would be. It was hard to imagine what could top this beautiful auditorium.

Rosemary walked out into the hallway with Susannah right behind her. I seized the opportunity to check out Susannah's ass.

I was not disappointed.

Well, it might have been nice to see her wearing a tighter outfit so I could really see what she had to offer, but what I could see was impressive. She wore a flowing blue dress that showed more in front than in the back, which was fine by me. The blue of her dress set off her eyes, which were lovely. It was more than just the color, though. That look of excitement in her eyes as she toured the place was what really made her irresistible. Her enthusiasm was contagious.

Rosemary stopped in front of a door, then turned to Susannah and smiled. She used both hands to gesture dramatically at the sign on the door. It read, *Dance Studio*.

Susannah gasped. "Oh, no way."

Rosemary smiled. She flung open the double doors, giving us a wide view of the place.

I glanced briefly at the room, and then I turned to watch Susannah's reaction as she saw the dance studio for the first time.

Susannah stepped inside, looking a bit dazed at first. Then her light blue eyes opened wide as she scanned the room. The studio was huge—large enough to run several dance classes at once. The dance floor itself was made of high-quality polished wood, and a long mirror ran the length of the room. The mirror made the generously sized room appear even larger. The studio was located on a high floor, and the large bank of windows opposite the mirrored wall offered an incredible view of the city. From this height, even Brooklyn looked beautiful.

I never took my eyes off Susannah as she wandered around the room. She walked over to the mirrored side and reverently touched the bar attached to the wall. She turned around, and for a moment I was afraid she would catch me staring. She didn't. Instead, it was like she looked right through me, still entranced by the dance studio. Normally it would be a blow to my ego to have a woman ignore me, but Susannah looked so happy, that I didn't mind. I understood why Johnny was thrilled to be able to give Rosemary this theater space to fulfill all her dreams. I had only just met Susannah, but I suddenly had the powerful urge to give her everything she wanted.

We all watched Susannah in silence for a few moments. It

was incredibly touching to witness her quiet joy. Finally, she turned to Johnny and said, "This is so beautiful." She covered her mouth, and I saw tears glistening in her eyes.

Rosemary walked over to her and gently placed her hand on Susannah's back. "It's gorgeous, isn't it?"

Susannah nodded, and the two friends stood there for a moment. There was an unspoken understanding between them. It was like they were sharing their dreams without uttering a word. Rosemary let Susannah bask in the beauty of the place for a moment more, then spoke up.

"Girl, you know you have to try it out."

"Really?"

"Of course. You can do any dance you want, and I can find the music for you. The sound system is amazing."

"Wow," Susannah said, clearly thrilled at the idea of performing a dance in this incredible studio. "Lemme think a minute."

While Susannah thought about what dance she wanted to do, she started stretching a bit. It was a glorious sight to see. I hoped Rosemary and Johnny didn't notice that I was practically salivating as I watched their good friend stretch out her arms and her lovely long legs in preparation to dance. I swallowed hard when she flung her leg up on the bar attached to the wall. The mirror showed *everything*, including her white lace panties.

I jerked my head away and forced myself to look around the room. Good thing my suit jacket hid what was going on below my belt.

"Okay, I know what I want to do," Susannah said. "Do you have "Buenos Aires"?

"Girl, I can find you anything you want," Rosemary said. "What version? Elena Roger? Patti LuPone? Madonna?"

"Patti. *Obviously*," Susannah said.

Rosemary laughed and cued up the music. Susannah took

off her sandals and walked to the center of the dance floor. Again, I was impressed with her commanding presence; she even *walked* with confidence. It was clear to me that she was truly in her element on the dance floor. I couldn't wait to watch her dance.

The music began, and I found it vaguely familiar. Rosemary had mentioned Madonna, so I figured the song was from *Evita*. I'd seen the movie years ago but didn't remember much about it.

Susannah launched into her performance, and I was enraptured from the moment she began to move. Her ability to sing loud and with confidence while dancing so rigorously was astonishing. It was an up-tempo number, and she performed it with a dramatic flair that teemed with sexuality. The song basically said, Look out Buenos Aires because here I come.

I was captivated by her sensual performance. Hair flying, skirt fanning out, she *owned* that dance floor. It was dazzling to watch the radiant woman dance with wild abandon against the backdrop of this shining, polished studio. My heart pounded along with the music, and I was stunned to discover that I was panting as I watched her.

Literally. I was literally panting with desire.

I realized I had better get a grip before I made a complete fool out of myself in front of my friends, not to mention the most breathtaking woman I had ever set eyes on. I felt like one of those goofy cartoon characters with his tongue hanging out.

I straightened out my suit jacket in a vain attempt to look unaffected by Susannah's blazing sexuality on display before me. Just then, she spun around and happened to make eye contact with me. She smiled seductively, further fanning the flames of my desire. She twirled back around, continuing the song with lyrics that boasted about having "star quality." That was a vast understatement, as far as I was concerned.

I glanced over at Johnny, expecting him to be as spell-bound and aroused as I was, but instead he smiled at Susannah like she was his little sister. I shouldn't have been surprised. There was only one shining star for him—the pretty redhead for whom he'd built this paradise theater foundation.

I watched, mesmerized as Susannah completed the saucy number with a dramatic flourish. Johnny applauded and whistled, and I clapped as hard as I could. Susannah stood in the middle of the dance floor looking ravishing as she panted hard from the exertion of her dance. Once again, I conjured the image of her on her back, sweaty and panting after a vigorous romp in bed with me.

My mind whirred as I struggled to find the right words to tell her how magnificent her performance had been. It wasn't often that I was lost for words, but this time, I had no idea where to start.

"That was amazing, Susie," Johnny said. "Just amazing!"

Amazing? That's all you got?

Well, it was better than anything I could come up with as I stood there, frozen and tongue-tied.

"Come on, David. We should let the girls play. I'll show you the rest of the place."

That was the last thing I wanted to do. All I wanted was to stay and bask in Susannah's light.

The feeling was, apparently, not mutual as Susannah was busy chatting with Rosemary and hadn't even turned around to look at me.

Reluctantly, I followed Johnny out into the hallway.

I felt like I was losing my mind. I already felt empty without Susannah. I half-listened to Johnny as he showed me around the rest of the building. All I could think of was lovely Susannah and her beauty, talent, and passion. I was desperate to see her again, but Johnny had made it clear that dating her was out of the question. I tried to put her out of my mind, but it already seemed impossible. I'd always been a grounded, logical man. I didn't believe in idiotic notions like love at first sight.

Until now.

CHAPTER 6

I'd thought about Susannah Peters every single day for the last two months. I'd lost count of how many times I had jerked off just thinking about her stretching on the bar in front of that mirror. *Dear God.* It didn't seem to matter how many times I'd had sex with other women; Susannah was the only woman who really turned me on. I fantasized about her every time I had sex with somebody else. I couldn't stop thinking about how beautiful she looked onstage when she sang to Johnny. And that sensual, exotic dance she'd performed was burned into my memory. I'd never forget the way she made me feel when she made eye contact with me from the dance floor. I often wondered if she ever thought about me, or if I was just some guy she met once and immediately forgot about.

There were so many times I'd wanted to ask Johnny about her. Was she still single? Washington, D.C. wasn't that far from New York, and I'd have been glad to spring for a fancy car to bring her to me, any time. But how would I even go about it? I'd been wracking my brain to think of a way to reconnect with her, without coming off as either stalkerish or completely pathetic.

Then, one day out of the blue, Johnny casually mentioned that Rosemary's friend was moving to New York.

We were eating lunch at the usual steakhouse in Chelsea when he said it, and I had to take care not to choke on my filet mignon. My heart lurched in my chest, but I tried to play it cool. Rosemary had lots of theater friends, so it could be any one of them who was moving to New York.

I took a sip of scotch and asked as casually as I could, "Is this the same friend I met that day at the foundation?"

"Oh, yeah. That's right. I forgot you met Susie. Yeah, that's her."

Susannah is moving to New York.

"Do you know if she's seeing anyone?" Shit. So much for playing it cool. I'd been wondering about her for so long that I was desperate for answers. I honestly didn't know what I would do if Johnny said she was dating someone else.

Johnny eyed me curiously. "Really? You're still interested? I remember you asked about her when you first met her."

I suddenly felt quite vulnerable; like my feelings were exposed. I didn't do well with vulnerable. Or feelings, for that matter. Susannah had had me tied up in knots for months, which was unnerving to say the least. The last thing I needed was for my friend to know how I felt about her.

"She is one damned fine woman, Johnny," I said with what I hoped was a sly grin. "I don't think I'll ever forget the way she looked when she stretched out those luscious legs of hers. She's a dancer, so you know, she's gotta be flexible."

Johnny chuckled, which was the reaction I'd hoped for. It was easy for me to play the sex angle and make it seem like I was only interested in Susannah for her body. I remembered the passion in her eyes as she danced and sang, and a sharp bolt of guilt shot through me. Yes, I was aroused beyond all reason by Susannah, but for once in my life, it wasn't just a woman's body that made me crazy. It was her vivaciousness, her color, her light. I didn't think I'd ever regretted treating a woman as a sex object before, but now I felt terrible. Most of the women I bedded were lazy and with little ambition of their own. They were willing to put out because I was an attractive, wealthy man. Those women would do anything I wanted, so long as I kept doling out the cash. Susannah was different. She had her own ambition and drive. She was a strong, dynamic woman who had barely even glanced in my direction.

Which only made me want her more.

"Susie is beautiful, that's for sure." Johnny's words agreed with me, but his overall tone was still that of a proud big brother. "No, I don't think she's seeing anyone."

"When is she moving?" I asked, forcing myself to take another bite of steak. It was hard to pretend I wasn't screaming on the inside. *Tell me everything you know about Susannah Peters, goddammit.*

"Next week. She's moving into an apartment in Brooklyn, not too far from the foundation."

"Not exactly a safe area." I pictured Susannah walking around that awful neighborhood alone, and my heart sank.

"Tell me about it," Johnny said grimly. "I offered to get her a place. I told her she could even move into our luxury apartment building in Chelsea. She wouldn't bite. Wants to pay her own way."

I wasn't surprised. It was just as I had suspected; Susannah was a strong, driven woman who refused to be given a handout. It was kind of sexy, the notion that I couldn't buy my way into her bed. I remembered Johnny saying the same thing about Rosemary.

"She'll be working at the foundation as a teacher, though, and I plan on paying her *very well*," Johnny said in a firm voice, indicating he would not take no for an answer on that one.

"That's good," I said. "So, what do you say? Will you hook me up with her?"

Johnny grimaced. "I don't know, man. She's a good girl, ya know? Not exactly the type you usually hang around with."

I realize that. That's why I want her so badly.

"Besides," Johnny said as he stabbed his steak with his fork. "You don't seem to have had any problem finding women in New York."

I nodded. I was usually proud of my conquests, and I'd loved bragging to Johnny about the hot women I had bedded since I moved to the city. That was backfiring on me now, as it made me look like a bad fit for Susannah.

I let out a deep sigh, and Johnny looked up at me curiously. He'd probably expected me to let the whole Susannah idea go, but I couldn't.

"Look, can I level with you here?"

"Of course," he said, eyes wide.

I ran my fingers through my hair, hating that I had no choice but to explain myself. "The truth is, I haven't been able to stop thinking about Susannah since I met her. I know it sounds incredibly stupid to feel that way about somebody I just met, but I really think I'm falling for her."

I clenched my teeth so hard, my jaw muscles started to ache. How I abhorred having to admit something so personal out loud, but I knew it was the only way to get Johnny on my side. If he thought I was only out for sex with Susannah, he'd never help me pursue her. I forced myself to look into Johnny's eyes, fully expecting him to laugh in my face.

His gray eyes softened. "Of course it doesn't sound stupid. I felt the same with Rosemary. I mean, I was a total fucking dumbass and ignored her for three years when she worked for me, but when I got to know her outside of work it was a different story. Man, when I saw her perform onstage, I swear, it was like I fell in love right then. Something about seeing her onstage ..."

"I know. It's insane," I said, both relieved and frustrated at the same time. It was nice to know Johnny understood exactly where I was coming from, but it was still uncomfortable for me to feel this way. This never happened to me. I never developed real feelings for the women I dated. I liked sex, they liked money, so it was a win for everybody. With Susannah, I felt like a lovesick teenager.

"It's not a bad thing, David," Johnny said, an amused twinkle in his eye.

"It is if it doesn't work out." Susannah barely took notice of me that day. What if she was only interested in artsy-theater types? I could never be that kind of guy. Then again, she had dated a doctor for a long time. A doctor she eventually dumped. My jaw started aching again. I was making myself crazy.

"I can definitely help the two of you get together," Johnny said with a grin. "I gotta talk it over with Rosemary, though. I need to make sure she's on board with this whole thing."

"But she can't tell Susannah how I feel about her," I blurted out, sounding like a middle-schooler begging his friends not to tell a girl that he *like*-likes her.

"I'll ask her not to say anything, David. Look, tell you what. When Susie gets into town, I'll arrange for us all to have dinner. It won't be an official set up or anything. At least not as far as Susie knows. All four of us will go to dinner together and just kind of see what happens. That way, she can get to know you a little better with no pressure. Sound good?"

"Yes, that sounds great, Johnny. I really appreciate it."

Johnny looked at me for a moment, and then laughed.

"What?"

"Relax, dude. It's gonna be fine," he said.

I realized how tense I must have looked, so I relaxed my shoulders and let out a breath.

"Don't be afraid of your *feelings*, David. Let your love shine for the whole world to see!"

"Shut up, ya dick," I said, tossing a napkin at his face.

We both laughed. I took a healthy sip of my scotch.

"Just, you know, take it slow," Johnny said with a look of concern in his eyes. "It hasn't been that long since she broke up with the guy she thought she was gonna spend the rest of her life with."

I nodded. "I promise I won't pounce on her right away. I just want a chance with her."

"Cool," Johnny said with a grin. "Good luck."

He lifted his beer and we clinked our glasses.

Okay, I can do this. Susannah's still single, and Johnny will make sure I get a real shot with her.

The trick is not to blow it.

CHAPTER 7

I'm doing this. I can't believe I'm really doing this.

It was hard to wrap my mind around the fact that I was really moving to New York. Johnny had offered to fly me in first class, but I opted to take the bus instead. I wanted a genuine New York experience, and it just seemed more romantic to take the bus.

I did let him pay for my moving expenses, however. Johnny had arranged for a moving van to haul all my stuff to my new apartment in Brooklyn, which was perfect. That way, I was able to bring only my backpack and my purse on the bus, making it feel like a real adventure.

I could hardly believe that I was headed to the musical theater capital of the world where, for the first time in my life, I could focus entirely on performing. Between teaching at the foundation and preparing myself for auditions, my days would be consumed with all things theater. I was also excited to be moving so close to Rosemary. She would help me learn my way around the city, and we'd be there to support each other through this crazy journey.

The odd thing was that I didn't miss Carl *at all.* He was

like a tumor that was removed from my life with surgical precision, to use a metaphor from his line of work. Now that he was gone, I realized how toxic he had been. I no longer had to hide my enthusiasm for the things I was passionate about. Things he thought were stupid and a waste of time.

I gazed out the window as the bus rattled its way up I-95, through Pennsylvania and New Jersey. I reflected on Broadway's long and storied history, and how I would soon be a part of it. I wasn't naive enough to assume that I would actually get a part on Broadway, even though I wanted it with all of my heart. Even if I tried and failed, I would know I gave it everything I had. Giving up my life in D.C. and moving to New York was a huge step, but I knew I would never regret taking this chance. No matter what the outcome.

I saw the sign saying we had entered New York City, and that's when my tears finally spilled over. I had visited the city lots of times, but this time was different. This time, it would be my home.

Ready or not, Broadway here I come.

I drew in a deep breath and vowed not to take a single second of this incredible journey for granted.

I WAS fortunate enough to have two full weeks to run around New York before classes with my kids would start at The Creel Foundation for the Arts. Rosemary and I had an absolute blast. She showed me the best places to eat, shop, and she helped me figure out the NYC subway system. Of course, we walked up and down Broadway, looking up at the marquees in wonder. Neither one of us could quite believe we were *here.* I was beyond excited at the prospect of teaching theater all the time instead of having to teach regular school, and I was thrilled to see Rosemary fulfill her dream of getting her theater degree. In a way, I felt like my dreams had already come true.

I was looking forward to having dinner tonight with Johnny and Rosemary near their apartment in Chelsea. Some friend of theirs would be joining us, too, which was nice. I didn't know too many people in the city yet, so it would be good to make a new friend. As always, Johnny offered to send a car to pick me up, but I declined. He was already over-paying me to teach at the foundation, and that was all my pride could handle.

I arrived at the elegant Webber's restaurant in Chelsea at around 8pm. I drew in a breath as I took in the opulence of the place; crystal and fine china place settings, lace table-cloths, and dark wood tables. This was hardly the first time Johnny had treated me to a five-star meal, but I still hadn't gotten used to glitz and glamour of it all. Honestly, I hoped I never would. Johnny spoiled all his friends rotten, which was so sweet, but I never wanted to get used to such treatment. It would be all too easy to get lost in that world. Rosemary never seemed to be jaded, though, even after dating a billion-aire for several years. She was still the same sweet girl she always was.

"Hey there."

I turned as I heard Johnny's friendly voice. He grinned as he walked toward me.

"Wow, you look terrific!" Johnny looked me up and down approvingly. I was wearing a dark blue dress that brought out the blue in my eyes. It was nothing fancy, but it was the most extravagant dress I owned.

"Thanks," I said with a smile. "So do you."

He wore dress slacks and an expensive maroon-colored shirt, but it was the warmth in his gray eyes that made him so handsome. Like Rosemary, Johnny had gone out of his way to give me a warm welcome to New York, and I loved him for it.

"Right this way," he said as he led me toward our table.

My heart sank when I saw who Rosemary was sitting with.

Oh. It's that stuffy friend of theirs that I met at the foundation.

I felt guilty for being disappointed, but I'd hoped their friend would be somebody cool to hang out with. This guy—Daniel I thought his name was—seemed so snooty. He was wearing another super-expensive suit that probably cost more than my monthly rent. I plastered on a smile as I approached the table.

The guy stood up to greet me. It was gentlemanly of him, I'd give him that.

"Nice to see you again. Daniel, right?"

"David," he said, looking put out that I had forgotten his name. Sheesh, he really was wound tight. I remembered the way he'd tensed up when I dared to touch his arm last time. I was tempted to lean over and mess up that perfectly slicked brown hair of his, just to see what he would do.

"Oh. Sorry." I resisted the urge to shake my head in annoyance. I looked over at Rosemary and said, "Hey, girl."

Rosemary glanced at David, then smiled at me.

Johnny pulled out my chair, which was right next to Rosemary, and I got myself settled.

"Would you like a drink?" Johnny asked, his warm smile a stark contrast to David's coolness.

"That would be great. Thanks," I answered.

"The usual?"

"Please."

Johnny signaled the waiter and then ordered a Prosecco for me. I noticed that David was looking at me rather intently, which was a tad off-putting.

"Susannah," David said. "I must say, I was glad to hear that you moved to New York. Whatever you were doing in D.C. was a complete waste of your time."

"What?" I asked, not bothering to hide my shock at his rudeness. Seriously, what was with this guy?

"After seeing you sing and dance, it's obvious you belong in New York. With talent like yours, I wouldn't be a bit surprised to see you performing on Broadway in no time."

It took me a moment to process his words. The tension in my body relaxed a little. "Oh, that is so sweet of you to say. I forgot you saw me dance that day."

"I haven't forgotten about it," David said, still looking rather intense. "How could I? It was an incredible performance. The song was from *Evita*, no?"

"Yes," I said with a smile. I couldn't believe he remembered the song I had performed, and I was impressed that he knew what show it was from.

The waiter arrived and asked if we were ready to place our orders.

"I know what I want," Johnny said, then looked at the rest of us. "Guys?"

Rosemary and David said they were ready, but I hadn't a clue about what I wanted.

"Gosh, I haven't even looked at the menu yet," I said, feeling a bit flustered. I didn't want to hold everyone else up.

"Not a problem, Miss. I'll come back when you've decided," the waiter said in a friendly tone.

"No, no, that's okay. You guys go ahead and start ordering," I insisted while I quickly scanned the menu. Rosemary and Johnny gave their orders while I tried to decide what I wanted. I felt David's eyes on me the whole time, which was rather strange. I was tempted to look up and meet his gaze, but I resisted.

"The grilled pork with lime and salsa *verde* is terrific," David told me.

I glanced up at him with a smile. "It's funny; I was just looking at that. That sounds lovely." I looked up at the waiter and said, "I'll have that, please. Thank you."

The waiter nodded, and then looked at David.

"The same," David said.

He met my gaze, and I found it difficult to look away. He didn't smile, but that was no surprise. Unlike Johnny, he didn't seem like the warm, affectionate type. Still, there was a hint of gentleness in his dark brown eyes. I got the feeling there was a softer side to David, one that he didn't like to show. He studied me for longer than was comfortable, then finally broke eye contact when he reached for his scotch.

"This place is beautiful, Johnny," I said.

"It is gorgeous, isn't it?" Rosemary said, taking in the ambiance of the restaurant as if it were her first time there, though I knew it wasn't. She had grown up poor, and I knew she would never forget what that felt like.

"So, Susannah," David said. "How are you enjoying New York?"

"You can call me Susie," I said with a smile. "And I promise to call you David and not Daniel."

He nodded. Still no smile, but there was a twinkle of amusement in his eye.

"And to answer your question, I am absolutely loving New York. I still can't quite believe that I'm here." I could hear the excitement in my own voice.

"I know what you mean," Rosemary said. "It's been two years for me, and sometimes I still can't believe it."

"Have you started teaching at The Creel Foundation yet?" David asked.

"Not yet. I start Monday. I've spent a lot of time over the summer preparing my lessons and all that. I used to teach high school, but now I'll get a chance to work with some preteens and even some younger kids. I've always loved teaching, but I used to get restless having to teach English Lit and grammar and all of that. Now I'll get to teach theater-related stuff all the time. Dance lessons, singing lessons, acting, that sort of thing."

My heart did a happy flip as I said those things out loud. *I was living in New York to teach theater.* I'd never been so excited about anything in my life.

"I'm sure you'll be a wonderful inspiration to your students. You're passionate about theater, and that will shine through to your kids," David said, the warmth showing in his eyes again.

I was so touched by his words that I hardly knew what to say in response. It wasn't only his words that were moving; I felt like he really meant what he was saying, like this was more than just polite dinner conversation. I barely knew this guy, and yet he was already taking more of an interest in my life than Carl ever did.

"Thank you," I said, meeting his eye. "I hope you're right."

"You look beautiful when you dance, Susannah. I could tell simply by watching you that that's what you were born to do."

We gazed into each other's eyes for a moment, and I felt a strange connection to David.

After a long moment, I said, "Thank you for saying that, David. I really need to hear that. I just got out of a long-term relationship with a guy who thought theater was stupid and a waste of time."

"Well, he's a fucking idiot," David said so bluntly that it made me laugh. It was fascinating to see him get angry for once. He drew in a deep breath, straightened his suit jacket, and coolly took a sip of scotch in an effort to regain his composure. I was again tempted to reach over and mess up his hair.

"Yeah, I guess he was kind of an idiot," I said.

"Clearly, if he was dumb enough to let you go without a fight. He's obviously too dim to understand how brave performers are to express themselves so publicly like you guys do." David nodded in Rosemary's direction, and then looked back at me.

"Well, Carl's a doctor, so he figured saving lives was much more important than what I do. Hard to argue with that logic, I suppose," I said wearily.

"He might save lives, but people in the arts give people something to live *for*," David said.

Such a simple statement, yet so eloquently put. I had never thought of it that way, but he was right.

"That's a lovely sentiment, David. I agree," I told him.

We gazed into each other's eyes again, but this time I was more self-conscious. Poor Rosemary and Johnny hadn't gotten a word in edgewise since we'd sat down, and Johnny was footing the enormous dinner bill.

"I'm sorry, Johnny. I've been monopolizing the entire conversation," I said, reaching for my wine. I took a sip to give them a chance to talk.

"Ah, who cares," Johnny said with a grin. "I'm lucky enough to live with Rosemary, so I get to talk to her all the time." He reached across the table and took her hand in his. She smiled warmly at him, her pretty, green eyes filled with adoration. "And this guy," Johnny said as he jerked his head in David's direction. "I meet him for lunch all the time. So go on, talk!"

Johnny wasn't stupid. He could see that David and I were attracted to each other. It occurred to me that I didn't know for sure if David was single, but I then realized that he must have been. It finally dawned on me that it was no accident that Johnny had introduced the two of us.

"Well, you know a lot about me already," I said to David.

59

"Tell me about you. You used to live in D.C. too, right? What made you move to New York?"

"I plan on starting my own line of men's clothing."

"Oh, that sounds so cool. No wonder. You're certainly a very snappy dresser," I said. This particular line of conversation provided the perfect opportunity for me to check out David's body. I ran my eyes over the suit he was wearing. It was a dark blue with pinstripes—the perfect color to show off his dark brown eyes and dark brown hair. A renewed ripple of attraction went through me as I noted how broad-chested he was. I found myself wondering what he looked like underneath all those fancy clothes. I was fully aware that David watched me as I surveyed his clothing. He probably realized I was undressing him with my eyes, and I found I didn't care. It was fine by me if he knew I was attracted to him.

"Thanks," David said, looking a tad smug when I finally lifted my eyes from his terrific form.

"What kind of clothes do you want to make? Are you planning to design your own, or are you gonna hire people to do that?"

"I'm designing the clothes myself. Right now, I'm working on a bunch of sketches and ideas, and I'm working on getting some investors together."

"Nice," I answered. "So, I guess you're working on a line of super casual men's clothes, like T-shirts, shorts, and culottes, right?" I could tell by the way he was dressed that he wouldn't go near clothes like that, but I couldn't resist teasing him.

David slapped his hand over his heart dramatically. "Culottes? You *wound* me, woman."

I laughed heartily, and David's eyes twinkled. I'd even managed to coax a sexy partial smile from him.

"So I'm guessing it'll be men's suits, trousers, that kind of thing," I said.

"Precisely. I'm finishing up some suit and shirt designs now, and I've found some great fabrics over at the garment district. I should have several designs ready to go for Fashion Week."

"What's Fashion Week?" I asked.

David looked at me curiously for a moment, then I noticed his facial expression relax the tiniest bit. He seemed surprised and pleased that I was asking more questions.

"It's held twice a year in New York. February and September," David answered, eying me intently as he spoke. "It's technically about a week and half. It gives designers a chance to show off their collections to fashion buyers and the public."

"That sounds really exciting," I told him. David was hardly the excitable type, but I could see the interest gleaming in his eye. I recalled the way I felt on the bus ride to New York. I had cried like a baby just thinking about working toward my dream of being on Broadway. David clearly had a similar passion, even if he showed it in a completely different way. I found him more alluring by the moment. "Here's to your designs becoming a huge success."

I lifted my glass of Prosecco and he toasted me with his scotch. I was rewarded for my efforts with another sexy half-smile that made my knees go weak.

Our meals arrived, and Johnny and Rosemary joined the conversation a bit while we all ate. We talked about places to shop and eat in New York, and how things were going at the foundation. Throughout the meal, David and I stole glances at one other. A delicious tingle of excitement ... and arousal ... went through me every time he caught my eye. His calm and cool demeanor was annoying at first, but now it was utterly enthralling. I found myself thinking of all the things I could do to make him lose his cool.

Things like having sex with him.

Nobody could stay that calm and suave during sex, especially if it was good sex. I pictured David on his back in bed, naked, while I rode him. How thrilling it would be to watch that slick, controlled expression of his give way to pure ecstasy as I made him come.

My erotic thoughts made me feel flushed, as if everyone at the table could read my mind. I took off my wrap and placed it around my chair. I was overheated and needed a second to compose myself. I took a sip of wine and avoided David's gaze. It would be too embarrassing if I glanced at him only to see that smug look of his. Here I was fantasizing about making him lose his composure, but all it had done was get me hot and bothered.

The waiter cleared our dishes and inquired about dessert.

"Ladies?" Johnny asked, looking at Rosemary and then at me.

"No, I'm good. Thanks, honey," Rosemary responded.

"I don't think I could eat another bite, but thank you," I said.

"I'll bet you could eat more if you saw their French silk pie. It's delicious," David said to me.

"I doubt it. I'm already so full I can hardly move."

"Fine. I'll take a slice, and we'll see how long you can resist," David said so seductively that it made me blush.

"And I'll take a crème brûlée. Thanks!" Johnny said.

"Excuse me just a moment," I said, standing up. David did that halfway standing up thing that men sometimes do when a lady rises. I felt my knees go weak again. David's half-smile and half-stand made me absolutely *melt*. I swallowed, and it took a second to find my voice again. "Rosemary, do you know where the restroom is?"

Rosemary shot me a knowing look. "Yeah. I'll come with you."

The two of us hurried off to the ladies' room. The moment the door to the huge, fancy bathroom was shut, I turned to her and put my hands on my hips.

"Was this a fix-up?"

"Yes," Rosemary answered immediately.

I burst out laughing and Rosemary giggled with me. "Why didn't you tell me?"

"Because I was sworn to secrecy. By both of them."

"Really? You mean David knew?"

"Oh, yeah," Rosemary said with a smile. "It was his idea."

"You're kidding," I said.

"Apparently, you made quite an impression on him when he first met you at the foundation. He was glad to hear that you were moving to New York, and asked if Johnny would arrange a little get-together."

"Wow." A thrill went through me. I couldn't believe David had remembered me after all this time. I had forgotten all about him.

"Well, what do you think?" Rosemary asked, eyes wide.

"At first I thought he was totally weird."

"And now?"

I couldn't help grinning like an idiot. "Now he seems kind of wonderful."

"Oh, I'm so glad. It's funny. He and Johnny are tight, but I really don't know him all that well. This is probably the most time I've ever spent with him. He does seem like a great guy. He's a hell of a lot more supportive of you than Carl ever was."

"I know," I said, dreamily recalling how David had told me I was beautiful when I danced. "I love that. I admit I'm interested in him, but ..."

"But what?"

63

"I always thought I might go for a blue collar kinda guy after being with Carl so long. He was such a snob. And David, well, he seems kind of ..."

"Highbrow? Stuffy? Like he has a huge stick up his ass?"

I laughed. "Yes. Exactly."

"I understand. I always thought that way about him, too," Rosemary said. She glanced into the mirror and fluffed up her hair, then freshened her lipstick. She turned back to me. "I feel like I know him a little better after spending time with him tonight. He seems much nicer than I thought."

"I think so, too." Tingles of excitement fluttered in my stomach. I hoped David would officially ask me out before the night was over. The idea of being alone with him thrilled me.

By the time Rosemary and I got back at the table, dessert had arrived. Johnny was chowing down on his crème brûlée, but David hadn't touched his chocolate pie. He did the half-stand thing when I got to the table, and I smiled warmly at him.

"You've got to try at least a bite, Susannah," he said, gesturing at his dessert.

"Okay, if you're gonna twist my arm," I said. I picked up my fork and leaned over the table, offering him a shameless view of my cleavage. He took advantage of the opportunity, stealing a glance at my breasts before looking back at my face to watch me eat. I savored the bite, closing my eyes and letting out a low, sensual moan of pleasure. It wasn't like me to be so flirtatious, but David brought out that side of me. He'd made it clear that he found me attractive, and it had been a while since a man made me feel desirable.

"Delicious, isn't it?" David said, eyes twinkling. He offered me a sexy half-smirk before finally taking a bite of his own. "Go on, take more. You know you want to."

I leaned over and took another forkful. Even if it had

tasted like garbage, I still would have leaned over the table again, but it really was incredible. "Thanks." I moaned again when I took a bite, but this time it was unintentional. The rich chocolate was the most decadent dessert I'd eaten in a long time.

"I'm happy to share, but I'd be glad to get you your own, if you like," he told me.

"No, don't you see? Calories don't count if they come from somebody else's plate," I said with a sly grin.

"Ah, I see. Well, in that case, *bon appétit*."

"Thanks. Okay, one more bite. I swear. Then I'm done." I took my time leaning over to take one last forkful. It honestly was hard to stop because the pie was so good. I savored the last bite, then put the fork down in front of Rosemary. "Get this away from me. Save me from myself."

Rosemary giggled, then she used her own spoon to steal a bite of Johnny's crème brûlée.

After dessert, Johnny paid the tab and it was time go. A ripple of nervousness and excitement went through me because now came the moment of truth. Either David would ask if he could see me again, or I would go home and spend the rest of the night second-guessing myself and wondering if the intense attraction between us was all in my head.

We all stood up. I went over to Johnny first and gave him a big hug. "Thanks so much, Johnny. This was wonderful."

He hugged me warmly and said, "Any time, Susie. Is it pointless for me to offer you a ride home?"

I nodded. "I appreciate it, though. I'm good with the subway."

Johnny sighed and nodded, knowing I was just as stubborn as Rosemary when it came to being pampered. She'd arrived at the restaurant by subway because of an earlier audition, but she would go home with Johnny in his limo. It was a good compromise, I thought.

65

"I'll make sure she gets out safely," David said, as the two men exchanged knowing looks.

After I gave Rosemary a hug, David and I were finally alone. I picked up my wrap from the back of my chair and headed toward the exit, acutely aware that he was following close behind. When I got to the door, I took a moment to put my wrap on.

"Here. Allow me," David said, taking it from me. I delighted in the simple touch of his fingers on my arms.

Once I had my wrap on, I looked up at him; he was a good head taller than me. He gazed down into my eyes for a long moment. Then, before I knew what was happening, his lips were on mine. His kiss was slightly more forceful than I was used to, but it was powerful and electrifying. Heat surged through my body as I relished the longest first kiss I'd ever had. David eventually lifted his lips from mine and regarded me with an expression of sheer confidence and poise. I'd wanted it as much as he had, and he damn well knew it.

"I promised Johnny I wouldn't pounce on you right away. I guess I lied."

"I guess you did," I said, breathless.

"My limousine is waiting outside. I can take you home."

"Oh. Oh, I—I don't know, David." He was a dear friend of Johnny's, so I knew I could trust him to get me home safely. I just didn't want to give him the wrong idea. I found him irresistibly attractive, but I wasn't about to go to bed with him on the first date.

I saw that subtle hint of gentleness in those dark brown eyes again, and he seemed concerned that I was uncomfortable.

"Only a ride home, Susannah. A chance to spend more time with you, and to make sure you get home safely. I'll worry about you all night if you take the subway."

"Oh, that's so sweet of you." The idea of spending time alone with him in the back of a limo was simply too much to resist. "That would be lovely."

He snapped his head in a sharp nod, pleased with my decision. He walked ahead so he could open the door for me. Sure enough, a sleek black limousine was double-parked just outside. Before approaching the car, he turned to me.

"Don't get me wrong. I would take you to bed in a second, but not until you're ready."

I stared into those rich brown eyes that were filled with unwavering self-confidence. He spoke as if my having sex with him was a foregone conclusion. Which it probably was, but definitely not tonight. Tempting as it was, I needed more than a brief double-date with David before sharing my body with him. Besides, I'd been with the same man for years; being with someone new would take some getting used to.

David approached the limo and the driver stepped out. I had expected an older man—somebody like Alfred from Batman or something—but this guy was maybe thirty-five or so. He had light brown hair and friendly blue eyes.

"Stewart," David said in a commanding voice that was slightly too bossy, yet sexy at the same time. "We're going to give Ms. Peters a ride home. Susannah, you can give him your address, and he should be able to find it on the GPS."

"Hi, Stewart. It's nice to meet you," I said, offering my hand. Stewart looked surprised that I had spoken to him, but graciously smiled and shook my hand.

"Very nice to meet you as well, Ms. Peters."

I was about to tell him to call me Susie, but he spoke again before I could. "May I have your address, please?"

"Sure. I'm sorry. It's all the way in Brooklyn."

"No problem at all, Miss," Stewart said, sounding like he meant it.

I gave him the address. He didn't write it down, but

simply nodded. Then he opened the limo door and helped me inside.

David followed me and took a seat at the back of the limo. "Sit wherever you're comfortable, Susannah."

I knew I should choose the seat right next to David, but I wasn't ready to, for some reason. If I sat next to him, we would start kissing again, and I might end up going farther than I intended. In my heart, I knew I wouldn't have sex with him yet. Still, it was all too easy to imagine myself on my back on the floor of the limo with my legs wrapped around this gorgeous hunk of a man.

I chose to sit on the side seat. He looked more amused than offended that I was sitting so far away from him.

The limo started to move, and I looked out the window for a moment, acutely aware that David was watching me.

"So," he began, and I turned in his direction. "I did have an ulterior motive for giving you a ride home."

David's tone was serious, but it was always serious. I wasn't worried.

"Is that so?" I asked.

"I want you to sing for me." It sounded like a command. I found myself a tad annoyed.

"Is that an order? Payment due for a ride home?"

He must have heard the irritation in my voice because I saw that tenderness his eyes again. "Of course not. It's a request. I want to hear your lovely voice again. Will you sing for me?"

My heart melted as I gazed into his eyes. When Carl was around I sang all the time. At home, in the car, wherever. He never even lifted his head. Of course, I wasn't singing just to entertain my man. I sang because I loved to sing. Still, it would have been nice if Carl had noticed once in a while and told me I sounded good. He never did.

"I'd be happy to sing for you."

"Good." He reached over, pressed a button, and the privacy screen up front lowered. "Stewart. You're in for a treat. Ms. Peters here is a professional singer, and she's agreed to grace us with a song."

I watched Stewart's kind blue eyes in the mirror, and I could tell he was smiling. "Sounds wonderful."

I thought it was kind of sweet that David wanted Stewart to hear me perform, and I certainly never minded having an audience.

"What would you like me to sing?" I asked David.

He carefully considered my question. After a long moment, he said, "Why don't you sing something that expresses how you feel about being a theater performer?"

I stared at him in wonder. That was probably the most beautiful song request I had ever gotten.

"Okay," I said softly. "I know a good one." The words to the song were exquisite; they truly expressed what it felt like when I performed. "You've heard of *Billy Elliott*, right?"

"The movie about the little boy who did ballet?"

"Yeah, that's the one. They did a Broadway musical version of it, and there's this incredibly beautiful song that he sings when somebody asks him what it feels like while he's dancing."

"Sounds perfect," David said. As usual, he didn't smile, but he looked intrigued.

I did a few quick vocal warm-ups to get myself ready, and then began to sing. Oh, how I loved this song. The lyrics were perfect, and they expressed the passion I felt about performing better than any words I could ever find myself. And, of course, singing was one of the best ways I had of expressing myself.

The song talked about how dancing—dancing and singing, in my case—is like hearing a special music in your head. Like an explosion within you, and sometimes it feels like flying. It was like being angry, scared, and confused, all mixed up, and mad as hell at the same time. My favorite line explained that it was the way you feel when you've been crying—empty and full all at once.

David never took his eyes off me. I met his gaze as I sang, and I had a feeling deep in my soul that he truly understood my passion for performing. He may not have been the emotional, artistic type, but somehow, he understood anyway.

I sang with all the emotion and fervor I possessed, using my hands and arms to dance as much as I could while sitting down. I focused on David most of the time, but I occasionally checked on Stewart as I performed. His eyes, in the rearview mirror, looked soft and sweet. His boss was forcing him to listen, but he seemed to genuinely enjoy my song.

The song's finale came when I sang about simply feeling *free* when performing. I studied David's reaction when I sang that last note.

First, he pressed the button to roll up the privacy screen. He was silent for a moment, and then he said, "That was absolutely stunning, Susannah. Thank you."

I smiled warmly at him. Like any performer, I constantly craved attention, and in that moment, David's attention was all the mattered to me.

"Can I come sit by you?" I asked.

Cracking that half-smile of his, David said, "Of course."

He reached out and helped me move over next to him on the back seat. I breathed in his sexy, and probably quite expensive cologne. The way he dressed and spoke and smelled, David was just so *manly.*

David wasted no time. He placed his huge hands on my face, then dipped his head down for another forceful, highly charged kiss. As I lost myself in the sheer bliss of feeling his lips claim mine, I had the most magnificent realization.

He's turned on by my talent.

All the other men in my life had merely tolerated my zeal for performing, but David was aroused by it. I was suddenly grateful that I had performed "Buenos Aires," an exotic and somewhat sultry song and dance number, on the day David first laid eyes on me. Had he been this turned on then? Was that why he asked Johnny and Rosemary to set him up with me?

Oh, David.

Kissing passionately, I couldn't say the words out loud, so I settled for a sensual moan instead. I ran my hands all over his broad chest, feeling the crisp fabric of his finely tailored suit. I slid my hands under his jacket to feel his arms. David looked dapper and refined in his suit, but I wished I could touch his bare skin instead.

David brushed my hair out of the way to kiss the sensitive skin on my neck. I shivered at the sensuality of his touch. He kissed farther down my throat and made his way close to my left breast. I tensed up ever so slightly. It wasn't that I wanted him to stop; I loved what he was doing. But I hadn't changed my mind about going to bed with him. It was too soon for me.

He must have sensed my hesitation because he stopped short of kissing my breast. His lips traveled upward and found my mouth again. I ran my fingers through his hair as we kissed. I moaned again, deep in my throat. I started to wish I *was* the kind of girl who slept with a guy on the first date.

The limo began to slow down and then stopped. I glanced out the window and saw we had arrived in front of my apartment building in Brooklyn. I broke off the kiss and sat back a bit. My eyes darted toward the door of the limo, worried that Stewart would open it and find us both in an awkward and disheveled state.

"Stewart won't get out of the car until I tell him," David informed me.

"Oh," I said breathlessly. I straightened out my blouse and my hair, trying to pull myself together. I was soaking wet between my legs, and I figured David must be uncomfortably hard between his. "I—I'm sorry."

"Sorry for what?"

I looked at the window of my apartment and then back at him. "I feel like such a tease. I know I should invite you in, but you know, I'm just not …"

David's eyes softened. "I wanted to get you home safely, Susannah. Hearing your beautiful voice and being able to kiss your lovely lips were extra bonuses for me. Nothing further is expected."

I let out a breath and nodded.

Then he added in a husky voice, *"Desired,* but not expected."

I desire you too, David. I probably should have said that out loud, but I couldn't seem to find my voice.

"Just tell me I can see you again, Susannah. As soon as possible. May I take you to dinner tomorrow?"

I was pleased to note he'd already learned that ordering me to do something wouldn't work. I was sure his wealth had other women eating out of his hand, but not this woman. I didn't care how rich he was; I was never going to come running when he snapped his fingers. A simple "please" and "thank you" would go a long way with me.

"That would be lovely, David. Thank you," I said with a smile. I leaned over to kiss him again. His lips were warm and inviting. The kiss went on longer than a goodnight kiss should have, and I was breathless again by the time I broke it off. I pictured my vibrator sitting in my bedroom drawer, knowing I would need it tonight to relieve some of my sexual tension.

"Goodnight, David," I said reluctantly.

"Goodnight," he said. He pressed another button and within seconds, Stewart had the limo door open for me. He took my hand and helped me step outside.

"Thank you so much, Stewart."

"My pleasure, Miss."

Stewart stood outside the limo, keeping watch over me until I was safely inside.

CHAPTER 8

I sat at a table alone, nervously sipping scotch and waiting for Susannah's arrival.

Nervous. I was actually *nervous*. I never felt that way, especially around women. I was used to being the one in control, but Susannah Peters had me feeling completely off balance. The girls I dated usually did whatever I commanded, knowing I would take them on a shopping spree and give them anything they wanted. They treated me like I was a royal prince with enough money to sweep them off their feet and whisk them away to my palace. For the night, anyway.

Susannah didn't take orders from me, and I found that exciting beyond all measure. I never realized how boring those other girls were, before I met her.

There was a downside, however. It had been quite some time since I had gone home to an empty bed after a date. I'd had to take care of my own needs last night, and it was a tad unnerving how quickly I came once I started jerking off while thinking about her. I prided myself on my stamina and endurance in bed; women were usually amazed at how long I lasted. I figured if they weren't sore afterward, I hadn't done my job. But last night Susannah had me so riled up, I'd barely touched my dick and I had an orgasm within seconds. *Seconds.* It was barely ten minutes later, and I was ready to try again. It was rather pathetic, frenetically rubbing myself in the shower like some horny teenager. I couldn't help it. *She was making me crazy.*

It wasn't only my uncontrollable attraction to Susannah that had me feeling so unbalanced. We hadn't known each other long, yet I cared deeply for her already. That never happened to me, either. I met a woman, picked her up, we fucked at my place, then I went and bought her pretty things so I could fuck her again. That was how I operated. I never got *attached* to the girl.

Susannah had wanted to take the subway here, but I already felt fiercely protective of her. The thought of her on that filthy subway was unbearable. She was a strong, independent woman, but she was small in stature and no match for a mugger. Or worse. So I managed to talk her into letting Stewart pick her up, arguing that she would be all dressed up and wouldn't want to get dirty by navigating the subway.

I sipped my scotch, scanning the room for her. I'd had a meeting nearby earlier, which was why I got here first. Once again, I felt like a pathetic, horny teenager waiting for a girl to show up. I shook my head, then drank more scotch. I needed to get a grip already.

My heart seized in my chest as I saw Susannah enter the restaurant; she was arm-in-arm with another man. After a moment of blind panic and unbridled rage, I realized it was Stewart. He must have walked her into the restaurant to make sure she found me.

Good God. So much for getting a grip.

I stood, and Susannah sent a dazzling smile my way. She

turned to thank Stewart, then headed toward me. I swallowed hard. She was resplendent in her short black cocktail dress and high heels. I couldn't help picturing that cocktail dress in a heap on my bedroom floor.

"You look lovely," I told her as I took her hand and kissed it.

"Thank you. And you look terrific," she said, taking in my dark blue Emporio Armani suit.

Susannah looked up at me, and I bent down and gently kissed her lips. It was unlike me to display affection in a public place, but I couldn't resist. I pulled out her chair, and she sat down.

Taking my seat across from her, I watched her get settled. She put her purse down and took off her wrap, revealing the plunging neckline of her dress. I bit my lip and fought the urge to moan out loud.

I quickly composed myself and drained the last of my scotch. The waiter arrived at my side almost instantly.

"Shall I get you another?" he inquired.

"Yes. And a Prosecco?" I asked, looking to Susannah for her confirmation.

"Yes, please," she said. After the server walked away, she said, "Thanks for remembering what I like to drink."

I'd called ahead to make sure we got a table right by the window, as the restaurant offered an incredible view of the city. Lansbury's Restaurant was located on the 12th floor, and the city positively glowed from this height. I watched Susannah as she admired the view. She appeared to be lost in the wonder of it all; it was refreshing to see her enthusiasm.

"This is beautiful, David. Thank you so much for bringing me here," she said, focusing her pretty, blue eyes on me. Perhaps I was imagining it, but she seemed to bestow upon me the same look of wonder she had for the city of New York.

"It's absolutely my pleasure, believe me."

She smiled at me, then picked up the menu. She scanned it for a moment or two, appearing a tad overwhelmed. A wave of affection washed over me; she was so unlike the other women I dated. She wasn't used to being pampered like this.

"Find something you like?" I asked.

"I'm trying to find something I *recognize*," she responded.

"I'll help you. What are you in the mood for? Steak?"

"No, I don't eat much red meat."

"Do you like fish?"

"Yeah."

"All right then," I said, getting up from my seat. I walked behind her and looked at her menu, putting my hand on her bare shoulder as I did. "This one here? That's halibut. That's salmon, and this one is yellowfin tuna."

"I wish you could order by number like at McDonald's," Susannah said dryly.

That got a chuckle out of me, which was no easy feat. She was adorable.

"Okay, I want this one," Susannah said, pointing to the perilla seed-crusted yellowfin tuna, with sumac, red wine, and port sauce.

"Excellent choice, madam," I said, squeezing her shoulder before returning to my seat.

The server returned with Susannah's wine and another scotch for me. I placed our order, and Susannah appeared to be relieved that she didn't have to say anything. I loved the idea of spoiling her rotten, and I hoped someday she would be more comfortable in my world. Johnny had said it had taken Rosemary a bit to adjust, but she was doing well now.

I watched Susannah's eyes as another waiter passed by with a tray full of artfully presented food. She looked at me and asked, "Do you ever just eat plain old pizza?"

"No."

"Hmm. We'll see about that."

It sounded like a challenge. I liked challenges.

"So, how was your meeting?" Susannah asked before taking a sip of her wine.

"It went pretty well," I said, figuring she was making polite conversation and didn't really care how it went.

"What was the meeting about?"

"Just meeting with a potential investor, that's all."

"Someone who might invest in your new design business?"

I nodded.

"That's good. So, you think it went well?" she persisted, and it seemed as if she genuinely wanted to know.

"Yes, I believe it did. I showed him my sketchbook and some samples, as well as some swatches of the fabric I plan to use. He seemed interested in what I presented. Said he'd have to check with his business partner, but he was impressed with my designs and seemed optimistic about my chances of success."

Susannah's beautiful eyes opened wide. "That's so exciting!"

"Yeah, it is," I said with a hint of a smile. The meeting had gone even better than planned. I'd worked hard on those designs, and it was always scary to put work out there for others to critique. It had been truly gratifying to get high praise from an investor, and it meant a lot to me that Susannah cared enough to ask about it.

"Takes a lot to get you excited about anything, huh?" Susannah observed, shaking her head. I was excited, I just didn't like to show it.

"You get me excited, Susannah," I said with a raised eyebrow.

She smiled, then gazed seductively into my eyes. I didn't want to pressure her, but I wondered exactly how long she was going to make me wait until we could have sex.

"How is life in the theater?"

"Glorious," Susannah said in a breathy voice. "I've gotten to use The Creel Foundation space a lot in the last few weeks, and it's been incredible. That huge stage, and oh, that *beautiful* dance studio!"

Susannah's face radiated with pure joy. I pictured her in the dance studio, recalling the sexy number she had done the day I met her. Watching her dance had been incredibly erotic, and it wasn't just her lovely dancer's body and sultry performance. It was the unmitigated passion and drive she displayed while performing. The same passion that shone in her eyes now. I hoped to God that her dream of performing on Broadway would come true someday, and I found myself wondering if there was anything I could do to help. Use my money to get some Broadway producer connections or something.

"Tomorrow is my first day actually teaching at the foundation. I can't wait. I can't get over the fact that I can teach theater all the time."

"You're going to be a magnificent teacher, Susannah."

"Thanks," she said. "I do love it. It's always so rewarding to teach kids and watch them grow up. I used to teach high schoolers, and I cried at every single graduation ceremony."

She had a look of tender wistfulness as she spoke of her students. Her dedication to those kids endeared her to me even more.

We chatted all through dinner, never running out of things to say. It was the longest time I had spent on a date with a woman in years. With other women, I usually sprung for the obligatory dinner and a shopping spree before moving the party to the bedroom. But Susannah was such a pleasure to talk to. She was intelligent and animated, and had interests of her own that weren't related to spending my money. And she *listened* to me. I hadn't realized how little I tended to talk about myself before, and it was because no one ever *asked*. Susannah asked me thoughtful questions and cared about my responses.

The server arrived to clear our plates, and I asked Susannah, "Shall I order a dessert for you to steal?"

"No, thanks. I can't keep eating like this if I want to retain my dancer's body."

The mere mention of her body made my cock go rock hard. It wouldn't be easy keeping my hands off her once we were alone in the car. I found myself fantasizing about spreading those shapely dancer's legs of hers and just taking her right there the floor of the limo.

I settled the bill, and then asked her, "What do you want to do next?"

I was willing to do whatever she wished, but all I could think about was getting her alone in the limo. I knew I wouldn't really have sex with her there, even if she agreed to it. Not for our first time together, anyway. Susannah was a classy lady, and I planned on making love to her in my comfortable bed in my posh penthouse. That was what she deserved.

"I want you to take me shopping," Susannah said decisively.

I didn't know what disappointed me more; the fact that she hadn't even hinted at sex, or that she wanted to go shopping like every other woman I knew.

I put on my best poker face and replied, "Sure. I'll buy you anything you want."

I certainly didn't mind indulging her, and I wanted her to

have everything she desired. Still, I couldn't help but be disappointed at her request. Our date had been so unlike any other I'd ever had, but it seemed it would end the way all my dates ended. With me buying her clothes, shoes, jewelry, and whatever else caught her eye.

"No, not shopping for *me*. Shopping for *you*," Susannah said with a sweet smile.

"What?"

"I want you to take me to some of your favorite men's clothing shops in the city. You're always dressed to kill, so I know you must go to those places all the time. Plus, I'm sure you're always poring over the clothes to get ideas for your designs and to check out the competition. You've seen me in my world—the theater, and now I want to see you in yours."

I was utterly dumbfounded.

Her simple request was the sweetest thing anyone had ever asked of me, and I felt an actual lump in my throat. As always, I composed myself before answering.

"Sure. If that's what you want."

"It's definitely what I want," she assured me.

I walked over and held out my hand to help her up.

"Then let's go," I said, feeling an excitement that I didn't dare show on the surface.

Once we were in the limo, Susannah alternated between making out with me and looking excitedly out the window. Her enthusiasm was so endearing that I didn't even mind when she got distracted by something outside.

As we drove through the streets of Manhattan, I pointed out several spots where famous movies had been filmed. She eagerly looked out the window each time like an excited child. She was so different from me in that regard. I rarely got all worked up over anything, but her enthusiasm was a joy to behold.

"See that there?" I asked, pointing out the window at the Macy's department store in Herald Square. "That's where they have the Thanksgiving Day Parade."

"Really? Oh, that is so cool. I watch that every year on TV!" Susannah's eyes got wide as she peered out at the landmark department store. She looked at me and giggled. "I'm sorry. I'm acting like some dumb tourist, aren't I?"

"Not at all. I like seeing you enjoy yourself."

"I am. I really am," she said with a smile. She shook her head in wonder. "How did I get here?"

"What do you mean?"

"I just keep thinking how in the hell did I get here? Living in New York, so close to Broadway. Teaching theater for a living. In this limo with you."

"I don't know how you got here, I'm just grateful you did."

"Me too," Susannah said as she leaned in for another kiss.

The limo slowed to a stop, and we took a moment or two to compose ourselves before stepping out of the car.

Our first stop was Barney's New York, on Madison Avenue. Stewart helped Susannah out of the limo, and I got out behind her and watched her face. She took a deep breath and surveyed the busy street. She looked exhilarated, which was exactly how she made me feel.

After giving her a moment to take in the sights, I took her hand and led her toward the store.

"Thanks, Stewart," Susannah called over her shoulder as we walked away. I chuckled inwardly. She was way too polite to be a New Yorker. She'd learn, eventually.

As we walked through the store, we saw plenty of gorgeous dresses, blouses, skirts, and other women's clothing. "Let me know if you see anything you like. Anything at all, and I'll be happy to get it for you."

"That's so sweet, David. Thank you."

I half-expected her to abandon the whole idea of looking

at men's clothing with me once she caught sight of the women's clothing and shoes, but she didn't. She took in the whole atmosphere of the store as we walked, but she never made a move to get a closer look at anything for herself. She held my hand and followed my lead, so I took her to the men's department.

The salesclerk glanced up at me and smiled. "Let me know if I can help with anything."

"I sure will," I responded.

The usual sales lady, Amy, knew I didn't need help, because I came in here frequently to look and sometimes to buy. I knew exactly where everything was and needed no assistance. Even so, I always used her name when making a purchase, so she would get credit for the sale. She was knowledgeable and attentive to my needs, so she deserved the commission, whether she happened to assist me on a specific purchase or not.

Susannah let go of my hand and began wandering around, looking at all the men's suit jackets, trousers, and ties. She stopped to admire a mannequin dressed in wool two-button suit.

"Oh, this one is beautiful," she murmured. She took a peek at the label and then exclaimed, "Oh, it's Armani!"

"Yes, this is a nice one. Classic fit, flap side pockets, lined with silky plain-weave."

Susannah rubbed the sleeve between her fingers. "This fabric is amazing. It even *feels* expensive. How much does this go for?"

"About three grand."

Her eyes opened wide. "Dear God." She let go of the suit sleeve like she was afraid she would damage it. "I've heard of Armani suits, but I've never seen one up close."

"Sure you have," I said, holding out my arms and showing off the suit I was wearing.

Susannah smiled and walked over to me. She ran her hands over my sleeves. The trouble with wearing a suit was that there were multiple layers of clothing between her delicate, feminine fingers and my skin. I imagined what it would feel like to have her unbutton my shirt and run her fingers across my chest. Even better, I imagined her unzipping my pants.

"Tell me about this suit," she said, admiring the way I looked in it.

The corner of my mouth turned up in a partial smile. I was proud of my wardrobe, but nobody ever asked me about it.

"This is an Emporio Armani. Made in Italy."

"What's it made of?"

"Wool, mostly. The inner lining is made of cupro. Cupro is a kind of rayon that's made from cotton linter."

She smiled at me, looking impressed with my knowledge. "What is cotton linter?"

"It's a downy kind of fiber you get from around cotton seeds."

Susannah nodded. "And the rest of the suit is just wool?"

"Yes. Mostly virgin wool."

"And what is virgin wool?"

"It's exactly what it sounds like. It's wool that has never been used before. It didn't come from recycled yarn."

Susannah tilted her head. "So, if it's never been used before, it's automatically better? More precious, more valuable?"

"Oh, yes. Definitely. It should be fresh and unspoiled. Virgin wool is the best. What man would want anything to do with old, used wool? A man needs something he can claim entirely as his own; something no man has ever worn before."

"Is that right?" Susannah said, narrowing her eyes.

I gazed at her, amused. "Absolutely right. Virgin is best. Period."

She stared at me.

I arched an eyebrow and said, "It's *wool*, Susannah."

Susannah threw back her head and laughed. She opened up my suit jacket and ran her fingers along the soft, silky lining. "Cupro, huh? Very nice."

She let go of my jacket, then wandered around the men's department for a bit. She asked lots of questions about the brand names, the materials, and the prices. The cost of each article of clothing never failed to surprise her. I had been around wealth my entire life, but I could see how it might be quite a shock to see how the other half lived. I wondered if she thought it a terrible waste to spend so much money on clothing, especially when she was about to start work teaching underprivileged children. If she did think that, she didn't say it. I didn't feel like she was judging me.

I was pleased at how much time she spent in the men's department with me. Susannah should have been bored out of her mind looking over men's clothes, but she wasn't. The fact that I was interested in the topic seemed to be enough for her.

Once we'd finished with Barney's men's department, Susannah said, "So where to next?"

"Where do you want to go?"

"You tell me. Take me to another one of your favorite stores."

I studied her for a moment. "You're an amazing woman, Susannah."

She laughed, then took my hand and we walked through the store. Her eyes got big as we walked past the shoe department—the same one she had ignored on the way in.

"Do you want to look?" I asked her.

"Do you mind terribly?"

"Of course not," I said, and I meant it.

Susannah spent a few minutes poring over Barney's shoe selection, and she found two pairs that she fell in love with. I insisted she let me buy them for her.

"Thank you, David." She stood on her tiptoes and kissed me, and then smiled as she looked at me. "These shoes are so cute!"

She squealed with excitement, and I loved that I could make her happy. Sure, she was spending my money, but she didn't make me feel like a human ATM, like other women did.

We left Barney's and visited two more stores: Blooming-dale's, and then Desmond's—a men's boutique shop near my penthouse on Park Avenue. At Bloomingdale's, I asked Susannah if she wanted to visit the women's clothes or shoes department, but she declined. At both stores, the sales clerks greeted me by name.

"Good evening, Mr. Groff," said Richard, the salesman at Desmond's.

"Good evening," I responded.

Susannah and I wandered through the store and studied the suits on display.

"It's funny how everyone knows you, David," she said with a smile.

I nodded. "Yes. I come to these stores a lot, and it's always a good idea to get to know the staff. It's important to develop a personal relationship because that makes it more likely that they'll be willing to carry my designs someday."

Susannah looked at me. "Can you imagine? It would be so exciting to see your name on a fancy label with all these others. Giorgio Armani, Gucci, Saint Laurent, and David Groff."

"It would be pretty cool," I said as casually as I could, feeling nervous excitement in my stomach. It was both intimidating and thrilling to try to compete with some of the world's most famous designers. I'd spent of lot of time fantasizing about what it would feel like to see my own designs in a store, and it was like Susannah completely understood how I felt.

I nodded to Richard on the way out, as Susannah and I headed toward the limo. We'd had a terrific evening together, and now the moment of truth was at hand.

Was Susannah ready to have sex?

Stewart helped Susannah into the limo, and she sat right next to me. The privacy screen was up, and the car didn't move; Stewart was waiting for me to tell him where we were headed next. And *I* was waiting for Susannah to tell *me*.

"So where to now, Susannah?"

She bit her lip and took her time answering. "Well..."

I was disappointed that she didn't seem as eager to share my bed as I was. We'd had such an intense connection from the start, and we were incredibly hot for each other. Still, I didn't want her going home with me until she was really ready.

"It's all right if you're ready to go home, Susannah."

She looked relieved. "Oh, David. I'm so sorry. It's just that tomorrow is my first day at the foundation, and I'm a little nervous. I want to get a good night's rest, you know?"

"Of course. I understand."

"Besides," she said, leaning close and brushing her finger across my lips. "I don't want to rush. I want ... I *need* to take my time with you."

Susannah looked at me with a sultry gaze that set my whole body aflame. She had an excellent point; we didn't want to do it when she was feeling rushed or stressed. Those blue eyes, filled with desire, told me everything that I desperately needed to know. *She wanted me as much as I wanted her.* It simply wasn't the right time.

I pressed the button to talk to Stewart. "I'd like to take Ms. Peters home now."

"Sounds good, Mr. Groff."

With any luck, next time I would be telling him to take Susannah and me back to my penthouse on Park Avenue.

CHAPTER 9

J snuggled close to David in the limo, hoping he understood why we couldn't spend the night together. At this point I was ready to be intimate with him, even though it was sooner than I usually went to bed with a man. I normally dated a guy for at least a few weeks before having sex with him, but it was different with David. I was already serious about him, and I got the feeling he felt the same way. He was hard to read sometimes, but I was getting better at picking up his subtle clues. He wasn't particularly expressive about his emotions, but the arch of his eyebrow and that sexy half-smile he let slip occasionally, gave him away.

He seemed happy that I wanted to learn more about his design business, and I loved spending time with him and hearing him talk about his hopes and dreams. He never gushed about all the things he wanted to accomplish, but I felt honored when he shared little details about his designs and plans for his business. I got the feeling that it was a big step for him.

I snuggled closer to him and felt his body relax. David's

physical aloofness took some getting used to; we were total opposites in that regard. Still, it made me feel warm all over when I felt the tension in his muscles ease when I touched him. I lifted my head and gazed into his eyes, hoping for a kiss.

David needed no further invitation. He dipped his head down and pressed his lips against mine. Our kisses quickly grew more passionate, and intense desire tingled between my legs. *Oh, why does tomorrow have to be my first day teaching at the foundation?* If only it was Saturday night instead of Sunday. I could have gone home with David and had glorious sex all night, and it wouldn't matter what time I got home.

David's hand slid down across my breast, and I let out a moan of desire and longing. I thought of my vibrator in my bedroom drawer, frustrated at the thought of having to use it again. *I didn't want a piece of machinery satisfying my needs. I wanted David.*

I figured it would have to wait until next week, but it soon became apparent that David had other ideas. He slowly, sensually slid his hand down my silky black cocktail dress, then he began sliding his hand up between my legs. He pushed me down so I was pressed against the edge of limo seat as he towered over me.

David's dark brown eyes were filled with intense desire and purpose. There was power and control in his expression as those eyes bored into me, all the while his hand traveled further up my dress. He cupped the outside of my panties with his huge hand, and I let out a small gasp. Eyes still locked on mine, he slid my panties to the side. Then waited.

"I should tell you to stop," I whispered.

"Probably. But I don't think you will," David responded in a commanding tone. That cool demeanor that had annoyed me when I first met him now aroused me beyond all reason.

He gazed at me intently for another moment, giving me ample time to say no. I just lay there, practically salivating as I looked up at him. I opened my legs the tiniest bit wider, and David's face split into that cocky, half-smile of his. It was slightly embarrassing, having him know how desperately I wanted him. I hardly cared, as long as he gave me what I needed.

David thrust two deliciously thick fingers inside me. I cried out and threw my head back. I opened my legs wider, and David obliged me by pushing his fingers farther inside.

"Oh, David. Oh, God," I moaned, relishing the sharp vibrations of pleasure rippling through me. He kissed down my neck, reaching as far down my blouse as he could with his mouth. He couldn't pull my dress down farther because he had one hand around my back and the other one between my legs. I pulled my dress down for him, exposing my lacy black bra. That elicited a delicious, manly growl from him.

He teased and tortured me for what seemed like hours with those fingers of his. I began to wonder if he was planning to make me beg for an orgasm. I had never needed sexual release so badly in my life.

"David. David, *please*," I cried, and he chuckled.

"I'll take care of you, Susannah. I promise. There is one condition, however," David said in an authoritative voice.

I stared into his eyes. He had me right where he wanted me, and he knew it.

"What?" I asked, eyes wide.

"I'm going to make you come, Susannah, and come *hard*."

I let out a tortured gasp as he moved his fingers in and out of me.

David leaned closer to me, those commanding, dark eyes boring into my very soul. "When you come, I want you to look at me. Don't close your eyes. Look at me. I want to watch. Can you do that?"

"Yes," I whispered.

David nodded. Eyes still locked on mine, he pushed his fingers in and out faster.

"Pull your blouse down," he ordered. "I want to see your beautiful chest."

I did as he asked—well, *commanded.* I was exposed, my breasts bare and my legs open as he fucked me hard with his fingers. I was nothing like the poised, put-together woman who had entered that five-star restaurant tonight. I didn't care.

Just when I didn't think David could drive me any more insane, he shifted his fingers ever so slightly to the right. I closed my eyes, threw back my head, and cried out so loud that Stewart must have been able to hear me, even with the privacy screen closed.

David had found *the spot.* The one it had taken Carl months to find.

"Hmm, you like to be touched there, don't you?" David said smugly. *Like* was an understatement of epic proportions.

"Yes. Yes, *please. Please don't stop, David.*"

"I won't, but you closed your eyes. You'll have to break that habit if you want me finish you off." His tone was teasing, but I took him at his word.

"Okay. Okay, I promise," I managed to say.

David leaned in even closer, and I kept eye contact with him. It was harder than I had anticipated because whenever I started to climax, closing my eyes was a reflex. Still, I was determined to keep my promise.

David stared into my eyes. Then he pressed my special spot with his fingers and circled my clit with his thumb at the same time, giving me the most powerful, satisfying, earth-shaking climax I had ever experienced.

I didn't cry out with delight like I usually did when

having an orgasm. Instead, I gripped David's shoulders tight. "Oh ... oh," was all I could say.

David's eyes grew wide as he stared deep into mine as he watched me during the most intimate moment any human being can experience.

When the shattering vibrations of sheer blissful pleasure finally subsided, I collapsed back against the limo seat and finally closed my eyes. I lay there for a moment before realizing how utterly exposed I still was. I opened my eyes, closed my legs, and started straightening up my dress.

With an amused expression, David helped me put myself back together. I suddenly felt shy looking at him, but I forced myself to meet his gaze. I expected to see cockiness, and there was some of that on David's face, but there was also that hint of tenderness in his eyes. I felt a rush of affection and instinctively wrapped my arms around him. I couldn't help myself. I needed that closeness after he'd touched me so intimately. It didn't matter that he wasn't the affectionate type. When we finally made love, he was going to hold me afterward whether he liked it or not.

"That was *incredible,* David," I murmured in his ear and hugged him close to my chest.

"My God, you're beautiful when you come, Susannah," David said huskily.

"Mmmm," I said, still savoring the complete relaxation and relief that comes from utter sexual satisfaction. I realized that David must be feeling the opposite. He was probably rock hard and quite uncomfortable.

I stroked his chin and said, "You have to let me return the favor."

I found I rather liked the idea of kneeling before him in this fancy limo, unzipping those expensive trousers of his, and then teasing and pleasuring him until I finally made him lose control. He couldn't keep up that cool demeanor forever. Not while I was driving him out of his mind with pleasure.

"You will, baby. But not tonight," David said definitively, still looking annoyingly calm and collected.

"Why?" I asked, feeling hurt. Didn't he find me attractive? Moments earlier, I had been on my back, legs spread, breasts exposed, and moaning with pleasure. Any other man would have reached the limits of his self-control by now, but not David Groff. He sat there, composed as always. He might as well have been drinking scotch instead of fooling around with a woman in his limo.

"Because you have more important things going on right now," David said, for once unable to conceal the affection in his voice. "Tomorrow is a big day for you, and you need your rest." He glanced out the window. "We're almost to your place. I want you to go home and get a good night's rest. You can … take care of me soon, just not now. Not tonight."

I smiled as I traced his lips with my fingers. His sexual restraint was still a tad annoying, especially considering how quickly I had given in to my desires. Still, it was sweet of him. I knew this was his way of showing that he cared.

"Are you sure?" I hated the idea of sending him home feeling sexually frustrated, though he appeared to be doing fine at the moment. I still wanted to please him, and I wanted him to *want* me to please him.

The car slowed to a stop, and David said, "I'm sure. Rest, Susannah. I'll see you soon."

He kissed me gently, then leaned over and pressed the button to alert Stewart that we were ready for him. Within seconds, the limo door opened.

"Ms. Peters has bags she'll need help with," David said.

"Certainly," Stewart said with a smile. He held out a hand to help me out of the limo, and reached back into the car to get my bags of shoes.

"Thank you so much, Stewart," I said, wondering if he had any idea what we were up to while he was driving. If he had heard me crying out David's name and pleading with him not to stop, he certainly gave no indication of it.

Stewart waited until I was safely inside, then he drove away.

I let out a deep sigh and as I took off my high-heeled shoes, feeling happy, sexually satisfied, and like I was falling in love.

CHAPTER 10

I was so turned on I could hardly see straight. *Good God, that woman drove me insane.* Now that Susannah was gone and I could let my guard down, I realized I was panting. Panting with desire like a cartoon dog, just as I had when I saw Susannah dance at the foundation.

I took off my suit jacket, then reached into the bar for a scotch.

You have to let me return the favor.

I kept hearing that sultry voice of hers in my head. It had taken every ounce of restraint in my body to turn that offer down. I did want her to get a good night's rest, but it was mostly my own stubbornness that kept me from letting her pleasure me. I wanted her so desperately that I felt like I was completely losing my self-control. I felt that way every time I was near Susannah, and I wasn't sure how to handle it. There was nothing wrong with being attracted to a beautiful woman, but I was always the one who took charge in the bedroom. I decided when the woman would climax. I called the shots. With Susannah, I needed her so badly it was scary.

What would she have done to return the favor?

I couldn't help thinking about it. Would she have slipped her delicate hand down my pants? Would she have made me look into her eyes when I came? *Would she have taken me in her mouth?*

I groaned aloud and took a sip of scotch. It was a relief not to have to hide my pent-up sexual frustration. I wished Stewart would hurry up and get me home, so I could be alone and relieve at least some of my sexual tension. It wouldn't be the same as having Susannah do it for me, but it would still feel good and help me relax. She had given me plenty to think about, that was for sure.

I closed my eyes and remembered what she looked like when I had my fingers deep inside her. The way she had called my name and pleaded with me not to stop, and the way she had cried out when I stumbled upon her G-spot. And oh God, the way she looked when she was having an orgasm.

I had nearly come in my pants without her touching me.

I had fought to appear unaffected, but watching Susannah as I pleasured her was one of the most erotic experiences of my life. Those *sounds* she made. Moans of ecstasy, soft whimpers of pleasure, and her cries of *David*. Watching those blue eyes of hers widen as her climax began to build, and the way she gripped my shoulders as her orgasm took hold, nearly pushed me to the edge.

On the outside, I was the alpha male who took charge and made sexual demands on a whim. On the inside, I felt like a teenage boy peering over the fence at a naked woman sunbathing, uncontrollably aroused with only his right hand to relieve his tension.

Susannah had made it clear that she was ready to go all the way with me.

Go all the way with me? Good Christ, now I was even starting to think like a pathetic teenage virgin.

Knowing that Susannah was ready to have sex with me left me feeling happy, nervous, and scared to death all at once.

* * *

BY MONDAY NIGHT, I had at least begun to get a grip on myself. This was due, in no small part, to my *getting a grip on myself* several times. Now that my sexual needs had been relieved somewhat, my head began to clear.

I had thought about Susannah all day, wondering how her first day at the foundation went and hoping she was happy. She had been so excited about moving to New York, to teach and concentrate on theater, and I hoped the experience would be all that she had dreamed of, and more. I called her Monday evening to find out how it went.

"Hey, you," Susannah said as she answered the phone. I could hear the joy in her voice, and I knew the day must have gone well.

"I've been thinking about you all day," I said before I could stop myself. It was true, but I hadn't meant to admit that to her. "I mean, I've been wondering how everything went at the foundation."

"Oh, it was perfect," Susannah gushed.

I smiled and lay down on my king-sized bed. I closed my eyes, enjoying the sound of her voice. I knew exactly how her face looked as she spoke; those pretty, blue eyes lit up with excitement.

"I had this absolutely adorable class of ten-year-olds. They were so sweet. Most of them just started fourth grade this year, and they are beyond precious. Oh, David, they're so poor, though."

I could hear the sadness and the compassion in her voice.

"Some of them have shoes that are completely worn

down, and you can tell that some of their parents aren't taking good care of them. It breaks my heart."

"I know, Susannah," I said. I couldn't begin to imagine what it was like to grow up like that. "But you're giving them a warm and bright place to go after school."

"Exactly. The kids were so excited to be there, and they really wanted to learn how to dance. I started teaching them this song and dance routine from *A Chorus Line*. It's called 'I Can Do That,' and I kept telling them to remember that. You *can* do that, if you just keep trying and don't give up."

I opened my eyes and my grin grew wider. Susannah was such a wonderful woman, and I was so proud of her.

"That's great. I'm sure they can do anything with you as their teacher."

"Thanks," she said. "I can't wait to see you again, David. Last night was wonderful."

"Yes, it certainly was," I said, visualizing Susannah moaning as I touched her between those lovely legs of hers. Of course, that wasn't the only part of the evening I'd enjoyed. I still couldn't believe she had let me drag her to a bunch of men's clothing stores. The remarkable thing was she enjoyed it because it was important to me. I never dreamed I would meet a woman like her. I didn't know they existed.

"I want to take you out Friday night," I said firmly.

"And I want to let you," she replied firmly back.

I chuckled. "Good. Since we've already covered the Manhattan tour of men's designer clothes, it's your turn to choose where we go. Do you want to go to a Broadway show, or do you want a break from the theater on the weekend?"

"Oh, I always love going to shows on Broadway."

"All right, then. What do you want to see?" I asked her.

"What do I *want* to see, or what is it humanly possible to get tickets for is the question."

"The answer to both is the same."

She laughed. "I doubt it. Some of these shows have been sold out for months."

"I'll make it happen. Now, what do you want to see, Susannah?"

"Okay, big shot. I *want* to see *Dear Evan Hansen*. Oh, that show has the most beautiful music in it. I would love to see the original Broadway cast while they're still performing, but it's impossible. Seriously, it's even hotter than *Hamilton* right now."

"Done," I said, making a mental note of the show's name. After we saw that one, I would get tickets for *Hamilton* for next time, if that's what she wanted.

She giggled; it was clear she didn't believe me. That was fine. It would be all the more satisfying when I came through not only with tickets, but *good* tickets. It would be a joy to see a Broadway show with Susannah. She would be so happy, and it made me smile just thinking about it.

"It honestly doesn't matter where we go or what we do," Susannah said. "I just want to see you again."

I felt the same about her, but I found it difficult to admit it out loud. I swallowed, realizing I would be pushing her away if I didn't tell her. I wasn't about to serenade her in a crowded restaurant like Johnny had done with Rosemary, but Susannah deserved *something* from me.

"I feel the same, Susannah."

"Good," she said, sounding relieved. "See you soon."

CHAPTER 11

*T*he week had flown by; I couldn't believe it was already Friday. I'd had so much fun at the foundation, it hardly seemed like work. There was plenty of time to rehearse my auditioning song and dance routines after I'd done all my lesson planning and before my students arrived for their after-school program. Johnny was basically paying me a full-time salary for part-time work. I felt slightly guilty about that, but I knew he could afford it. It was a similar situation to Rosemary's—she struggled with having Johnny's wealthy father pay her way through school, but she was working incredibly hard and getting good grades. I tried to do the same. I was lucky to have this job, so I put a lot of planning and effort into teaching those precious children.

My stomach fluttered with excitement just thinking about seeing David. It was funny; I would never have imagined myself with someone like David. If he hadn't had Johnny set us up, I never would have given him a second glance. On the surface, he had seemed rich and snobby—far too much like my ex-boyfriend for comfort. Now I knew he wasn't like that at all. Okay, so he wasn't the warm and fuzzy type like Johnny, but he was thoughtful in his own way. It had meant a lot to me that he called on Monday to see how my first day of teaching went, and when we spoke on the phone, I got the impression that he was really listening to me. He actually cared how my day went.

We texted back and forth all through the week, usually starting by talking about our day, then gradually moving on to more X-rated territory. Though we didn't come right out and say it, it was clear we would be fully intimate this weekend.

I was nervous, but I could hardly wait to have sex with David. After what he did to me with his fingers, I couldn't begin to imagine what he could do with the rest of his body. I looked forward to getting him out of his fancy suit, that was for damned sure.

When I got home from the foundation, I got all dolled up in a shimmery dark blue dress that dramatically showed off my bright blue eyes. I also wore the matching pumps I got at Barney's last week. I thought of this dress the moment I laid eyes on the shoes, knowing they were a perfect match.

I glanced out my apartment window just in time to see David's limo pull up. I shook my head. I could hardly believe I was dating such a wealthy man. I'd always heard that having money can change you, and I was determined not to let that happen. Working with those beautiful, yet utterly impover-ished kids certainly helped keep things in perspective.

I hurried down the stairs, not wanting to keep David waiting. When I opened the door Stewart was there, poised to ring the doorbell. I gasped as I nearly ran into him.

"So sorry, Ms. Peters! I didn't mean to startle you."

I laughed. "My fault. I shouldn't have been rushing around like a madwoman. And you can call me Susie, by the way. I keep meaning to tell you that."

Stewart smiled and nodded, but somehow I doubted he

would. We walked down the sidewalk together, and he opened the limo door for me. David graced me with a sexy half-smile, and I was acutely aware of him checking out my legs as I climbed into the car and slid down next to him.

"You look lovely, Susannah," he said, looking me up and down.

"Check it out. I'm wearing my new shoes," I said, seizing the opportunity to lift my leg for him. I heard a small moan escape his lips.

"Very nice," he said.

"You look so handsome, David," I said, eying him up and down. He wore a black suit and looked dapper as always. The suit reminded me of the one we saw at Barney's.

"Is this Armani?" I asked, touching his sleeve.

"It *is*," David said, surprised and pleased. I loved that he was such a clothing expert, and I wanted to learn what I could, in order to keep up.

He pressed a button and the limo began to move.

"So, where are we going?" I asked.

"To see *Dear Evan Hansen*, of course," he replied nonchalantly, as if we were headed to McDonald's.

"You're joking," I said, staring at him. I figured we were going to a show, but I put the idea of seeing *Dear Evan Hansen* completely out of my mind.

"That's what you wanted to do, right?" David couldn't hide the twinkle of amusement in his eyes. "So, we're headed to the Music Box Theater."

"Oh my God, David. Oh my God." I threw my arms around him and embraced him. He chuckled and stroked my back. I let go of him and grabbed his shoulders. "I'm so excited!"

"I can see that," David said with nearly a full smile.

"How did you ever manage to get tickets? The last I heard, they were sold out through January."

He shrugged and said simply, "Money."

"How much — no wait. Don't tell me. It's rude of me to ask, and I don't think I want to know." I couldn't begin to guess how much this had cost, and I would probably feel guilty about it for the rest of my life if I knew. David could easily afford it, but I couldn't help but think of my students and the food and comfort that kind of money could provide them. Still, I couldn't help but be excited. I rationalized it by thinking that I could have a great evening tonight and be there for my kids on Monday. It wasn't an either/or proposition.

I leaned back in the limo and put my hand over my heart. "I cannot believe I actually get to see this show. Thank you so much, David."

As we walked into the Music Box Theater, I drew in a deep breath. It wasn't my first time there, but I was thrilled every time I walked into any theater. Whether a dirty dinner theater or a gorgeous place like this, theaters were like palaces to me. As we got ready to find our seats, I paused a moment like I always did.

David stood at my side, silently watching me as I drank in the view of the theater; the seats, the stage, and the ornate ceiling. Carl would have nudged me to get going, but not David. He seemed to know that to hurry me would be to break the spell I was under. His silent patience spoke volumes.

I finally turned to him and whispered, "Thank you for bringing me here."

"You're so welcome, Susannah." He gently brushed my hair out of my face and kissed me softly.

"So, where do we go?"

David signaled to an usher and showed him our tickets, and the man nodded for us to follow. Down, down, down we walked, my eyes growing wider with each step we took. I could only ever afford tickets in the balcony. *Exactly where were we sitting?*

Fifth row. The answer was the fifth row. *Good God.*

"Oh, David," I said, staring up at the stage as we stood in front of our seats.

"Nothing but the best for you, my shining star," he said.

Shakily, I took my seat and he sat down next to me. I wrapped my arm around his neck and pulled him close. Every moment with David felt like a dream come true.

The show was astonishingly, breathtakingly beautiful. It was a modern tale about the struggles of anxiety, bullying, and even suicide, yet the show's message was one of hope. The story followed Evan, a teenager stricken with anxiety, who is advised to write letters of encouragement to himself, hence the title of the musical. One of his classmates, a terrible bully named Connor, gets ahold of some of Evan's letters and kills himself shortly after. After finding the letters, Connor's family thinks they were written from their son to Evan. Evan embraces the lie that the two were close friends, and soon Connor's family becomes Evan's surrogate family. Evan goes on to start an anti-bullying campaign that soon goes viral.

The music was heartbreaking, soothing, and inspirational all at once. I lost count of how many times I cried during the show. It didn't matter whether it was a serious show like this one, or if it was *Oklahoma*; the sheer power and beauty of the shared theater experience never failed to touch my soul.

The actor who portrayed Evan, a guy in his early twenties named Ben Platt, was simply stunning. It was no wonder he won the Tony for his performance. Seeing him perform on the awards ceremony was the closest I thought I would ever get to him, yet here I was.

The song he performed after Connor's family uncovered the lie, called "Words Fail," was hauntingly lovely. I couldn't understand how Evan could weep and sing at the same time, yet somehow, he managed. The show ended with a feeling of hope and inspiration, with the idea that all those who are lost would someday be found.

It took me several moments to dry my eyes after the show ended. As always, David waited in silence next to me. Not judgmental, impatient silence; sweet, understanding silence.

Finally, I turned to him. "Thank you so much, David. This was amazing. What a powerful performance. I didn't know it was possible to sing and cry at the same time, but Ben Platt did it somehow. Wow."

"Yes, he is an incredible performer. I'd heard bits and pieces about this show, but I wasn't too familiar with it. It was phenomenal," David said.

I nodded, glancing back up toward the now empty stage.

"That'll be you up there someday."

"Can you imagine?" I whispered.

"Yes," he said definitively, as if he was sure of it. *He believed in me.*

"Are you hungry?" he asked.

"Starved."

"We'll go anywhere you want for dinner. Your choice."

"Sounds good," I said.

David held out his hand to help me up, and we made our way through the theater and back outside. I still couldn't quite get over the luxury of having a limo waiting for us everywhere we went. Back in D.C., I either took the Metro or had to park in crowded parking garages. In New York, I would have had to stand around and wait for a taxi if not for David. Instead of all that hassle, there was Stewart, smiling warmly and waiting to open the door for me. I was again struck with the thought, *How in the hell did I end up here?*

I bit my lip and smiled, then turned to David. "You said we can go anywhere I want for dinner, right?"

"Of course."

I leaned over and whispered in Stewart's ear. He shot an amused look over at David and then nodded.

"What are you up to?" David asked suspiciously.

"Nothing at all," I replied with mock innocence.

I snuggled up to David in the limo as we sped toward dinner. I couldn't help but wish David would initiate physical contact a bit more. To be fair, he had certainly initiated contact on our last date when he had given me a spectacular orgasm. I was the touchy-feely type, and I always had to be the one to wrap my arms around David or affectionately stroke his hair. He never seemed to mind when I touched him, but he would never do it first. That wasn't his way, and I knew I needed to accept him for who he was. Overall, he was wonderful, and I certainly wasn't perfect, either.

The place I had chosen for dinner was close by, so we didn't have too much time for physical togetherness.

That will be after dinner.

My whole body tingled with excitement just thinking about it. I could hardly wait to finally see David's place, especially his bed. The idea of finally having sex with him was wonderful. Just being *near* him was wonderful.

David frowned, looking out the window as the limo slowed to a stop. I giggled wildly at his expression.

"Where are you taking me, woman?"

"You said we could go anywhere I wanted," I reminded him. Louie's Pizza was located in midtown Manhattan, not too far from the theater. It was still in the touristy areas, but slightly off the beaten path, and a favorite of some of the locals.

David looked at me hesitantly, like he wasn't sure he wanted to get out of the car.

"Come on, be a big boy now," I said. I leaned over and

pressed the magic button that would soon make Stewart appear.

"What I am going to do with you?" David asked, shaking his head.

"I guess we'll find out later tonight."

The door to the limo opened before David could respond, but it was clear from his expression that I had gotten his attention. Stewart took my hand and helped me out of the car.

"Louie's is an excellent choice, Ms. Peters," Stewart said with an adorable smirk. He knew my choice of restaurant was making his spoiled boss squirm. "They make a mean cannoli."

"I know, right? Everybody loves Louie's." I smiled at Stewart and he grinned back, both of us enjoying our fun with David. It was hilarious seeing the all-business, Armani suit-wearing David Groff have to set foot in a dirty, greasy pizza joint.

David and I walked to the front door and he shot me a wry look. He opened the door for me, and I watched him grimace as he spied the brightly lit neon menu plastered up on the wall. I got in line and he followed just behind me.

"What do you want?" I asked him.

"Does it matter?" he asked grimly.

I turned around and shot him a look.

"Sorry. That was obnoxious, even for me. All right, so I helped you with the menu at the last place. Now you tell me what you recommend."

"I say we go with good old-fashioned pepperoni pizza."

"Sounds divine," David said, kissing his fingers with a flourish.

I smiled, happy to see that he could be a good sport about slumming it with me.

Soon it was our turn. "Hi," I said to the older man behind

the counter. He looked like the stereotypical New York City pizza owner, like he'd just stepped off the boat from Italy. "We'd like a large pepperoni pizza."

I turned to David and asked, "What do you want to drink? Can you live without scotch?"

"Got some in the limo. Thank God," he said, murmuring the last part. "Coke," he said to the old Italian man.

"It wouldn't kill you to say please and thank you once in a while," I admonished. "It's not a sign of weakness, you know. We'll take a Coke and a Diet Coke, too. Thanks!"

"You'll never be a real New Yorker with those manners."

I laughed, knowing he was probably right. Out of habit, I reached for my wallet.

"I got this, Susannah. You go ahead and find us a seat."

"I feel bad making you pay all the time."

"It's silly to have you pay," David told me as he handed Chef Boyardee his gold card.

I knew he was right. He was a ba-jillionaire, and I was on a strict budget. It still felt odd to never pay my way, but it didn't make sense to use my money when he had so much.

David paused when he got to the booth where I sat.

"Would you like me to have Stewart fetch you a towel to sit on?"

David snorted. "That won't be necessary."

He sat down across from me, looking amused and annoyed at the same time.

"It's like being on an adventure, isn't it? Not being in a five-star establishment. This must be like camping for you."

David chuckled at that. It wasn't long before our pizza number was called.

"I'll get it," I said, standing up.

David looked at me like he didn't know what I was talking about. I picked up the receipt from the table. "Number 96. That's us."

"Oh, I—" He started to stand up.

"I got it. It's okay." It was adorable that he didn't know how these places worked. I brought the pizza back to our table, and David jumped up to help me with the food and the drinks.

Once we were settled in our seats, I stared at him.

"What?"

"Go on, take a bite."

David sighed. First, he took off his suit jacket, rolled up his expensive shirt sleeves, and then flipped his tie over his shoulder. I laughed. He scowled at me, but I could see the humor in his eyes. He picked up a plastic knife and fork from the tray.

"Oh, come *on*. Don't be *that* guy," I said.

"Fine." Grudgingly, he put down the utensils and picked up the slice of pizza like a normal person. At long last, he took a bite. He savored it for a moment, then took another bite.

"You like it. Admit it!" I picked up the plastic fork and aimed it at David like I would stab him if he didn't fess up.

"Okay, okay. I admit it. It's really good, okay?" He smirked. "Reminds me of my college days. We lived on pizza in the dorm." After he gobbled the first slice, he reached for another. I hadn't even started on mine. I took a bite.

"Mmmm. This *is* divine," I said.

"It is nice not to have to wait long for the food, I'll give you that." He was reaching for a third slice already.

"Why? Are you in a hurry?"

"Depends on what's next on our agenda, I suppose."

You are next on my agenda, you gorgeous hunk of a man.

"I was kinda hoping we could go back to your place," I said.

"Anything you want, Susannah. Anything."

"That's what I want."

"Good," he said with his trademarked half-smile.

We finished our meal and I got up to bus our tray. David stood up, again looking guilty for not doing it for me. I knew he hadn't realized that's what you were supposed to do. He was so adorably clueless.

"Oh, wait," I said, tugging on his sleeve as we headed for the door. "I wanna get some cannoli for Stewart."

"Why?" David asked, looking genuinely confused.

"Because he likes them, and he's a very nice man. An order of cannoli for take-out, please," I said to the old Italian guy. I turned to David expectantly. He sighed and fished out his wallet. I knew I should have paid for it, but it amused me to make David buy something for Stewart. As generous as David was with me, I doubted he ever gave Stewart a second thought.

"You can give it to him, David," I said as we walked outside.

"No, you do it. He'll know it was your idea anyway."

Stewart was already standing outside the limo waiting for us. It was uncanny how he always seemed to know the exact moment we were ready to go.

"Hey, Stewart," I called to him as we walked up to the car. "We got you some cannoli."

Stewart's blue eyes opened wide. "Aw, that's so nice of you. Thank you!" His smile was so kind and genuine that it truly warmed my heart. He seemed like such a nice guy, and I'd bet David hardly knew a thing about him.

Stewart opened the door so he could put down the cannoli, and I caught sight of his limo license on the dashboard. It read "Joseph Stewart."

"Wait a minute. Stewart is your last name?" I asked.

"Yes, ma'am."

I glanced over at David. "Ugh, you can be such a snob sometimes!"

"What?" David asked, eyes wide.

I shook my head. I guessed it was rich-guy protocol to call butlers and limo drivers and whatnot by their last names, but I hated the idea.

"So, your name is Joseph? Do people call you Joe?"

"My friends call me Joey."

"May I call you Joey?"

"Of course, Ms. Peters," Joey responded with the sweet smile of his.

"Good. Joey it is. And *please* call me Susie." I jerked a thumb at David. "He's the only one who insists on calling me Susannah."

Joey pressed his lips together, stifling a laugh at his boss's expense.

"All right, then. Susie it is."

"Good," I said with a smile. I turned toward the passenger door and Joey jogged ahead to open it for me.

"Thanks," I said as I stepped inside.

I snuggled up next to David, noticing right away that his body was a bit tense.

"Do you really think I'm a snob?" he asked, sounding slightly wounded.

I touched his face gently. "Sometimes. I'm sorry, David. It's just my ex-boyfriend was snobby, and I'm a little sensitive about it. And I've waited tables in the past, so I've been on the receiving end of that kind of attitude. People like us, we're not just 'the help,' you know. We may be poor, but we have feelings, too."

"I know," David said, sounding a bit guilty. "I'll try to be better. I'll even try to remember to say 'please' and 'thank you.'"

"I appreciate that." I traced his lips with affection. "You might be a snob sometimes, but you also happen to be a pretty terrific guy. And guess what?"

"Tell me what."

"I'm crazy about you," I told him, before pressing my lips to his. He wrapped his arms around me, returning the kiss. It seemed no matter how tense he was, he relaxed at my touch. I *loved* that about him.

He nuzzled my neck and murmured in my ear, "I'm crazy about you, too."

We made the most of the drive over, our hands and mouths all over each other. My stomach tingled with excitement when the limo finally stopped. I couldn't wait to be alone with David at his place.

Stewart—or rather, *Joey*—helped me out of the car, then gestured at the building right in front of us, indicating that this was the place. It was an incredibly tall building; I looked up and up as it kept going. I could feel Joey's eyes on me, and I knew he was smiling. I think he enjoyed the fact that I wasn't jaded by David's wealth. I still found it exciting and a tad overwhelming.

David stepped out of the car and stood beside me. He saw me looking up at the building and gently put his hand under my chin, lifting my head higher and higher, until I was looking at the very top of the building.

"There. That's the place."

"Wow," I said, feeling slightly dizzy. "I could faint just looking up at it."

"Go ahead. I'll catch you," David said in that deep, sexy voice of his.

"I wanna see. I wanna see it!"

Both Joey and David chuckled at my excitement. Joey walked us to the door of the building where the doorman took over.

David turned to Joey and said, "Thank you. Have a good night."

Joey looked surprised, then tipped his cap. "My pleasure, Mr. Groff. You have a good night as well."

David turned to me and nodded sharply as if to say, "There, I said thank you. Are you happy?"

I giggled and said, "Good job. I'm proud of you."

"Evening, Mr. Groff," the doorman said.

"Good evening, Jeffrey," David responded.

The doorman's name tag said "Jeff," so at least David had called him by his first name. I wondered if David ever called anyone by their nickname. I'd never heard him call Johnny "Jonathan," though.

The elevator took us right to David's penthouse.

"You'll love the view, Susannah," he said. He seemed excited to show me his apartment. David Groff didn't get excited about much, so I took it as a compliment.

I gasped as I stepped off the elevator and straight into his living space. David watched me as I took it in.

It was *huge.* The living room alone was about the size of five apartments like the one I rented in Brooklyn. And he wasn't kidding about the view. The lights of the city over-whelmed me, and I felt like a child experiencing the wonder of Christmas for the first time.

"Oh, David," I whispered. The living room walls were basically all windows, and everywhere I looked, I could see the wonder and the excitement of New York City. David walked over and stood next to me for a moment. As always, I found peace in his silence. He was content to stand with me and let me take it all in, and I was fully aware of his quiet affection. He enjoyed seeing me happy, which filled my heart to the brim.

I turned to him and said excitedly, "Show me the rest!"

"With pleasure," David said, taking my hand. "I should warn you, though. There are other people here."

"What?"

"I have a housekeeper and a cook. And also a, well, a ..."

"A what?"

"You're going to call me a snob again."

I giggled, and then stroked his cheek with affection. "No, I won't. Oh, let me guess. You have a *butler!*"

"A little bit," he admitted.

I laughed aloud. "Oh, this is so surreal!" I looked around as if expecting one of his many crew members to pop out at any second.

"Would you like to meet her?"

"*Her?*" I had been picturing Alfred from Batman again. I had never heard of a female butler before. What if she was beautiful? And what about the housekeeper and chef? Did David have a bunch of beautiful women working and *living* here?

"Sure," I said, though I wasn't at all sure I wanted to meet her.

David pressed a button and spoke into an intercom. "Katherine? Could you come to the front, please?"

The front. David sounded business-like, as if he were in an office or something. It made me feel better. He didn't exactly sound like he was telling this Katherine to *come hither.*

"So, she lives here?" I asked, hating the uncertainty in my voice. David gave me that tender look of his, which calmed me instantly.

"On the weekends she stays here. Tuesday through Thursdays she works only in the evenings when I'm at home. She's off Mondays."

Katherine emerged from a long hallway and walked up to David. Sure enough, she was sharply dressed in a butler uniform just like the ones I had seen on television. I was relieved to see that she was a woman in her fifties or so, her gray hair tied up neatly in a short braid at the back.

LINDA FAUSNET

Katherine glanced at me curiously and then turned to David. "Good evening. What can I get for you, Mr. Groff?"

"Nothing at the moment. I just wanted to introduce you to Susannah Peters. I think you'll be seeing a lot of her around here."

Katherine's gray eyes softened. She smiled at David, and seemed pleased with this news. I got the distinct impression that David rarely introduced his dates to his staff.

"Well, it's very nice to meet you, Ms. Peters," Katherine said. She offered her hand, and I shook it. She met my gaze and smiled warmly. I could tell by the way she looked at David that she cared about him. She was professional, yet somehow motherly at the same time. I liked her immediately.

"Please, I would like you to call me Susie if that's okay," I told her. She looked at David, who shrugged.

"Of course," Katherine said.

"And do you really go by the name Katherine, or is that just what he calls you?" I asked with a side nod in David's direction. "Do your friends call you Katie or something?"

"Kate, actually."

"Is it all right if I call you Kate, then?"

"Of course you may," Kate said with another warm smile. "Is there anything I can get for you? A drink, perhaps?"

"No, I'm good right now. Thanks, though."

Kate glanced at David, who shook his head. "That will be all for the moment."

"All right, then. Don't hesitate to let me know if you need anything, Susie."

"Thank you so much," I said with a smile, now glad that I had met her. Not only was she not young and totally gorgeous, she was kind, and she took good care of David.

Kate turned and walked back down the hallway and into a room somewhere back there.

"That's the servant's quarters," David said.

I laughed. I couldn't help it. *Servant's quarters.*

"Well, it is," David sniffed.

"I'm sorry. I'm just not used to being around ba-jillion-aires, even though I've known Johnny for years. It's still weird."

David chuckled. "I'll show you the rest of the place."

He led me through the huge kitchen, his office, the guest rooms, and he showed me where all the bathrooms were. David's penthouse apartment was like a mansion. I could literally have gotten lost in it without David as my tour guide. Still, he hadn't shown me what I wanted to see the most.

I wrapped my arms around his neck and gazed into his eyes. "Aren't you going to show me your bedroom?"

With that half-smile of his, David murmured, "I thought you'd never ask."

CHAPTER 12

I took Susannah's hand and led her to my bedroom. My palms were sweaty, which I hoped she attributed to my wearing a three-piece suit in the middle of the summer. I took women to bed all the time, so why was I so damned nervous?

I knew why, of course. Because Susannah Peters was nothing like any other woman I had ever known, and I desperately wanted to please her. I never had trouble pleasuring women, but then again, I never cared about the women I slept with. I'd had lots of one-night stands and was never with a woman for more than a few weeks. This time was completely different. I wanted Susannah Peters in my life for as long as she was willing to put up with me. For our first time together, I needed to prove myself to her. I wanted to pleasure her longer and harder than any other man ever had. I wanted—no *needed*—to be the best lover she'd ever had.

And I wasn't at all confident that I could do it.

I knew how to feign confidence, even when I didn't feel it. It was quite a useful skill in the business world. This was the first time I'd ever needed that skill when it came to sex. I used to feel in control in the bedroom, never failing to bring a woman to orgasm before gratifying my own needs. Susannah had me feeling completely off balance. I tried to not to think about how quickly I came while jerking off to thoughts of her.

Would I be able to last long enough to satisfy her when we were having sex?

Susannah wandered around the room with the same look of awe she'd had while looking around the rest of the house. There was a small table with two chairs, a large sitting area with a red velvet couch and matching chair, a large mahogany desk, and a king-sized bed with a black bedspread and satin sheets underneath. I hoped Susannah would get to see those sheets soon, but I wanted to give her all the time she needed to explore first. My bedroom offered as perfect a view of New York as my living room did. She walked over to one of the huge windows and gazed out at the city.

"It's all so beautiful," she murmured. She turned around and looked at me with uncertainty. "You do have a way to cover all these windows, right?"

I arched an eyebrow. "Why? Thinking of doing something in here that you don't want the whole city to see?"

"Maybe," she said in a sensual voice.

I took that as an invitation. I walked over to her and leaned down to press my lips to hers. She wrapped her arms around me and we kissed passionately for a few moments. Susannah broke off the kiss, then glanced nervously again at the windows. I had had sex in here plenty of times with the windows uncovered. When the lights were off, I doubted anyone could see anything. Besides, the women I usually took to bed found the idea of being watched exciting. Like in every other regard, Susannah was unlike all those other women.

I chuckled. "Don't worry. I've got this covered. Literally." I walked over to my nightstand and picked up the remote for the window covering. Susannah watched with fascination and relief as the shades came down, giving us complete privacy.

"Better?"

"Much," she answered. I stayed over near the bed, hoping she would join me.

She did.

Susannah sat on the bed. She smiled up at me, then grabbed ahold of my tie, pulling me down for a kiss. She moaned softly as our lips met.

"I guess I should be careful with this tie," she said. "It probably cost more than my rent."

"Cut it off. I don't care."

She laughed softly and then went to work on carefully taking it off. She slid off my suit jacket just as carefully, and I grabbed it from her and tossed it aside. I didn't care if my suit got wrinkled; that's what dry cleaners were for. She gazed into my eyes, her pretty, blue ones sparkling.

"I love these broad shoulders of yours," Susannah said as she ran her hands over my white Armani shirt. She was tantalizingly slow about unbuttoning it, but she finally got my shirt open and ran her hands over my bare chest. I watched her face as she admired it. Her eyes opened wide, and I could see her getting aroused by looking me.

I took her hands and pulled her to a standing position so I could slip off her dress. My breath caught in my chest. She was wearing a matching black lace bra and panty set. I cupped her face and kissed her, pushing her down onto the bed. Her moans were already making me crazy; I couldn't imagine what sounds she would make when I pounded in and out of her.

I could hardly wait to find out.

Susannah unbuckled my pants and slid them off, and I helped her with my underwear. I reached behind her back and took off her bra.

"My God, you're beautiful," I said as I ran my hands over her naked breasts. I slipped a hand down her panties and she gasped slightly. I looked deeply into her eyes as I slipped a finger inside her, thrilled to find she was soaking wet.

"I need you," she whispered.

"I can tell," I said with a smirk. "Don't you worry, baby. I'll take care of all your needs. First thing's first. Do I need protection?"

She shook her head. "IUD."

"Good."

I slipped her panties off. She opened her legs, biting her lip with eager anticipation. I planted my hands firmly on the mattress and slid my cock partway inside of her.

"Oh, David," she moaned. She gripped my shoulders tightly, waiting for me to thrust myself all the way in. It took every ounce of restraint I had, but I made her wait a few seconds.

No matter what, I had to remain in control at all times.

I felt like a young man finally losing his virginity, scarcely believing that this glamorous, dynamic woman was letting me have sex with her. But I needed to be David Groff—businessman. Billionaire. Alpha male lover.

I rammed inside of her, and she threw her head back and cried out my name. My own burst of pleasure was so strong, I had to bite the inside of my cheek to keep from groaning out loud. I was supposed to make the woman scream, not the other way around.

Susannah opened her eyes, and in her gaze I saw both

desperate sexual need and tender affection. She was not the type who slept around, which meant this was probably an emotional experience for her. I was determined to satisfy her sexual needs, but I knew I had to tend to her feelings, too.

I was even less confident I could do that.

I bent and kissed her lips, and she ran her fingers through my hair. Her whole body softened at my touch, and I realized that kissing was the best way to reassure her that I cared. After a while, I lifted my lips so I could look into her eyes.

"Oh, David. Oh, God you're good," she moaned, gripping my shoulders tighter. "You're so ... good ..." she panted as I pounded into her over and over again.

Sex with Susannah was even more exciting than in my numerous fantasies. She was so damned beautiful, her brown hair splayed out on my bed, those gorgeous eyes filled with desire. I reveled in her beauty and vibrant presence, my pleasure intensifying with every thrust. Between her loveliness, her perfect dancer's body, and her cries of passion, I really didn't know how much longer I could hold on. I could last all night with other women, but no one had ever aroused me to the point of near insanity like Susannah.

She kept crying out my name, but I couldn't tell if she was close to orgasm. Breathing heavily with the effort, I thrust into her over and over, trying to grab ahold of any image I could to keep from coming before she did.

"David, David, oh David," she cried, her eyes still pleading with me to satisfy her. "Don't stop, *don't stop.*"

I couldn't stop or slow down, not with her begging for more, but I knew if I kept going, I would have an orgasm. I knew I would never get over the humiliation of finishing before her.

Just when sheer panic began to set in, I suddenly remembered that I had found her G-spot when I fingered her in the limo. I shifted slightly to the right, and pounded hard.

She gasped and dug her fingers deeper into my shoulders. "David," she whispered, which was somehow even more erotic than her screams. "Oh G—god. Right there. David, David, right *there.*"

Susannah let go of my shoulders and dug her nails into my back instead. It was perfect, because the slight pain from her fingernails brought me back from the brink of my own release.

She looked up at me, those sweet blue eyes of hers pleading with me to give her what she needed. "David, *please don't stop.*"

I gazed down at this dazzling woman I had somehow been lucky enough to find and was struck with a sudden realization.

I was completely and utterly in love with Susannah Peters.

And I would not let her down.

"Look at me," I growled.

She obeyed, staring deeply into my eyes. She seemed afraid I would stop my thrusts if she refused my demand. Just like in the limo, I wanted her to look at me when she climaxed.

"Yes," she whispered. "Just don't stop. *Please.* Oh, David ... oh ..." It was fascinating to watch her as she experienced ultimate pleasure. At first, her eyes began to close as they had in the limo when she started to come, but she remembered my command and opened them wide so I could see.

"D—David ... oh ... oh ..." Her cries of release were soft and sensual. It drove me wild, the way she could hardly speak when she finally reached orgasm. "Ah ... ah ..."

I stared deeply into her eyes as my cock licked that sweet spot inside of her, reveling in her pleasure until her body eventually stopped shaking.

Only then did I allow myself to let go. I closed my eyes

and shifted my body in a way that maximized my own pleasure. I rammed in and out of the most beautiful woman I had ever known. It took mere seconds for a powerful orgasm to rock me to the core. I let out a deep, primal groan as I emptied myself inside of her. I *never* made noise during sex, but the pleasure and relief was so intense that my grunting had become completely involuntary.

When I opened my eyes, I realized Susannah had been watching me while I orgasmed. It made me feel vulnerable and cherished at the same time.

"Oh, David, that was *incredible*," she said, looking relaxed and utterly satisfied.

I was thrilled with her reaction to our frenetic lovemaking, but I was still gasping for breath, so I couldn't respond.

"Hmm," she said. "I have to say, it's nice to finally see you sweat a bit."

"You certainly make me sweat, Susannah. You've been driving me out of my mind since the moment I first laid eyes on you."

I hadn't meant to confess that much. It was a weak moment, and it just slipped out. I was physically and emotionally exhausted by her.

Her pretty face softened. "Wow. Usually the most reaction I can get out of you is a raised eyebrow and that sexy half-smile you do." She laughed, gently touching my slightly upturned lips. "Yeah. That one."

After I finally caught my breath, I bent down and kissed her. I pulled out of her and lay down on the bed.

"I guess you're not exactly the cuddle-after-sex type, huh?" she asked.

"Not really."

"That's too bad. Because I am."

Susannah moved over to my side of the bed and snuggled up close to me, her head resting on my bare chest. She couldn't see my face, so I allowed myself to smile. A real, full smile. A sensation of total relaxation and contentment washed over me, and I began gently stroking her hair. It was still awkward for me to try to express my feelings for her through touch, but I was trying my best. Growing up in an emotionally distant environment, I just hadn't learned how to express emotions verbally or physically. I cared deeply for Susannah, and I knew how much she needed to be held after sex. She was an emotional person, and she craved intimacy. She deserved a man who could give her everything she needed, so I had to figure out how to be that kind of man.

"Mmm," she murmured. It was such a sweet, happy sound, and I knew I was doing okay.

We lay there for a while, cuddled up together. Warm, content, and sexually satisfied. Eventually, she lifted her head to look at me. My heart squeezed in my chest when I saw that sweet, lovely face. Oh, how I adored this woman.

"This was the perfect evening, David. *Perfect.*"

"Yes, it certainly was."

"I'm so comfy. I hate to leave."

"Then don't," I said, shocked that she would even think of such a thing. It was warm and comfortable in my bed. Why on earth would she want to go?

Susannah sighed wearily and sat up. "Well, you know. I don't have any of my stuff with me to stay the night."

"I have everything you need for a shower. You can wear one of my shirts to bed." Dear God in heaven, would Susannah look gorgeous in one of my shirts.

"I know. But I still need stuff like my makeup remover, and I wear contact lenses and all. I need my lens solution and my lens case and all that."

"Write down a list of anything you need, and Katherine will run out and get everything for you."

"At this hour? That's crazy."

"No, it's not. It's New York City. It won't be hard to find open stores."

"I know you're loaded, David, but it seems like such a waste to go buy all that stuff that I already have at home."

"Susannah," I said sternly. "Do you want to stay tonight? Or are you just making excuses not to?"

"David," she said. "Of course I want to stay with you."

"Then it's not a waste. Besides, I think it would be nice if you kept some of your things at my place, don't you?"

"Yes," she said with a smile that lit up her whole face. "When you put it that way, how can I possibly refuse?"

"You can't," I said, sitting up in bed. I pulled out a sketch pad from my nightstand and flipped past the pages filled with my design sketches. I handed Susannah the notepad and a pen.

"Write down anything and everything you need. Makeup stuff, contacts, underwear, whatever you want. Consider it done."

Susannah took the notepad, shaking her head. "You spoil me, David."

"I know. And I love it."

And I love you too, my darling Susannah. Someday, maybe I'll even be brave enough to say it.

CHAPTER 13

*D*avid's bed was the most comfortable thing I had ever slept on. Soft and warm, with silky satin sheets; it was like sleeping on a cloud. I had used his broad chest as my pillow for half the night, and it felt good to be snuggled up close to him. He never reached out to hold me, but he never seemed to mind me hanging all over him.

After I woke up in the morning, I sat up in bed and watched him for a few moments. It was fascinating to see him when he was asleep. He looked relaxed and vulnerable for once. David Groff was all business on the surface, but I knew there was a softer side to him. He let it slip once in a while. A tender gaze, a smile he couldn't quite hide, the way the tension in his body eased whenever I touched him. It was funny; I was always kind of jealous of the relationship Rosemary had with Johnny. He was so outwardly affectionate with her. After breaking up with Carl, I had hoped to someday find a man like that—one who wasn't afraid to express his feelings for me.

David was nothing like that. And yet, somehow that was okay. David was not at all the kind of man I had pictured myself with, but that didn't matter. I adored him just the way he was.

When it became clear that David wouldn't wake up any time soon, I decided to take a shower. The bathroom attached to his bedroom was enormous. It had a full-sized jacuzzi, a double sink, and a shower that sprayed water from all directions. Kate had bought my favorite shampoo and conditioner for me. I used those to wash up, but I couldn't help but pick up David's body wash and inhale deeply. It smelled manly and clean, just like him.

David was still passed out when I got out of the shower. Kate had gotten me clean underwear as requested, but I didn't ask for any other clothes. I walked into David's huge closet and picked out a blue, button-down shirt to wear for the time being. I put it on, and it went down to my knees. Good thing, seeing as I didn't have any pants to wear underneath.

I waited a little while longer for him to wake up, but he was still sound asleep. I wanted him to wake up to be with me, but he was so damned cute when he slept. I figured I'd wander out into the living room and take in the view of New York City in the morning.

I took my time gazing out the window for a while. It was lovely and peaceful, and it gave me time to contemplate just how lucky I was just to be here. Just to be in New York City pursuing my dream was so much more than other people ever got to do. And meeting David so soon after arriving was almost too good to be true. I lingered for a while at the window, then headed toward the kitchen in search of coffee.

I walked in to find Kate and another woman already there. Kate smiled warmly at me, so it was too late to turn around without being seen. My face got hot as the two women looked at me. Being dressed only in David's shirt practically screamed *I had sex with your boss.* I wondered if they had heard us going at it last night. I had completely forgotten there were other people in the house, once I finally got David alone in his bedroom. *Had they heard me screaming his name?*

If they had, they certainly didn't let on. I reasoned that the hallway where all the staff's rooms were located was pretty far away from David's bedroom. I wasn't *that* loud.

"Good morning," Kate said with a kind smile. "Would you like some coffee?"

I could hear it brewing, and it smelled so good that it almost made the embarrassment of standing there in my walk-of-shame clothes worth it. Almost.

"Oh. Uh, well, I don't know," I stammered, glancing down at my clothing and then back up at Kate and the other woman. The other lady had dark brown skin and dark eyes. She was stunningly lovely, and I couldn't help feeling a twinge of jealousy knowing that David lived with an attractive woman.

"I'm so sorry that's all Mr. Groff had for you to wear," Kate said, her soft eyes filled with empathy. She knew I was embarrassed. "We seem to be about the same size. I have some black yoga pants that might fit you, if you like."

"Oh, that's really sweet of you. But I don't want to be any trouble."

"It's no trouble at all," Kate insisted. She met my gaze and added, "I know Mr. Groff wants you to feel at home here. May I get them for you?"

"Sure," I said, feeling relieved. Standing here with no pants on felt like some kind of nightmare you have about showing up to school naked. I really did want to cover up.

"Wonderful. I'll be right back."

Kate headed off to get her pants for me, which of course left me alone with the other woman I had yet to meet.

She walked over to me and held out her dainty, perfectly

manicured hand. "Nice to meet you. I'm Dina, Mr. Groff's chef."

"Nice to meet you, too. I'm Susie."

Dina smiled at me. "You're a dancer, right?"

"Yes. Dancer and a singer."

"Very nice. Mr. Groff's told us a lot about you," Dina said, her gorgeous eyes twinkling. "And he never talks about the ladies he dates."

Though I didn't want to think about other women David had dated before me, I appreciated Dina's candor.

Kate emerged with the pants, and I quickly slipped them on.

"Thanks so much," I said, feeling less self-conscious.

"Would you like some breakfast?" Kate asked. "We've got ingredients for pretty much everything around here, and Dina can make you anything you like."

"Oh, I think I'll wait for David to get up. I would love some coffee, though, if you don't mind."

"Of course. Coming right up."

Kate poured a cup of coffee for me.

"Do you drink coffee?" I asked her.

"Sure," Kate responded, surprised at my question.

"Will you sit down and have a cup with me?"

Kate smiled. "Okay." She brought over two cups of coffee, plus the cream and sugar.

"Dina? Do you want some?" I asked.

"Not right now. I have a lot of work to do, but thank you," Dina said with a smile. She left the kitchen, which gave Kate and me a chance to chat.

I took a sip from my mug. It was easily the most delicious cup of coffee I had ever had in my life. Knowing David, he probably had it flown in directly from Colombia.

"Oh my God, this is amazing," I said, taking another healthy sip.

"Oh, I know. One of the many perks of this job," Kate said, enjoying her drink as much as I was.

"How long have you worked for David?" I asked, glancing down at her crisp black and white uniform. I still couldn't quite believe I was dating a man who had a *butler*.

"Since he moved to New York a few months ago. Dina worked for him back in D.C., and he paid for her to relocate. Said he'd never find another chef like her."

Jealousy fluttered up in me again, but I tried to ignore it. Dina was lovely, but she was just an employee. I worked with hot guys all the time in the theater, and though some were gay, plenty of them weren't. So far, I had never dated an actor I worked with. It was only a matter of time until David saw me in a play where I kissed another man. If I expected him to be cool with that, I had to chill out about his attractive chef.

"How do you like working for David?" I asked.

"I like it a lot. He's not really a demanding boss. I've had some in my day, believe me. Mr. Groff's not hard to take care of. I pride myself on anticipating his every need, while staying out of his way at the same time. Now that I know his likes and dislikes, things run smoothly around here."

"That's good," I said. I inhaled the fragrant aroma of the coffee again. If the coffee was this good, I couldn't wait to try the food.

Kate was staring at me contemplatively.

"What?" I asked, suddenly self-conscious.

"I think he's quite taken with you, Susie. It's nice to see him so happy."

I smiled warmly at her. "He makes me happy, too." *In case you didn't hear last night.* I blushed just thinking about it and took another sip of coffee. "I can't believe he's still asleep."

"Oh, he's quite the night owl. He's up 'til all hours working on his designs."

Kate jumped up suddenly from her seat, startling me. "Good morning, Mr. Groff."

"Good morning," David said, looking directly at me. His eyes traveled down to where I had the first three buttons of his shirt undone. He seemed pleased to see me in his clothes.

David glanced at Kate and said, "Consider Susannah as much your boss as I am. Sit and chat if that's what she wants to do."

"Thank you, sir. May I get you some coffee?"

"Yes," David said gruffly. He glanced over at me, then added, "Yes, *please.*"

I giggled and nodded approvingly. David walked over to where I was sitting, cupped my face, and kissed me tenderly. He straightened up and gazed down at me fondly. "This one's got me wrapped around her pretty little finger already."

"I can see that, Mr. Groff," Kate said, clearly amused. "I think she might be good for you."

He grinned that half-smile that made my knees go weak.

"I think so too," he said.

We gazed into each other's eyes for a moment, just happy to be near each other. I looked him up and down, then smiled. "A suit. Really? On a Saturday?" I teased.

"I like wearing suits. And it's not like this is a fancy one."

I laughed. The lighter brown suit he wore was only slightly less fancy than his usual suits. "I want to see you in jeans sometime."

Kate chuckled, then bit her lip when David shot her a look. He tried to look stern, but I could see the amusement in his eyes.

"Sorry, Mr. Groff. It's just that I would like to see that too, someday."

"Don't hold your breath," David muttered, picking up his coffee mug.

132

I exchanged a look with Kate; she and I both took David's words as a challenge.

David and I had breakfast and proceeded to spend the rest of the weekend together. He wanted to buy me new clothes, but I told him that was silly. We stopped by my place so I could grab some stuff to wear, instead. On Saturday night we went to another five-star restaurant, then we came home and made love in his bed again. Now that he knew exactly where my sweet spot was, it took David no time at all to drive me completely out of my mind. He pounded me hard and fast, over and over again until I reached orgasm. He didn't even make me look him in the eye when I came. I dug my nails into his back, closed my eyes, and cried out his name until my spasms of pure ecstasy eventually subsided. I was past caring if his staff heard us having sex; that kind of pleasure was worth any next-day awkwardness.

I loved every moment I got to spend with him. Then, Sunday night came, and I finally had to go back to my place. We lingered outside the limo in front of my apartment, kissing and not wanting to let go. Joey stood off to the side, politely averting his eyes.

"I have to go," I said reluctantly.

"I know. I'll see you soon, baby," David said tenderly.

I finally walked up the stairs to my apartment feeling warm and cherished, knowing David and Joey were watching to make sure I made it safely inside.

CHAPTER 14

*D*avid and I had been dating for several weeks, and I woke up each morning still not quite believing what my life was like these days. Living in New York City, doing what I loved all day long, and dating the most handsome, exciting man I had ever known, who happened to be extraordinarily wealthy. I felt like I was living in the middle of a fairytale.

I absolutely adored my work at The Creel Foundation. Most of the teachers only worked there part time in the afternoons and evenings, holding down other full-time jobs to pay their bills. Since I had more time, I was able to work with Johnny to create lesson plans and to map out the future of the foundation. I had both teaching and theater experience, so I had plenty of ideas we could try. He had the means to do anything I suggested, and I was excited about all the wonderful things we could do with the place. Johnny and I were such great friends, that working with him never felt like work at all.

Rosemary helped out when she could, but she was busy with school and auditions. I hadn't been to any auditions yet, but I hoped to soon. I wanted to make sure I was prepared when I finally performed in front of real New York producers.

"Ahh, so close, Miggy. You've almost got it," I said to Miguel, one of my ten-year-old dance class students. "Okay, I'll show you one more time, really slowly, so you can see."

Miggy nodded, eagerly watching my feet. I was running through a routine from *Newsies.*

"Okay, okay, lemme try again," Miggy said, his little face screwed up with determination. He tried again, and this time he nailed it.

"Perfect, *perfect,*" I told him with a smile. My heart swelled. He had worked hard on this routine, and he looked so proud of himself.

"Hey, is that the guy who owns this place?" Miggy asked, glancing over at the door of the classroom.

I looked over to see David, sharply dressed in a pricey suit as always, watching me teach. He must have slipped in some-time during my lesson. His eyes twinkled, and he looked proud of me and the work I was doing. I didn't think I would get to see him until the weekend, and I was thrilled that he had come all this way to surprise me.

"No, the goofy blond guy who always wears jeans is the owner of this place. That's my boyfriend," I said.

"Oooooh," the kids said simultaneously, like they were in on a juicy secret.

I laughed and then told them, "Okay, let's take a break for a few. Use the bathroom and please be sure to get some water. Hydrate, hydrate, hydrate!"

The kids ran off, and I walked over to see David.

"What are you doing here?" I asked, wrapping my arms around his neck.

"I happened to be in the neighborhood, and I thought I would drop by for a visit."

"You were in the neighborhood," I said dryly. "In *Brooklyn*."

David frowned. "Okay fine. I missed you. You happy now?"

"Yes," I said softly. "I'm very happy."

I wanted to kiss him, but I figured I needed to behave around my students.

"You're doing great job with these kids, Susannah."

"Thanks. I love doing this, so much."

I watched the kids mill around a bit. Once they had all returned from the bathroom, I clapped my hands to get their attention.

"Okay guys, come on back. Let's sing a song for Mr. Groff here. What do you think we should—"

In his hurry to join the group, Jayden, one of my clumsier kids, ran right into David. In the process, he spilled half his cup of water on David's pants.

I gasped, knowing those trousers cost nearly a thousand dollars. David yelped and took a step back.

"Man, I'm really sorry!" Jayden said, his face flushing with embarrassment.

David looked sternly at him.

Oh David, please don't yell at him. He's just a little boy.

"You know what this means?" David asked. "It means someone must have turned on the *sprinkler system!*" With that, David dipped his hands in Jayden's cup of water and playfully splashed drops of water on him.

Jayden giggled and wiped his face.

David's smile lit up nearly two-thirds of his face this time.

Jayden grinned, but still looked worried when he saw the huge wet spot on David's leg. "Sorry. Hope I didn't ruin your fancy pants."

"Ah, it's water," David said, waving his hand dismissively. Then his eyes grew wide. "At least it wasn't grape juice. Or fruit punch. Then I mighta hadda rough you up a little." David pounded his fist in his hand, but his eyes made it clear he was only teasing. He turned to the rest of the group. "Come on, already. I came all this way to hear you guys sing. What have you got for me?"

I stared at David in amazement. I'd been sure he would be wildly uncomfortable around children. I met David's gaze and smiled, falling harder for him by the moment.

"Why don't we sing 'You'll Never Walk Alone'? We've gotten pretty good at that one." I assembled the kids together, made sure they were all looking at me, then directed them to begin. They sounded like sweet little angels, and it was such a lovely song. I glanced over at David; he seemed incredibly touched at hearing my little guys sing their hearts out. I loved having David see me in my element; in the theater with my precious students.

David applauded loudly when the song was over. I heard someone else whistling his approval, and I looked up to see that Johnny had walked in.

"Wow, that sounded great. Nice job, guys. I think you deserve a present for that," Johnny said as he set down the huge box he'd walked in with. The kids all rushed over to see what Johnny had brought them.

"Cool, T-shirts!" Miggy exclaimed.

Johnny started handing out the brightly colored *Creel Foundation for the Arts* T-shirts for the kids. David walked over and crouched down on the less-than-clean floor to help.

"Go long!" David called out as he bunched up a T-shirt and launched it at Jayden, who caught it in mid-air.

I watched with adoration as David and Johnny put smiles on the faces of all my kids. These little guys didn't have much, and a new T-shirt was a real treat for them. Once all the shirts were handed out, I went over to David and put my arm around his waist.

"You're so wonderful with kids, David."

"You sound surprised."

"That's because I am surprised."

There was a tinge of sadness in his half-smile. "I have two little sisters and a little brother. They didn't get much affection from our mom and dad, so I made sure they got it from me."

My heart ached for David, and I didn't quite know what to say. It was rare for him to open up about something so personal.

"Looking good, guys," David called to the kids who were putting on their shirts. He was done talking about his family for now, so I let it go. Still, I squeezed him a little tighter to show him that I cared.

"You know," I began. "I think *you* should sing for *us*," I said to David.

The kids cheered at that idea.

"Oh, no, no, no, no," David said.

"Yeah, Mr. Groff," Johnny said teasingly. "I want to hear *you* sing."

David's eyes opened wide with mock-terror. "Oh, no you don't. Believe me. I am a terrible singer. Just *awful*."

"Oh, come on," I prodded. "You can't be that bad."

"Come on, mister!" Johnny said in a childlike voice, making the kids laugh.

"Hell n— I mean, *heck* no. Look, Ms. Peters," David said, eyes twinkling, "I know all about how Mr. Creel performed *karaoke* for you and your friends, and surprised everyone by singing like a perfect little angel. And the whole world heard him sing when he serenaded Rosemary, and he sounded fantastic. There will be no such miracle with me. If I sing, all the windows will break, cats will run away, and you'll all have to go home early with a headache."

The kids giggled at David's exaggeration. I laughed, too,

but now I was more determined than ever to hear David sing. Before I could tease him further, the door swung open, and a very attractive man walked in.

"There he is," Johnny said with a grin. "Good to see ya, man. Susie, this is Luke Rannells."

"Oh, right," I said with a smile. I had seen his résumé when Johnny and I were looking for someone new to teach acting and voice lessons in the evenings, but Johnny had been the one to interview him. "So nice to meet you."

"Likewise," Luke said with a smile, shaking my hand warmly. "Wow, you guys are lookin' spiffy. Nice shirts."

The kids grinned with pride, and I found I liked Luke already. His résumé was impressive; he'd been in several off-Broadway productions and had taken voice lessons for more than a decade. He also happened to be knee-weakeningly gorgeous, with light brown hair, brown eyes, and a terrific build. Luke also seemed charming and charismatic. I was pretty sure I'd have made the same decision if I had interviewed him. *Damn, was he fine.*

I glanced over to see David scowling, and I bit my lip to keep from laughing. I didn't want David to feel bad, but it was cute that he was jealous of this hot stranger.

Serves you right. After all, you have that goddess of a chef living with you. Now you know how it feels.

"Luke, I saw by your résumé that you were in the off-Broadway production of *Bloody, Bloody Andrew Jackson*. That must have been wild," I said, ignoring David's frown. I would be working with Luke, so it would be good to get to know him. Besides, I really wanted to hear about the show. It was one of my favorites. It portrayed President Andrew Jackson as an emo rock star, and it was subversive and hilarious. I could easily see Luke portraying Jackson, who wore tight black jeans during the show.

"Oh, it *was* wild. I had a blast doing that show. Not often you get to really rock out like that in the theater, ya know?" Luke said, his eyes lit up with excitement. I looked forward to working with another theater person who shared my passion.

I glanced at David, feeling slightly annoyed at his irritated expression. *I'm allowed to talk to other men, Mr. Groff.*

"Luke, this is my boyfriend, David Groff."

There, I made it clear that I'm taken. Happy now?

"Good to meet you," David said, giving Luke a slightly too-firm handshake. I fought the urge to roll my eyes. Instead, I looked over at Johnny who was goofing around with my kids. I thought about gathering my students around so we could continue the lesson, but our time was almost up anyway. I figured I'd just let them have fun for now.

The door to the classroom opened. Johnny glanced up, and a look of panic crossed his face.

"Oh shit," he said as he rushed over to the door.

It was Rosemary. Her face was red and blotchy, and tears streamed down her face.

"Rosemary, what—" Johnny said.

She laughed. "It's okay. I'm okay, I'm fine. I'm sorry, I thought I could get myself under control by the time I got here." She took a deep breath and tried to compose herself.

Everyone in the room stared at her, waiting to find out what all the fuss was about. Johnny gazed at her, looking cautiously optimistic. These seemed to be happy tears, but we all needed reassurance from Rosemary that she was really all right.

"Okay, you all know that audition I did for the Broadway revival of *Hairspray*?" Rosemary asked.

"Yeah," Johnny said, eyes wide.

Oh, please tell me she got the part. No one deserves it more than she does.

"I got it," Rosemary said, her voice quaking with emotion.

"I got a part in the ensemble." She struggled to get the next part out, and barely managed to whisper, "I'm going to be on Broadway."

"Rosemary, Rosemary, oh my God," Johnny said, grabbing her and hugging her with all his might.

Rosemary laughed and cried at the same time. They held each other close for several moments, and when Johnny finally released her I could see his eyes were wet.

"Oh, Johnny," Rosemary said, clearly touched by Johnny's reaction. He loved her so much, and nothing brought him more joy than seeing her happy.

She turned to me. We locked eyes and shared a moment of mutual astonishment. All those years of working and planning and dreaming; all the hours of sharing our hopes and dreams and fantasies of what it would be like to finally get our big break. No words between us were necessary. I understood what she was feeling more than anyone else ever could.

"Susie," she whispered.

"Rosemary, oh my God," I said. I opened my arms and she rushed into them. We hugged as tightly as she and Johnny had, which only served to release a fresh torrent of tears from Rosemary.

I let her go and looked into her eyes. "It's happening, Rosemary. It's really happening. Everything you've ever worked for. I'm so happy for you!"

And I was happy for her, but I couldn't help but feel a twinge of jealousy.

Okay, maybe it was more than a twinge. It was more like a sharp stab, and it took me by surprise. Rosemary was my dearest friend, and I wished no less than for every one of her dreams to come true. Still, it brought to the surface every nagging doubt I'd ever had about my own chances of making it to Broadway. I hadn't even been on an audition, and here

Rosemary had already made it into the Actors' Equity Association, and now she had landed an actual role *on Broadway.*

I suddenly felt left behind.

I took a deep breath, knowing deep in my heart that the feeling would pass. Doubts like this were nothing new. Every artist had them, and real artists knew how to power through them. That's what I would do. Besides, this was Rosemary's moment. It was no time to indulge in a pity party for one.

Rosemary noticed Luke standing off to the side. Once she caught his eye, he grinned at her and strode right up to her.

"Hi. You have no idea who I am. Congratulations!" Luke opened his arms for a hug. Rosemary burst out laughing and then obliged. His hug was warm but brief. She was the boss's girlfriend, after all. After releasing her, he explained, "I'm Luke Rannells. The new voice lessons teacher."

"So nice to meet you, Luke. Welcome aboard," Rosemary said.

"Thanks. And congrats again. That's incredible. Johnny spent half my job interview talking about how amazing you are and how hard you've worked."

"Oh, that's so sweet," she said, glancing over at Johnny, who had never looked more proud of her.

Patiently waiting his turn, David finally approached Rosemary. "Congratulations, Rosemary. I can't tell you how happy I am for you."

David gave her a swift but warm embrace, surprising all of us.

"Thank you so much," Rosemary said. She and I exchanged looks, nonverbally saying, *I can't believe David actually hugged somebody.*

The kids had gone quiet, likely because they weren't sure what was happening. Rosemary was a mess and in no shape to explain, so Johnny gathered the kids around to talk to them. He explained the situation and why it was such a big deal. He mentioned that maybe I could teach them a song or a dance from the show *Hairspray*, which was a terrific idea.

I started running through the songs in my head; there were a number of good ones for kids. I couldn't help but wonder if doing a song from the show would be hard for me. A constant reminder every time we rehearsed it that Rosemary's dream had come true, but mine was still unfulfilled.

"You okay?" David asked with concern. I realized he'd been watching me and had picked up on my distress. I quickly put on my actress face.

"Of course. I'm just so happy for her. She deserves this so much. She's worked hard for it," I told David. And it was true. I knew that from the bottom of my heart.

Then why did I feel so lousy?

CHAPTER 15

*W*e had dinner at another one of Susannah's favorite cheap food places, and again I was forced to admit that the food was pretty damned good. We went to a Thai food place in her neighborhood where the employees knew her by name. She wasn't much of a cook, that lovely girlfriend of mine. Neither was I. It didn't matter. I was happy to take her wherever she wanted to go, and of course I had Dina at home to whip up whatever Susannah wanted to eat.

I was nervous about bringing Susannah back to my place, but it wasn't about the sex for once. Now that I had gotten to know her body so well, I knew exactly how to please her. She would never know how I close I came—pun utterly intended —to blowing it with her that first night. Now that I had my hormones under control, I could easily satisfy her.

No, this time I was nervous because I wanted to show her some of the designs I'd been working on. No one outside of the fashion industry had seen my designs, so this was a big deal for me. My parents knew what I was up to in New York, but I didn't think they really cared. I wasn't complaining, though. They were financing most of this, of course. My startup, my penthouse—everything. My brother and sisters were supportive, but none of them lived close by.

Besides, Susannah's was really the only opinion that mattered to me. I knew she would be kind when she saw my work. She was *always* kind. In keeping my emotions close to my vest, revealing my designs to her felt like a huge expression of emotion. It probably wouldn't be for anyone else, but it was for me.

I finally broached the subject when we got back to my place after dinner.

"So, I was thinking. Would you...maybe want to take a look at some of the designs I've been working on?"

Her pretty, blue eyes lit up. "Are you kidding? *Of course* I want to see them. I've been dying to, but I didn't want to put any pressure on you. I know I don't want anybody seeing my performances until I feel ready. Show me, show me!"

"Okay, keep your pants on. Well, strike that. You can take your pants off if you want."

"Later. I promise," she said seductively. "Now, show me your work."

I led her to my home office, my head quickly filling with images of all the places we could have sex in there. Having sex on an office desk surrounded by piles of designer clothing might not be every man's sexual fantasy, but it was certainly one of mine.

"Wow, this is beautiful," Susannah exclaimed as her gaze swept the room. This was the only place in my apartment that she hadn't seen. I hadn't been ready. Until now.

I watched Susannah as she took it all in. My office offered another terrific view of the city. She gazed out the window and smiled softly as she frequently did when looking out at the city of her dreams. Then she turned to the large mahogany desk. My cock twitched as I fantasized about swiping the desk clean of its papers and scraps of clothing and having my way with Susannah right there on top of it.

She drew in a deep breath. "Mmm, it even smells like you, David. That masculine cologne of yours. This place is lovely. I'm sure you do some of your best work in here."

I watched nervously as her gaze continued to roam, finally landing on the three mannequins in the back of the room. They were each dressed in my original designs. I'd spent hours obsessively putting the clothes together and getting them ready to show Susannah, hoping I would finally get the nerve to show her today.

"Oh, David, are these yours?" Susannah exclaimed, her pretty eyes going wide as she quickly crossed the room to get a closer look.

"Yes. Those are some of my designs." I was relieved to hear my voice portray a lot more confidence than I felt.

I walked over to join her as she looked over the suits I had so painstakingly designed. The middle mannequin wore my favorite: a slim-fitted charcoal suit with a royal blue silk tie.

"Did you actually make these?" she asked, admiring my work.

"Had them made, yes. I don't sew them myself. I hand-selected all the materials from different places—some from the garment district here in New York, others came from Europe and Asia. I get everything together and then hire seamstresses."

"David, these look amazing!"

Susannah spent a great deal of time looking over each mannequin and the design it exhibited. She lovingly touched the fabric, seeming to pore over every inch. She stopped at the second mannequin, examining the blue silk tie closely.

"Is that—"

She noticed, I thought, feeling excited. There was a hidden design on the tie—the one I was most proud of.

"They look like little circles, but they're ..."

"Smiley faces," I finished for her.

She glanced up at me, a look of amusement and surprise on her face. She seemed impressed, which thrilled me more than she would ever know.

"Yes," I said, lifting the tie. "We businessmen get a rap for having no sense of humor, but it's not always true. And here, look really close toward the bottom of the tie."

Susannah did as I instructed, squinting at the bottom. She suddenly laughed out loud. "Oh my God, *I love that.*"

Once of the tiny faces on the tie had its tongue sticking out; a secret for the guy wearing it. I loved it too.

"There are three of them like that. See if you can find the other two."

"Oh, that is so fun. Lemme see."

Watching her excitement over my designs made me happy. I allowed myself a smile when she wasn't looking. Susannah seemed to bring out that part of me. She made me so happy, it was hard to contain it sometimes. Not a bad problem to have.

"Here. Here's one," she said.

"Yes. That's two."

Susannah flipped the tie over and eventually located the third one.

I chuckled. "Good job. You did it."

"David, your designs are beautiful, just *beautiful.* I mean, I don't know anything about men's suits other than what you've told me, but these are just lovely. They're smart and attractive, and the design is so clever!"

Susannah was looking at me, but somehow, I couldn't bring myself to return her gaze. There was something I wanted—no, *needed* to say to her, and I knew I wouldn't be able to if I was looking into her eyes. I was just no good at this sort of thing.

"I'm really glad you like my designs, Susannah. I, well …" I stared at my suits instead of her. I took my time, knowing what I wanted to say. Susannah was a warm and loving woman, and I had no idea what she saw in me. But I knew she deserved to hear me express my feelings out loud once in a while, no matter how uncomfortable I found doing so. "These last few weeks, while I've been working on these designs, I kept thinking about you and what you might think of them. It felt like they wouldn't be real until I shared them with you."

I kept staring at the clothed mannequins. I thought that admitting my feelings out loud would be awkward, but the silence afterward was worse. I could feel her eyes on me.

"I know it sounds stupid," I added.

"David," Susannah began softly. "David, please look at me."

I swallowed and finally turned to look at her. Her gentle smile eased my anxiety in an instant.

"It doesn't sound stupid," she said, touching my arm with gentle affection. "I think it's probably the sweetest thing anyone's ever said to me. You should know you can tell me anything you're thinking or feeling. It's never gonna sound stupid. You're safe with me, David."

I did feel safe, gazing into those pretty eyes of hers. She was warm and affectionate, yet she understood and accepted that I wasn't.

"I know you have a really hard time talking about your feelings," she said softly. "Is it because of your family? You said they didn't give you or your siblings much affection growing up."

I sighed. I didn't like talking about my family, but Susannah deserved some kind of explanation for my bumbling when it came to my emotions. If nothing else, at least it would reassure her that it had nothing to do with how I felt about her.

"Yes. They weren't bad parents, I guess. They just weren't around much. We always had nannies and chefs, and people like that around to take care of us."

"Oh," Susannah said with a sad smile. "Is that why you like having Kate and Dina living here?"

"I never really thought about it, but probably. They take good care of me. Anyway, I come from a family that never hugged each other or talked about feelings. It just wasn't done. That's why I'm so terrible at expressing myself."

"You're not terrible. I think you're wonderful."

I gazed down at her, overwhelmed with love for her, with no idea how to articulate it. I knew the day would come when I would have to say *I love you* out loud, but I wanted the moment to be perfect—when I finally had the nerve to tell her.

Susannah let go of me and went back to admiring my designs. "I'm so proud of you. These look wonderful, David. Do you have a name for your designs? Or, like, a company name?"

"It's just going to be my name. You know, like Ralph Lauren or Tommy Hilfiger."

"Ralph Lauren, Tommy Hilfiger, and David Groff. The giants in the fashion industry," Susannah said.

"Not quite. Not yet, anyway. The company name will just be David Groff, and I've hired a graphic design company to develop a logo for me. They're going to provide several ideas to choose from; I would love to get your opinion on them when they're ready."

"Of course," Susannah said. "I can't wait to see what they come up with."

She looked at me for a moment.

"What?" I asked.

"I'm really proud of you for your designs and all," she said.

"But," I prompted.

"But I still wanna hear you sing."

"No," I said firmly. "No, you do not. Trust me on this."

She giggled. "I'll get you to sing yet. Just you wait."

I watched her carefully as she drew in a deep breath. She clearly had something on her mind.

"Are you all right?"

Susannah nodded, then said, "I have an audition tomorrow. It's for a new off-Broadway production. I'm scared, David. I suddenly feel so out of my league here."

"Baby, you're going to be wonderful. You've got this under control." This time I didn't have to feign sounding confident. I believed in her wholeheartedly.

"I hope so," she said.

"You're going to go into that audition and give it everything you've got, and you're going to blow them all away. God, I'll never forget the way you made me feel when I first saw you dance."

Susannah gazed up at me hopefully, needing to hear more.

"You were incredible, Susannah," I told her. "When I first saw you, I noticed how physically beautiful you were. There are lots of pretty girls out there, but then I saw you strut onto that dance floor like you owned the place. And you *danced* like you owned the place. Susannah, you were strong, powerful, *sensual*. I couldn't take my eyes off you. I was staring and practically drooling like an idiot, but I couldn't help myself. Not only was your technique flawless, but you have an incredible charisma—that elusive presence and chemistry that people talk about when explaining what it takes to be a star. Simply put, you have what it takes to make it, Susannah. You really, truly do."

She looked at me gratefully, as if she was about to cry.

Then she said, "When I met you that day, I thought you were a stuffy old snob with a stick up his ass."

I laughed out loud at that. It was just so unexpected.

Susannah wrapped her arms around me. "But when we met again at the restaurant, you were so sexy and charming, I thought, Where has this wonderful man been all my life? You talked to me about theater, and you actually listened to what I had to say." She looked deeply and hungrily into my eyes and said in a sultry voice, "I was so turned on, I hardly trusted myself to accept a ride home with you. I was afraid I might end up giving myself to you right there in the limo."

"And I would have gladly taken you right there in the limo."

She kissed me and then said, "Thank you for believing in me. I'm still pretty stressed out, though." She started nuzzling my neck. "So I need you to take me to the bedroom and relieve my tension."

"Yes, ma'am." I scooped her up into my arms. I still hadn't given up on the idea of having sex in my office, but for now, moving this party to my bedroom was fine by me.

CHAPTER 16

*S*ex with David last night certainly relaxed me. It always did, since he knew exactly how to please me. But it was more than that. We lay in his bed for a while, talking about my audition, and soon I was far more excited than nervous about it. The outcome honestly didn't matter—though, of course, a callback and getting a part was ideal. But the real thrill was to be auditioning for a show in New York City. After all, how many people actually got a chance to do that? I reflected on all the shows I had been in, from grade school through college. I had always dreamed of coming to New York to audition, and the day had finally come.

The audition was at Pearl Studios on Eighth Avenue, late in the afternoon. It had driven me nuts to wait half the day, but now it was finally time to leave. David had wanted Joey to drive me in the limo, but I adamantly refused. Any New Yorker worth her salt going to an audition had to take the subway. Besides, how snotty and privileged would I look if I showed up in a stretch limousine? The other actors would hate me, and the casting director might think I didn't really need the job.

I waited in line—or *on line*, in New York City speak—for my first audition. I drew in a deep breath as I looked around at the city, remembering my vow not to take a single moment for granted. The streets were teeming with people, and there was so much noise and activity all around me. Cars honking, people yelling. Everything in New York moved so fast. It was exhilarating.

I was hardly nervous at all anymore, but that might change once it was my turn. I was just so damned excited to be there. I clutched my audition book to my chest, finding it difficult not to tear up. I was so close to my dream, I could hardly believe it.

I chatted with other people in line who were all a lot nicer than I had expected. I figured they would mostly be rude New Yorkers or aloof theater pros, but instead, I found they were transplants like me. People who had hopped on a bus and headed to the Big Apple, hoping for their big break.

The line didn't move as quickly as I'd hoped. After several hours, I was still inching closer to my turn. At least I was inside the building now, and no longer standing outside in the bright sun. I flipped through my audition book, wondering what they might want to hear. The weird thing about auditions was that you were expected to know all your songs by heart, but they usually only asked you to sing a sixteen-bar cut. I had several songs prepared. My regular go-to songs were "Meet Me in St. Louis," which was a terrific one made famous by Judy Garland, and "When You've Got It, Flaunt It" from *The Producers*. I had recently added "Johnny One Note" to my repertoire. I hadn't thought much about that one in the past, but I realized how much fun it was to sing when I serenaded Johnny with it at The Creel Foundation. I also had a few pop songs prepared, like "The Power of Love" by Celine Dion, and "True Colors" by Cyndi Lauper. Naturally, "Buenos Aires" was my go-to dance audition

153

piece, but this audition was a musical comedy show that didn't call for dancing. It was funny that Rosemary had gotten a part in the *Hairspray* song and dance ensemble, even though dancing wasn't her specialty.

Rosemary was so lucky.

Well, okay. Maybe it wasn't fair to say she just got lucky in getting the part. But still, what I wouldn't give to be in her dancing shoes.

The line continued to inch closer, and a renewed thrill rippled through my body. I could hardly wait to get in there and give it everything I had. Sometimes the casting directors chose a song from the audition book, but if they left it up to me, I was pretty sure I wanted to sing "Johnny One Note."

The door to the audition room opened and they called in a girl about five people ahead of me. I was so excited, I wanted to scream. Even though I told myself that just auditioning would be enough for now, I couldn't help but think about what might happen if I actually got a part. I needed to log lots of hours in union shows to get into the Actors' Equity union and to get an agent. I needed an agent for any realistic hope of getting into a Broadway audition. This show, if I got a part, would help me earn hours toward becoming an Equity Membership Candidate, which was a critical step toward membership. That was how Rosemary had done it. She had worked on summer stock and other off-Broadway shows to get into the union. She'd also managed to get an agent, though she credited the crazy viral video for that stroke of luck. Her agent, Cynthia Bowles, had contacted Rosemary after seeing her in one of her shows, but she had mentioned the video when they met. Rosemary's fame had clearly preceded her, and being the girlfriend of infamous heir Johnny Creel certainly didn't hurt her chances any.

I honestly wasn't sure if that was a good thing. Sure, it helped her land an agent, but what if David had already been a famous men's designer, and I was known as David Groff's girlfriend? It might feel like I hadn't earned my spot on Broadway. I hoped Rosemary never felt like that. She was so talented and hardworking. Though I felt jealous of her, I was also incredibly proud.

And someday that might be me up there on the Great White Way.

The door swung open again. Now only three people waited ahead of me. I was so close, I could taste it. I flipped through my audition book for the umpteenth time, trying to kill a few minutes. The wait became more unbearable the closer I got.

At long last, the door swung open again and a weary casting director emerged. She flipped her gray hair back and said, "I want to thank you all so much for coming today. I'm afraid we're out of time, but feel free to leave your headshot and résumé on your way out."

I couldn't move.

My mind kept replaying what she said, but it was like my brain couldn't process her words. What? It was over, just like that? It wasn't just the hours and hours of waiting and anticipation, though that was bad enough. I had waited my whole life for my first audition in New York, and I'd thought today would be the day. Just like that, any hope of getting a part and working toward my union membership were gone in the blink of an eye.

With shaking hands, I took out my headshot and résumé and tossed them into the pile. I might as well have put them through a paper shredder, because I knew the casting directors wouldn't even look at them. They had clearly seen enough people's auditions for their needs.

I promised myself I wouldn't cry. At least not until I got out of there.

* * *

"So, how did it go?" David asked when he called me that night.

"It didn't," I said wearily. I was touched that he'd called to check on me, but I didn't feel like rehashing the day's events. I'd cried while riding the subway back home. I was just so damned disappointed. All I had wanted was to experience my first New York City audition. Regardless of how the actual audition went, I'd thought at least I would have accomplished that much. It never occurred to me that I wouldn't even be seen by the casting director.

"What do you mean?" David asked.

"I waited for hours for my turn and just when they were about to get to me, they said they had seen all the people they needed to see. I never even got in the door."

"Oh, baby. I'm so sorry," David said, sounding worried and sad.

I closed my eyes as I listened to his voice. I loved that I didn't have to explain how crushed I was. He knew. I opened my eyes again. "It's okay. I was pretty upset earlier, but I feel a little better now."

"That's good," David said, still sounding concerned. "I know it's a miserable experience, but it probably happens all the time. I'll bet it probably took Rosemary a while to get her first audition. You should ask her."

A wave a jealousy washed over me. Yes, I knew I probably should ask Rosemary for help. She had been in New York for two years, and she probably went through a lot of the same things I was going through. I probably should confide in her, but I just couldn't bring myself to do it. We had always been equals when it came to pursuing our shared dream, but now I suddenly felt inferior to her. Rosemary would soon be on

Broadway, and I couldn't even make it into an audition for a lousy off-Broadway show.

"Yeah, I guess I should," I said, knowing damned well that I wouldn't.

"I'm sorry it didn't work out this time, Susannah. Maybe if you get there earlier for the next audition, you'll get your chance."

"Oh, I will definitely get there a lot earlier next time," I said defiantly. I'd been kicking myself for not leaving my apartment sooner. When I thought of all the time I'd wasted just sitting around waiting to leave, I wanted to scream. "I'll get there at 3am if I have to."

"That's my girl," David said proudly. "Well, it was their loss. If they had stayed just a little while longer, they could have had a real star for their show."

"Thanks, David," I said with a smile. We talked for a little while longer and then reluctantly said goodnight. I found myself wishing I was with him. If he'd had his way, I would be. He kept insisting that Joey was available to drive me anywhere I needed to be, and it wouldn't have been a problem for me to stay at David's penthouse and be back at The Creel Foundation the next morning. It just didn't seem right to me. I was supposed to be a struggling artist, and today I certainly had felt like one. I was supposed to live in a crappy apartment and take the subway. It was called paying my dues.

Yeah. That's what this was. Paying my dues. A failed first audition was normal, and I was sure lots of Broadway performers got their start this way.

Missing my first New York City audition was part of the real New York City performer experience.

I laughed ruefully and shook my head.

* * *

FORTUNATELY, another opportunity to audition came up just a few days later. I was determined not to blow it this time, so I showed up hours earlier than necessary. There were already a few people in line, but not many. The odds were pretty good that I would at least get seen this time. I was nowhere near as excited as I was the first time, which was kind of a bummer. It was hard to muster up that same excitement knowing there was a still a possibility that it might not happen.

Once the line started moving, I found myself finally feeling hopeful. There really weren't many people in front of me, so things were looking good. I flipped through my audition book as the line inched closer and closer. Then the hardest part came; I was next. The door finally opened, and I drew in a breath.

The casting agent, a brunette in her forties or so, nodded at me to come in.

Oh, thank God.

I walked into the room with confidence, turned to greet the casting directors seated at the table in front, and smiled. My adrenaline surged, but I kept my expression even.

"Good morning," I said.

"Good morning," said a man at the table. "Okay, sixteen bars. Your choice. Go!"

I nodded. I handed the piano player the sheet music for my song, then I strutted back to the center of the room.

I drew in a deep breath and sang sixteen bars of "Johnny One Note." I was fairly pleased with how I sounded. It was always invigorating for me to sing in front of any audience, and performing for casting directors was thrilling.

"Okay, thanks very much for coming in," the brunette lady said crisply but politely.

"Thanks," I said with a bright smile.

I nodded at the casting directors, then hurried out.

I wasn't sure what to think as I headed back to the subway. I was relieved that I had finally had my first New York audition, but it was impossible to gauge what they had thought of me. It had all happened so quickly. Would they have asked for more if they were interested? Oh, well. I would find out soon enough if I got a callback.

I gazed up at the tall buildings and felt a tiny thrill ripple through my stomach. *I had just auditioned in New York.* It was probably the first of many, and that meant many more opportunities for success. It was crazy to expect to land a role straight away.

I smiled to myself as I took a seat on the subway, feeling like a real wannabe theater actress. Taking the subway, standing in line for auditions, running around New York. *I was actually pursuing this.* The worry of not getting in was over, as was the high I'd experienced when I got up to sing. Now I just felt happy and somewhat optimistic. I was on my way, working my way up, and paying my dues.

I was eager to talk to David, to share my experience with him. I thought about calling Rosemary, too. She'd understand my excitement, since I was sure she had felt the same way when she first arrived in New York. I was sure she would be happy for me.

But I couldn't help feeling that my news of going on an off-Broadway audition was small potatoes compared to Rosemary's situation. She was already in rehearsals for *Hairspray,* actively preparing for her role on Broadway. Rosemary would never belittle me, though, or make me feel bad, but I'd probably end up feeling bad anyway. I could tell her how my audition went, but then I would have to ask her how things were going with her. And she would tell me. And it would make my little audition seem, well, *little.*

No. I wouldn't call Rosemary. At least not today. I needed to enjoy my small victory right now.

I felt a twinge of sadness. I used to tell Rosemary everything.

* * *

I PEERED out the window at The Creel Foundation, reflecting over the last few weeks. I had been on several more auditions. It was still exciting to get up and perform for professional casting agents, but most of the time I didn't get to do much. So far, only one casting agent had asked to hear more than the usual sixteen- or thirty-bar cut. And still no callbacks.

Whenever I found myself feeling bummed out over not hearing back from any casting calls, singing and dancing and working with my kids at The Creel Foundation cheered me up. It always felt good to get up and perform, wherever I was. It was cathartic and healing every time.

Seeing David always cheered me up as well. I smiled when I saw David's limo roll up. I was looking forward to being with him tonight. We had no real plans yet. It didn't matter much where we went on the weekends. Just being with him made me happy.

"Gotta go, Johnny. My chariot awaits."

"See ya, Susie," Johnny said with a friendly grin. "You two kids have fun."

"We will," I said with a smile. "We always do."

CHAPTER 17

"There's my shining star," I said as Joey helped Susannah into the limo. I had to remember to call him "Joey" and not "Stewart," lest I get a disapproving look from my girlfriend. Susannah looked a bit tired, but her pretty face lit up when she saw me. I had never dreamed any woman would look at me the way she did. Good God, was I a lucky man.

Susannah snuggled up next to me on the seat, and I wrapped my arm around her. "It's been such a long week." I should have added that it was a long week because I missed her terribly when we were apart, but of course, I didn't. I sincerely hoped I didn't come off as cold and uncaring around her. Nothing could be further from the truth.

"It certainly has," she said, resting her head on my shoulder.

"Where do you want to go tonight? Do you want to see a show?"

"Nah, I'm sure it's too late to get tickets to see anything good."

"Silly girl. Of course it's not too late. Name the show and I'll get tickets. *Good* tickets."

Susannah smiled, but I could see the underlying sadness in her expression. "I'm sure you could. I don't really feel up to going to a show tonight."

"Okay. If you're sure," I said, studying her face. "Are you all right?"

"Yeah, I'm fine," she insisted.

I knew she wasn't, but I didn't want to make her talk if she didn't feel like it. She'd had several auditions lately and still no callbacks. She was probably feeling disappointed and rejected, and wasn't up for seeing a Broadway show full of successful performers. If somebody told me they didn't like my latest designs, I wouldn't exactly want to rush off to fashion show and see other successful designers. I understood completely how she was feeling. I just wished she would confide in me.

Easy for me to say. Not like I was great about sharing my feelings. Still, I wanted to help her feel better.

"Okay. What would you like to do then?"

Susannah paused to think for a moment. "Do you want to come back to my place? You've never even been inside."

"Sure, baby." I didn't know why she wanted to go back to her tiny apartment instead of my place, where I had a full staff to make us dinner and all that. I supposed it didn't matter. I was happy to do whatever she wished.

I pressed the button and told Joey to drive us to Susannah's place.

"Oh, there's something I wanted to show you," I said to Susannah. I reached over to the other seat and picked up a large manila envelope. "These are the logos for my company that my graphic designer came up with."

I pulled out the papers with four different *David Groff* designs on them. I watched her face as she glanced at them.

"They look nice," she said. She seemed distracted.

"Well, which one do you like the most?" I asked.

"Umm. Let me see. I think I like that one." She pointed to one of the designs.

"Oh, good. That was one of the two I had narrowed it down to."

"That's good," Susannah said without much interest.

I couldn't help but feel disappointed. I'd been excited all week to show her these designs and had imagined the two of us having a lively discussion about the logos. I thought we would talk about what we liked and what we didn't, and eventually come to a conclusion. Susannah was usually so supportive of my work, and I loved getting her involved in it. I swallowed my disappointment and put the designs away. I knew she'd had a rough week. It was time for me to focus on making her feel better.

I put my hands on her shoulders and started massaging them. She smiled, and I felt her relax. "Are you hungry? We could eat before we go to your place if you want."

"I'm not really hungry at the moment. Are you?" she asked.

I shook my head. "No, I'm fine."

I kept rubbing her shoulders and massaging her back until we got to her apartment.

"Thanks, David. I didn't realize how tense I was," she said, kissing me softly.

"I can think of other ways to relieve your tension."

"So can I."

I pressed the button, and within seconds Joey opened the door for us. After he helped Susannah out of the limo, I stepped out. I suppressed a grimace as I looked up at the dirty old building that housed my girlfriend's apartment.

"Home sweet home!" Susannah chirped, looking amused at my expression. She turned and headed up the steps. I looked at Joey, wide-eyed, and he chuckled. I followed Susannah up the stairs and into the apartment building.

By the time we'd hiked up three flights of stairs to get to her apartment, I was sweating inside my Brunello Cucinello suit. The hallway was dark and dingy, and the smells from multiple dinners cooking simultaneously, assaulted my nostrils. It would be a struggle to maintain my poker face throughout this whole ordeal, but I couldn't bear the thought of hurting Susannah's feelings. She worked hard to afford this place, and I needed to quit being such a snob.

I took a deep breath as Susannah slid her key into the lock, preparing to effusively praise whatever I saw on the other side of the door.

Good God almighty was her place tiny.

I had bathrooms in my penthouse that were bigger than this entire place. There was a small strip of a kitchen, a cramped living room area, and a door that must have been to her bedroom. My tie suddenly felt tight, and a wave of claustrophobia swept over me. *How did Susannah live like this?* I searched my brain for anything positive to say. Quaint, sweet, nice ...

"It's ... cozy," I offered.

Susannah laughed. "You're cute when you're trying not to look horrified."

"I'm not horrified. It's just ... you deserve better."

Susannah proudly looked around at the place. "Well, it may be a dump. But it's *my* dump."

I chuckled. "That's exactly what Johnny said when he was broke. When his dad's money got cut off, he had to move into a crappy apartment in D.C."

Susannah raised an eyebrow. "Crappy like my apartment, right?"

"N—no. I don't mean it like that. I just mean he had to work hard and pay for it himself. Look baby, it was a huge step down from his penthouse, you know? But he learned to be proud of it because it was his."

She smiled, letting me off the hook. She wasn't one to get offended easily, and she liked to tease me. "I know you what you mean. And yeah, that's how I feel. This is *my* place. In *New York*." She glanced out the dirty window and added, "It may not have the view that your place has, it might be Brooklyn and not Manhattan, but it's still my view. And I love it."

I nodded, proud of Susannah for her spunky attitude. I understood her need for independence, but more than anything, I wanted her to come and live with me someday. I was a bit worried that maybe she never would. Maybe living on her own while she pursued her dream was just something she needed to do. I respected that of course, but I still wished I could wake up with her by my side each morning.

Susannah looked thoughtful for a moment, and then gently asked, "Does your family, you know, pay for all your stuff?"

I could see that she felt bad asking, but she clearly wanted to know. I saw my displays of wealth as evidence of my power and influence, and I despised having to state the truth out loud. Still, I would not lie to the woman I loved.

After hesitating far too long, I nodded. "Yes."

Susannah smiled sympathetically, then walked over and put her arms around me. I didn't want to look her in the eye after my confession, but she forced me to.

"Well, that's how it is right now. Soon enough your design business will take off, and that will pay for everything. You're gonna do great things, David Groff."

How I loved the way Susannah looked at me. She didn't see me as some sap who lived off his dad's money. She gazed at me with affection and desire. She believed in me, and made me feel like a man. And right now, I wanted to make her feel like a woman.

I leaned down and kissed her, and she eagerly responded. I began nuzzling her neck, and she murmured, "I need you to do me a favor, David."

"And what's that?" I asked between kisses.

"I need you to help me christen my apartment. My bed. I haven't had sex in here yet, and we need to fix that. Give me some good memories for when we're apart during the week."

"Anything you want, baby. Anything."

Susannah cupped my face and kissed me again, then took my hand and led me to her bedroom.

Naturally, the bedroom was as small as the rest of the place. She had a double bed, which looked minuscule compared to my king-sized one, and I highly doubted there were silk sheets on it.

God. Sometimes I could be such a snob, that I even annoyed myself.

Even so, a terrible thought occurred to me. *Would Susannah expect me to spend the night? Have somebody from my staff run out and get supplies for me like I had done with her?*

Of course, I would honor Susannah's wishes if that was what she wanted. God knows she never asked for much. Still, I hoped I wouldn't have to stay overnight in this crowded, dirty, noisy place. Through the thin walls, I could hear her neighbors shuffling around, which probably meant they could hear us, too.

I tried to block out all the distractions and focus on the task at hand—pleasuring my lovely lady.

Susannah sat on the bed and pulled me down by my tie and kissed me. I always found it a turn-on when she grabbed my tie like that. This time she slowly untied it, then slid it around the back of my neck and pulled me toward her again.

The way she took control was incredibly sexy. And after all, we were on her turf.

She unbuttoned my shirt and took it off. I slid my hands under her blouse and rubbed the outside of her bra before I took off her blouse. I reached behind and unclasped her bra and slowly removed it. Susannah lay down on the bed so I could slide off her jeans and underwear. Our lovemaking was usually more frenzied, as we were both eager to get our hands on each other after being apart all week. But taking our time like this was rather erotic.

After we had slowly and sensually undressed each other I slid on top of her, but she had other plans. Susannah bit her lip seductively, then pressed her hands firmly on my chest. She wasn't strong enough to push me off, but I obeyed her command anyway. I rolled over and onto my back.

"That's a good boy," she said in a sultry voice.

I watched with desperate anticipation as she leisurely straddled me. She rubbed my chest for a bit before finally lowering herself onto my rigid cock.

An involuntarily groan escaped my throat, and Susannah smirked with pride. It was tough to get a reaction out of me, but she just looked and felt *so damned good.*

Her hands planted on the mattress, she thrust her hips up and back, riding me hard. I watched her face as she shifted her thrusts to hit her G-spot in just the right way. She panted faster, crying out softly with pleasure. She got close to orgasm, then pulled back to prolong the experience. It was fascinating and utterly erotic to watch.

"Oh, David, you're so *hard*," she moaned. She gasped as she ground against my cock, hitting her sweet spot again.

"I know," I said through clenched teeth. "You're making me *crazy*, Susannah."

Susannah bit her lip again and tossed her head back. She grabbed ahold of my ass and rode me harder. Her eyes closed and her breasts jutting forward, she was a vision; watching her pleasure nearly drove me over the edge. It was incredibly hot to watch her take control, but having her in charge made it harder to contain my own pleasure. If she kept grinding me like this, I was going to lose it.

"Baby, I can't hold on much longer," I warned her.

Susannah laughed seductively, which only turned me on more. She gripped my shoulders so she could get good traction, and I knew what she was going to do next. She was going to finish herself off, and I could hardly wait to watch.

She gazed deeply into my eyes as she rode my cock in the perfect spot to maximize her pleasure.

"David," she gasped. She usually cried out my name when she was close to coming, but this time it was more of a whisper.

"Trying to keep quiet because of the neighbors, are you?" I teased, enjoying her struggle.

"Yes," she whispered.

"You know that just makes me want you to scream even more, baby." I thrust my hips up suddenly, knowing just how to stroke her to make her crazy. Sure enough, she let out an involuntary loud cry.

"David," she hissed. "Stop."

"Hmm, usually you scream at me *not* to stop." With that, I thrust three more times. She dug her nails into my shoulders and bit her lip.

"David," she pleaded.

Well, there was no stopping me now. I thrust my hips over, and over, and over again until she cried out loud in ecstasy as she reached orgasm.

"Mission accomplished," I said cockily as she panted and tried to catch her breath.

Susannah was still recovering from her orgasm, but I was desperate for mine. I flipped her onto her back and rammed myself inside her. I watched her bite back another scream as I pounded her until I found my own release. I usually grunted a bit when I came, but not this time. It was a struggle, but I managed to ride the sharp vibrations of pleasure without uttering a sound.

"You bastard," Susannah said, then laughed while still trying to catch her breath.

I chuckled too. "At least now all your neighbors know you're spoken for."

She nodded. I lay down next to her, and she rested her head on my chest like she often did after we made love. As we lay there together, feeling happy and satisfied, I realized it really didn't matter where we slept tonight. As long as she was in my arms, I would be comfortable.

After a while, Susannah lifted her head and said, "You're so wonderful, David."

I gazed into her eyes and stroked her hair affectionately. She smiled, then put her head back down on my chest.

There were so many things I wanted to say to her. That I knew she was hurting because she hadn't been cast in any shows yet. That I believed wholeheartedly in her talent, and I knew she would do great things someday. That I wanted her to come and live with me in my penthouse. Most of all, I wanted to tell her that I loved her.

I knew this was the perfect moment. We had just been intimate. I was holding her. She wasn't looking at me, which made it easier for me. A bolt of fear shot through me because I knew I would really do it this time. I would say the hardest and most important three words I'd ever said to anyone.

Susannah suddenly sat up and looked down at me with a soft smile. "We can go back to your place now if you want. I know it's more comfortable there, and we can have Dina make us dinner or whatever. I just … David, I appreciate you coming here with me. Feels more like a home now that

I've had you here. And now that I've, you know, *had* you here."

I chuckled, both relieved and disappointed that I hadn't said "I love you" yet. I guess it just wasn't the right time after all.

$\mathcal{R}$osemary had been so busy with *Hairspray* rehearsals, that I hadn't seen her much over the last few weeks. She texted me and asked if we could get together, and of course, I said yes. I missed her, and I really wanted to talk to my best friend. Yet, at the same time, I was stressing out about seeing her.

It had been the same story over and over again with my auditions. I showed up, waited in line forever, sang a few bars, and then got shown the door. Those casting agents saw so many people, it was a wonder how they could even remember the individuals they had seen. It was so demoralizing sometimes, and as much as I loved Rosemary, I wasn't sure I wanted to hear about how well her career was going.

I felt like a horrible person for even thinking that. Rosemary deserved to be excited about landing a role on Broadway, and as her best friend, it was my job to support her and be happy for her. And that was exactly what I would do, even if it killed me inside.

David and Johnny went to their favorite steak joint hangout, so Rosemary and I decided to get together at her penthouse while the boys were gone. She greeted me with a sweet smile and a warm, loving hug.

"It's been way too long since we hung out," Rosemary said as she sat on the couch and I flopped down on the big fluffy chair next to her. "Moscato?"

"Please," I said, gratefully accepting a glass of wine from her. "So, how's it going? Tell me *everything*." My stomach clenched as I said the words.

"It's been amazing, Susie," Rosemary said, green eyes sparkling. "Just incredible. Every day when I show up for rehearsal I still can't believe I'm there, you know?"

I sipped my wine and nodded. It was nice to see Rosemary so happy, and I felt like a slightly less wretched person that it did make me feel good to see her so excited.

"Of course, it's also kind of terrifying. It's hard to wrap my head around the fact that in two weeks … *two weeks* … I'm going to be performing *on Broadway*. It's insane!"

"It is crazy, but crazy wonderful," I said, clutching my wineglass a bit tighter. "Do you like the people you're working with?"

"I do. I really do. There's a nice mix of actors who have already been in a few shows, and a few newbies like me. I'm kinda glad I'm not the only Broadway virgin, ya know?" Rosemary said with a laugh.

Ugh, if Rosemary was a Broadway virgin, what did that make me?

"That's good. I can't wait to see you onstage, Rosemary. It's going to be so amazing."

She nodded, squealing a bit.

"I'm so proud of you, Rosemary. I hope you know that," I told her, meaning every word. She had worked so hard for this and wanted it every bit as much as I did. Talking with her about this was less painful than I had expected. Seeing my best friend so happy was wonderful.

172

"Thank you, Susie."

"To Broadway," I said, offering my glass in a toast.

"To Broadway," Rosemary agreed, and I heard the catch of emotion in her throat as she toasted me. We drained our glasses, and Rosemary refilled them.

"So, how is everything going with you?" she asked.

"Oh, you know. The same old grind, going to a bunch of auditions," I said, not really wanting to talk about it.

"Yeah, I know how it is. I lost count of how many auditions I went on before I got my big break." I could hear the warmth and encouragement in her voice. I was tempted to ask her for details. It had only taken two years for her to get a part on Broadway, which was an incredible feat considering how many people never even get that far. I wanted to ask her how long it took to get her first off-Broadway part. She must have performed in lots of shows since she arrived in New York; otherwise, she never could have gotten into Actors' Equity. Did she get callbacks right away, or did it take her a while to finally find some success after auditioning? Did the casting agents ask her to sing more, or did they send her packing after she sang a mere sixteen bars? Did she question her talent and her very sanity for trying to attempt the impossible?

Did she ever feel like a talentless loser like I did sometimes?

I opened my mouth, but filled it with wine instead of asking the questions I had on my lips. What if Rosemary said she got tons of callbacks right away and had her pick of shows to do right off the bat? I didn't think my already shaky self-confidence could handle that kind of information.

Rosemary looked at me with concern, like she wanted to say something more, but then a woman in her fifties walked into the room and asked her, "Would you like some more wine, Rosemary?"

Rosemary glanced at the nearly two-thirds-empty wine

173

bottle. "Sure, that would be nice. Thank you. Oh, Susie, this is Barbara, our housekeeper and miracle worker. She keeps this place clean and tidy, even with Johnny living here."

"Oh, wow. That's no easy feat. Nice to meet you, Barbara."

"You too," she said with a friendly smile. She turned to Rosemary and asked, "Were you planning on dining here this evening?"

Rosemary glanced at me, and I nodded and said, "Sure, that would be nice. I don't feel like moving, do you?"

"No, I agree. Let's stay here. Johnny's cook, Stephanie, makes an incredible chicken parmesan dish. Whaddya think?"

"Works for me," I said.

"Okey doke. Sounds good," Barbara said. "I'll let Stephanie know, and I'll bring more wine in the meantime."

"Perfect," Rosemary said with a smile. She watched Barbara walk into the kitchen, then turned to face me.

"I live in a penthouse. In New York. With a housekeeper and a chef. How in the hell did I get here?"

I burst out laughing, feeling relaxed by the wine and being in the company of one of my favorite people on the planet. "I cannot tell you how many times I've asked myself the same question."

It felt good to laugh with Rosemary, but I also felt guilty about being so upset over my auditions when I was living a life of luxury. It was so much more than most people had, and I had absolutely no right to complain about anything.

Rosemary glanced around at her fancy living room, and then out the window at the incredible view of New York. "This is nuts. I don't think I'll ever get used to it. I kinda hope I don't."

"Do you know David has a *butler*?"

Rosemary giggled. "Are you serious?"

"Yeah. A lady butler, isn't that funny? I never thought

about women being butlers, you know? She's really sweet, though. Around Barbara's age, I think."

"That's wild," Rosemary said, shaking her head with wonder. "So how are things going with David?"

I sighed happily. "Wonderful. He's amazing. I can't get over how different he is from my first impression of him. He's incredibly talented, for one thing. He designs these beautiful suits and ties and stuff, and I'm just so proud of him. And he's supportive of everything I do, you know? He's the only guy—the only *person*, really—who isn't a performer but still gets me. It's like he understands what I do and why I want to do it. I always thought you had to be an actor or a singer yourself to understand."

Rosemary nodded. "I used to think that, too. Before Johnny."

"Johnny is so much fun to work with," I told her. "We're having a blast at the foundation together."

Rosemary laughed. "Who would have ever thought he would be good to work for?"

"I know, right?"

Johnny had been a horrible boss when Rosemary worked for him all those years ago. After they fell in love, he was like a completely different person. He was a modern-day Ebenezer Scrooge. A much younger, hotter version.

"Johnny said he's never seen David so happy," Rosemary told me, and her words made me feel warm all over. I wondered if David talked to Johnny about me the way I was talking to Rosemary about him. I rather doubted it, since David was hardly the gushing, effusive type. I couldn't see him telling Johnny how he felt about me, but it was nice to know that Johnny had noticed a difference in him.

"He makes me happy, too," I said, swirling the wine in my glass. "It's just …"

"What?" she prodded gently.

"He hasn't said 'I love you' yet, and I just wonder if he does love me."

"Do you love him?"

"Yes," I said.

Rosemary squealed like a teenage girl, which made me laugh. "Oh, that's so sweet. And how crazy is it that our boyfriends are best friends, too?"

I giggled like a schoolgirl myself. It was something lots of little girls say. *When we grow up, our boyfriends are gonna be best friends, and we're gonna have a double wedding and live happily ever after.*

"I know," I said. "I think maybe he does love me, but he has a really hard time talking about his feelings. He doesn't talk about his family much, but it sounds like they were neglectful parents. They pretty much let the servants raise their kids, and they never gave the kids much affection."

"That's so sad."

"Yeah, it really is. So even if he does love me, it would be really hard for him to say it out loud. He's just not like that."

"You could tell him first. I know it's hard, though."

"Yeah, I guess I could. Johnny said it first, right?"

"Well, yes. But you know how he is. He's like this warm, fuzzy puppy dog who's not afraid to show how he feels."

Rosemary smiled as she spoke, and I heard pure love in her voice.

"I mean, he *sang* to you," I said dreamily. I couldn't help but think of David's insistence that he would never, ever sing for me.

"Yeah, but that's not when he first said 'I love you.' That was when we first started getting close. He learned a song on the guitar as his way of telling me he had feelings for me."

"Then, how did he tell you he loved you?"

Rosemary paused, not wanting to make me feel bad.

"It was something perfect and wonderful wasn't it?"

Rosemary nodded, and I laughed. "Go on, you can tell me."

"Well, he stopped by rehearsal one night at the community theater. He brought me roses and stayed around until everyone else had left so we could have some privacy. We sat on the stage together, and he told me loved me." Rosemary looked me in the eye, then added, "And then we had sex on the stage."

I sat up in my chair and put my wineglass down on the table. "You shut up. You *shut up.* You did not!"

Rosemary blushed and nodded, and I burst out laughing. She laughed too, and I realized just how much I had missed hanging out with her these last few weeks. "I can't believe you never told me that."

She chuckled and said, "I know. I should have. It was just so crazy. The only person I told was Ryan, and I almost didn't even tell him."

"How's he doing, anyway?"

"He's doing okay. Lonely, I think. Jack's deployed for another few months, and I used to be the one to keep Ryan company while he's away."

"Well, tell his ass to come visit us in New York," I said. "I miss him too."

Ryan was a great friend. Hanging out with him and our other theater friends was really the only thing I missed about living in D.C.

"I will tell him to come for a visit," Rosemary said. "Johnny'll arrange for everything. Won't cost Ryan a thing."

We drank and talked for a while longer, and then Barbara reemerged from the kitchen. "Okay, ladies. Dinner's all ready."

"Awesome, thanks," Rosemary said. "Let's move the party to the dining room."

The time flew by as Rosemary and I talked and laughed

some more over dinner. Good thing David had a chauffeur, because I was in no condition to stumble to the subway after all the wine I'd had. I texted David when I was ready to go, and Rosemary and I had one more glass of wine while we waited for Joey to come and get me.

"What're you thinking about, girl?" Rosemary asked when she saw I was lost in thought.

"David. I love him, and I wish he would give me some clue about how he feels about me. There's no way he would ever show up with flowers or sing to me or do anything like that."

"He's a terrific guy, Susie, but he's just not like that. That's not his way. He hasn't said he loves you, but that doesn't mean he doesn't. My first impression of him was the same as yours. I thought he was cold, distant, and snobby, but he's none of those things. And he really is different when he's with you. The way he acts and even *sounds*. He's just happier when you're near him."

I smiled, knowing in my heart that it was true. David might not be overly affectionate, but I had learned to read his subtle clues. His half-smile meant he was charmed or amused. His muscles relaxed when I touched him, which meant he was comfortable with me and that he trusted me. And then there was the sweet, gentle look in his eyes—an expression that seemed reserved just for me. Did that mean he loved me?

"Do you think he loves you?" Rosemary asked, as if reading my mind.

"Yes. I think he does. I guess that will have to be enough for now."

"I'm so happy you two found each other."

"Me too." Just then my phone buzzed with a text from David, telling me he and Joey were outside waiting for me in the limo. I found myself looking forward to being in David's arms. Yes. That was more than enough for me.

"Okay, gotta go. This was so great, Rosemary. Thanks so much."

I squeezed her in a tight embrace. "I'm so proud of you, Rosemary. I can't wait to see you on Broadway."

It hurt like hell to say the words out loud, and I hated myself for that. There was no room in our beautiful friendship for my petty jealousy.

"Thank you, Susie," she said, her voice shaking a bit. "For everything."

I held her close for a moment, then let her go.

CHAPTER 19

I was actually quite excited once Rosemary's opening night finally arrived. After all, just going to a show on Broadway was a thrill for me that never got old. Performing on Broadway was my fairytale dream, and a New York Broadway theater was like the prince's castle. It was full of magic and wonder, and so much more now that I knew someone who would be onstage. I had been tearing up all day just thinking about it.

My best friend, Rosemary Sutton, was making her Broadway debut tonight. The woman with whom I'd spent countless hours rehearsing, dreaming, laughing, and crying would finally see her dream realized.

I waited in David's living room while he got ready. I teased him relentlessly about taking longer to get ready than I did, but I had to say, the ultimate result was worth it. Kate and Dina applauded when he walked into the room, and I slapped my hand dramatically over my heart. He looked stunning in his black suit and tie. I walked over to him and looked him up and down.

"And who are you wearing tonight, Mr. Groff?"

David's half-smile made my body tingle all over. He loved it when I talked fashion to him. I think it turned him on.

"Ermenengildo Zegna," he responded coolly, sending another delicious ripple of excitement through my body. Okay, so I found his fashion talk a turn-on, too. His knowledge and passion for the subject was rather alluring. And it didn't hurt that he was so irresistibly handsome in those suits of his. Someday I should have him make love to me while still wearing a suit. Hmm, maybe in his home office. I'd bet he would like that.

"If I ever make it to Broadway, I want you to wear one of your own David Groff designer suits to opening night."

David reached out his hand to take mine. "Not if. *When* you make it to Broadway, I'll wear anything you like." He kissed my hand, then took a step back to look at me. "You look ravishing, Susannah."

I spun around to let him get a better look at the gorgeous ensemble he'd bought me just for the occasion. I wore a lovely shimmery blue dress, which made my blue eyes stand out dramatically. Matching blue pumps, and a sparkling diamond necklace and earring set finished off the outfit. David spoiled me rotten, and I loved it. He made me feel beautiful, not just because of the clothes he bought me, but because of the way he looked at me.

We had excellent seats near the front of the theater, and Rosemary's friends and family members took up nearly the entire row. I doubted that ensemble members of a show were given great seats for their loved ones, even for opening night. Once Johnny and David got involved, there was no stopping them from buying up the best seats in the house. Rosemary's parents were there, as were Johnny's mother and father. Yes, even the big man himself, Walter Creel, was in attendance. It was easy to see how Johnny had grown up to be such a spoiled brat. Walter was a snob of the highest order and hadn't been thrilled when he heard his son was in love with his former secretary. He eventually came around, realizing that Rosemary made Johnny happy. Walter had paid for Rosemary to go to NYU for her college degree, and now he was grinning from ear to ear. Attending Rosemary's premiere was great publicity for him, since he'd proudly announced to the media that he had funded her school career.

The Creels also paid for all our theater friends from D.C. to attend, which was wonderful. Ryan and I practically cried when we saw each other, hugging like we would never let go. Luke and some of the other employees from The Creel Foundation were in attendance as well. It felt good to be surrounded by so many people I loved.

Finally, it was almost time for the show to begin. We settled into our seats. David was to the left of me, with Johnny to my right. Johnny was excited, but he was also a nervous wreck. I squeezed his hand and offered him lots of reassurance that everything would be just fine.

The lights dimmed, and a feeling of both peace and excitement washed over me. The stage was a happy and familiar place to me, and I loved being surrounded by the joy and wonder of it all. *Hairspray* was such an upbeat show, full of energy, and hope for a brighter future filled with peace and equality. It was about the civil rights struggles of the 1960s, and the healing power of dance and music.

It was amazing to see some Broadway actors up there who I recognized. It made me wonder if Rosemary knew any of them personally, and if perhaps she could help me network with some of them.

The first time we saw Rosemary was in a scene where a group of teenagers gathered onstage to sing and dance for a live after-school TV show called "The Corny Collins Show." I caught sight of her familiar red hair and gasped. *There she was.* She looked incredible wearing a poodle skirt, her hair and makeup done perfectly.

I looked over and saw Johnny scanning the stage looking for her. I squeezed his hand and pointed to Rosemary. He gasped.

"My God, she really made it," Johnny whispered as he gazed at the love of his life onstage. Tears formed in his eyes, and he turned to me and said softly, "I'm so proud of her."

I smiled at him and said, "Me too."

We turned back to the stage and watched in awe as Rosemary joined the group and sang "The Nicest Kids in Town," a snappy upbeat number that served to set up the main story of the show. Essentially, it was about some white kids and some black kids who were on the same TV show in Baltimore in the 1960s, but were not to mix. One day per week was "Negro Day," and the rest of the week was for the white kids. Naturally, all that would change by the end of the show when love and friendship won out, ushering in the new wave of integration.

I held Johnny's hand throughout the whole number, and I felt his tense muscles start to relax a bit when he saw how well Rosemary was doing. I wished I could say that I, too, felt better as the show went on.

As I stared at Rosemary singing and dancing her heart out on a real Broadway stage, I was suddenly struck with a horrible, painful realization.

That was never going to be me up there.

The odds of anyone making it to Broadway were infinitesimal, no matter how good you were. Rosemary was a terrific performer, but it was still nothing short of a miracle that she had made it. Hundreds of thousands of people flocked to New York to try to land a role. Out of all those people, what were the chances that any of them would wind up as one of the handful that appeared onstage?

And what were the odds for someone like me who can't even get a callback for small, WAY off-Broadway shows?

Every performer had these doubts. The life of an artist was a constant roller coaster ride between extreme highs and crashing lows, sometimes all in the same day. I thought I had been through it all over the years, but somehow this moment seemed different. The realization struck me like it was a foregone conclusion.

I'm not going to make it.

The pain of that thought, that *certainty*, hit me with stunning ferocity. Oh God, it hurt so much.

"Susannah?" David whispered. "Are you all right?"

I turned my head and realized he had been watching me as I stared at Rosemary performing. His brown eyes were filled with concern—alarm, even—at my expression.

I felt pathetic and awful for making Rosemary's special night all about me. Some best friend I was.

"Of course," I said, gazing back up at the stage. "She looks so beautiful. She's a natural up there."

And she really was. Rosemary looked like she belonged onstage. Maybe that's why it hurt so much. I knew she belonged up there, and I didn't.

I had wanted to be onstage for as long as I could remember. Performing was like breathing to me.

If I didn't belong onstage, then where the hell did *I belong?*

Rosemary's performance was flawless, and the show was terrific. I genuinely wished for a long and successful run on Broadway for everyone involved.

I celebrated with Rosemary and all our friends after the show. Everyone lavished love and attention on her, as they should have. It touched my heart to see how many people were there to support her, just as they had during all her days as a struggling actress. Her sweet smile and the joy in her eyes lit up the room, and I loved seeing her so happy.

And yet, I felt like a little part of me had died tonight. I smiled and laughed and celebrated with everyone, but I had to summon all my acting powers in order to do it. I felt like an utterly wretched person. How could someone else's success—especially the success of someone I loved dearly—hurt so much?

We got back to David's house after 1am, and he passed out almost immediately. I lay awake beside him, letting the tears flow freely now that no one was watching. I remembered the way I had felt when I first came to New York. I'd thought that I would be all right, no matter what happened. I would finally be in New York, pursuing my dream and giving it everything I had. I'd genuinely believed that I would be okay, even if I never made it to Broadway.

I didn't feel okay. That was for damned sure.

Maybe deep down I thought I would make it, and that's why I'd been happy just to be in New York. I had expected it be hard, but not this hard. Not this demoralizing. I'd been a big star back at the community theater in Washington D.C., but that was small time compared to New York. In New York, I was lost among the throngs of other wannabe actors. Here, I was a nobody.

Exhausted, I cried myself to sleep. As usual, I woke up earlier than David. Once again, I lay there in bed, driving myself crazy with my thoughts. Eventually, I came to the conclusion that I couldn't give up on my performing career, even if my odds of making it to Broadway were worse than getting struck by lightning twice. The idea of going back to teaching high school English was unbearable, when all I wanted to do was sing and dance.

Obviously, what I was currently doing in my career was getting me exactly nowhere. I had to shake things up. Try harder. I was never going to get into the actors' union or have any hope of getting an agent if I didn't get into some goddamned shows. I needed a ton of hours on *off*-Broadway productions, and I made up my mind that that was exactly what I was going to do.

I was going to get into a show in New York if it goddamned killed me.

CHAPTER 20

J sipped my scotch in the back of the limo as Joey drove toward The Creel Foundation to pick up Susannah. I'd been worried sick about her the last few weeks, and I was hoping I could get her to take it easy this weekend. She'd been running herself ragged and pushing herself way too hard lately. If she wasn't at The Creel Foundation rehearsing, she was at an audition. Susannah auditioned for *everything* these days, even parts she didn't want. I guessed she figured it would boost her odds of getting in a show.

We had spent Thanksgiving visiting her family in Washington, D.C. last week, and I'd hoped that getting away from New York would be good for her. I was afraid it may have had the opposite effect. I was honored to be introduced to Susannah's family, and we all got along well. But her parents and younger sister had peppered her with questions about Rosemary's Broadway debut, which was the last thing Susannah needed.

Seeing Rosemary's career take off while her own languished was killing her. I knew Susannah was in pain, and I did my best to gently prod her, but she wouldn't confide in me. I wanted very much to ease her sorrow, but I had absolutely no idea of how to help.

My own design business was coming along quite well. Just this week I'd scoped out several locations for an office where I could officially keep work hours and hire some staff. I had always hoped to include Susannah in decisions like that, but she seemed so overwhelmed lately. I'd scouted for locations on my own, all the time regretting that she wasn't right by my side during the process.

Susannah wasn't waiting outside the foundation when I got there, so I went inside to find her. Nowadays, it wasn't uncommon for me to come in and find her still dancing and singing onstage long past the time we'd agreed to meet. This time, I heard a man singing from the stage as I walked down the hall. Whoever he was, he sounded incredible. I even recognized the song. It was one of the tunes from *Dear Evan Hansen.*

I smiled, amused that I was starting to recognize showtunes because of my girlfriend. I had heard her practice "You'll Never Walk Alone" with her kids so many times that I practically had it memorized.

I walked into the auditorium to find the new guy, Luke, singing up on the stage. I spotted Susannah standing in the back watching him. She was clearly enraptured by his performance. She watched him as if she was in a dreamy trance; she didn't even notice me.

Luke was one hell of a singer. His voice was rich and deep, and he had an incredible stage presence, just like Susannah. He also happened to be quite attractive. He was tall and muscular, clad in a tank top that showed off his bulging arm muscles. Who knew theater guys could be so ripped? Maybe he was gay. I *hoped* he was gay.

Susannah gazed at Luke on the stage, her pretty, blue eyes

filled with wonder. She seemed more at peace than I had seen her in quite a while. A fierce bolt of jealousy bordering on fear, shot through me. Susannah was a beautiful, vivacious, talented woman who could have her pick of men. Why the hell would she want me when she could have a hot theater actor who probably understood her hopes and dreams better than I ever could?

Luke finally wrapped up his annoyingly pitch-perfect rendition of "For Forever," which I knew for a fact was Susannah's favorite song from *Dear Evan Hansen*. Susannah applauded loudly, and so did I. I clapped mainly to force her to notice that I was here.

She spun around, startled.

"Oh, David, I'm so sorry I kept you waiting. I guess I lost track of time."

"I can see why," I muttered irritably. She was too busy staring at her handsome coworker who could sing like an angel.

She rushed over and threw her arms around me. "Oh, it's so good to see you. It's been such a long week."

"I know." I felt the tension in my body ease when she touched me. I rubbed her back, trying to get her to relax. She was full of stress; I could feel it practically radiating from her. For the millionth time, I wished like hell I knew what to do to make her feel better.

Luke came down from the stage and walked toward us.

Great. Now I'll have to say something nice about his performance. Otherwise I'll look like the jealous boyfriend that I am.

"David, you remember Luke," Susannah said.

"Yes, of course. Good to see you again," I said, giving him a firm handshake and making sure I looked him in the eye. "You sounded great up there."

"Thanks," Luke said with a smile. There was a warmth in his light brown eyes that made me dislike him more. He was talented *and* nice. Why *should* Susannah prefer a stuffy guy like me over him?

"We're gonna do a show together with the kids," Susannah told me.

This keeps getting better and better, doesn't it?

"That's nice. What show?"

"*School of Rock*," she answered.

"Oh, like the movie?"

"Exactly," Luke said. "It's a really fun show with a bunch of great roles for the kids. I'm gonna play the teacher, and Susie is gonna be the principal."

"That sounds good," I said, and I actually meant it. It would be good for Susannah to be in a musical, even if it was just for the foundation. Performing was healing for her, and getting up in front of people and singing and dancing might boost her confidence. I tried not to think of all the time she would be spending with Luke.

"Thanks," Luke said. "Well, I'm gonna head out. See ya, guys."

"Have a great weekend. See ya Monday," Susannah said to him, then she turned to me and smiled. She looked tired, but I could still see the happiness in her eyes when she looked at me. She was glad I was here with her, and that would have to be enough for me. Sure, she had watched Luke with wonder while he performed onstage, but when she chatted with him casually, she looked at him like she would any other acquaintance.

I needed to get a grip on myself. The woman I loved was a theater performer, and having her co-star with gorgeous actors was a job hazard that I would have to learn to deal with.

Susannah slid her arm around my waist, and we walked out to the limo together.

* * *

THE FOLLOWING Friday I came to pick her up at the foundation a little early. It wasn't that I didn't trust Susannah, but I had been thinking about her working with Luke all week. I wanted to see how she looked at him while they were rehearsing. At the same time, part of me didn't want to know.

This time, I was pleasantly surprised to find Johnny in the auditorium with Susannah instead of Luke. Susannah was up onstage rehearsing, and Johnny was sitting in one of the audience chairs, playing on his phone. He looked up when he heard me come in.

"Hey, man," he said as I took a seat next to him. "She should be almost done."

I nodded as I watched Susannah onstage. I knew she had been working on a new song and dance routine to try for her dance auditions. She messed up a little, then sighed and went to rewind the music so she could do it over.

"She's a workhorse, that's for sure," Johnny said. I could hear the worry in his voice and see it in his eyes as he watched her rehearse. I realized I wasn't the only one concerned.

"She's wearing herself out," I said.

"I know she is," Johnny said, looking grim.

I was tempted to confide in Johnny that I strongly suspected it was Rosemary's success that was making Susannah push herself so hard. Johnny was a good friend and a compassionate person. He would understand and wouldn't judge Susannah for feeling that way. I opened my mouth to mention it, but then changed my mind. Susannah would probably be upset—embarrassed, even—if Johnny and Rosemary knew she felt jealous.

Susannah slowed her dancing suddenly in the middle of

the upbeat number. I frowned as I watched her. Something was wrong. She stopped dancing and stood in the middle of the stage for a moment.

Then she collapsed on the stage floor.

"Shit." I jumped out of my seat and rushed to the stage. Johnny was close on my heels.

My heart lurched in my chest when I saw her lying unconscious in the middle of the stage.

Good Christ, she was so pale.

I gathered her in my arms, and in that horrific moment I thought she was dead.

The only thought I had was *How on earth am I going to live the rest of my life without her?*

An overwhelming torrent of panic and grief washed over me. I was struck frozen, helpless with horror as I held her lifeless body in my arms.

Then I saw her chest move.

Breathing. Breathing. She's breathing. She's just fainted. Get a fucking grip on yourself and help her.

"Call an ambulance!" I shouted at Johnny. I glanced up and saw he was way ahead of me, his phone already to his ear. I cradled her in my arms. "Susannah, Susannah, baby please wake up. *Please, please.*"

I would have given anything in the world—my fortune, my future, my own *life*—to see those beautiful blue eyes open again. I gazed down at Susannah, my panic beginning to rise again. Her skin was cold and clammy, and her lips were dry. I hoped to God the paramedics would arrive soon, because I had absolutely no clue what to do.

What if she died right here in my arms?

She stirred slightly.

"David," she said in a weak voice.

"Yes. Yes, baby, I'm here," I reassured her. She opened her eyes and relief washed over me.

"What happened?"

"You fainted. It's all right. Everything's gonna be all right." I gently pulled her close to my chest and held her.

Moments later, the door to the auditorium burst open and Johnny came in with the paramedics. I hadn't even noticed he'd left.

I reluctantly let go of her so the paramedics could examine her. Her vitals checked out okay, and once they determined she was fairly stable, they took her out on a stretcher to the ambulance. I was relieved that Susannah seemed to be all right, but watching them load her into the ambulance was still a terrible sight to see. She wasn't out of the woods yet, and I was terrified of what the doctors might find wrong with her.

I told Joey to take Johnny to the hospital in the limo, and I rode with Susannah in the ambulance. The paramedic, a young guy in his late twenties or so, started an IV. After a few moments, Susannah seemed to get her color back a bit.

"My name's Alex," the paramedic said in a friendly but professional voice. He proceeded to ask her a few basic questions, and he listened closely to the answers. She seemed to be coherent.

"I want a private room for her in the hospital," I said firmly.

"That may not even be necessary," Alex said. "We'll take her to triage first and run a few tests. Depending on what we find, we may not have to admit her."

"Triage? As in that busy area full of sick people? No way. I want a private room. No arguments. I will pay *anything you want.* Just make it happen."

Alex nodded, looking annoyed.

"David, be nice," Susannah said softly. "I'm sorry about him. He's a little overprotective."

Alex smiled warmly at Susannah. "It's okay. I would do

the same for my girl. Well, you know, if I had that kind of money. Or a girl."

Susannah smiled at him, then she turned to me and held out her hand. I took her small hand in mine and squeezed gently.

"You're gonna be all right, baby," I told her.

She nodded.

When we got to the hospital, they took her to a private room and checked her out more thoroughly. They kicked me out of the room for a few moments so they could talk to Susannah privately. The doctor, a woman her late fifties, eyed me suspiciously as I walked out. I understood. My aunt was a doctor; she told me about the many sad cases of domestic abuse she had seen in the emergency room. They probably wanted to talk to Susannah, to make sure I wasn't hurting her. I tended to come across as fairly intense, and it was good to know they were looking out for her.

They called me back in, and I noticed that the doctor was watching Susannah's face carefully as she looked at me. Susannah's eyes softened when she saw me, and she smiled. She reached out her hand and I took it.

"Okay, it looks like it was dehydration that caused Ms. Peters to faint," the doctor told me. She turned to Susannah. "We're gonna keep you here on the IV for a little bit to make sure you're properly hydrated, then we'll release you. You need to drink plenty of fluids and get some rest. Try to avoid stress if you can, okay?"

"I will. Thanks so much," Susannah said.

I nodded my thanks to the doctor, and she left the room.

I collapsed into the chair next to Susannah and let out a deep breath, my adrenaline rush finally easing a bit.

"Are you okay?" she asked.

"I think you took at least two years off my life today. I *love* you, Susannah. Don't ever scare me like that again."

I didn't even realize what I'd said until I saw Susannah's eyes grow wide.

I sat up, feeling my face get warm. So much for waiting for the perfect moment to tell her how I felt.

"That's not ..." I let out a frustrated breath. "That's not how I wanted to tell you that. *Goddammit.*"

Not only had I screwed up the way I told her I loved her, now I was cursing. Beautiful.

"Never mind how you said it," she said, sitting up in bed, her eyes still wide. "Did you mean it?"

I couldn't ever remember feeling so vulnerable, so utterly exposed. I felt like *I* was the one onstage instead of her, with a spotlight shining right on my face. I pushed through my discomfort and told her the truth.

"Of course I meant it. Jesus Christ, when you collapsed I thought I might never get the chance to tell you."

I knew I'd never forget the image of Susannah, pale and limp, lying on the stage. I really thought I had lost her for a moment.

"Oh, David," Susannah said, reaching for me. I took her into my arms and closed my eyes. Then she said the words I had ached to hear. "I love you too, David. So much."

As tender as the moment was, I was tempted to pull away. Touchy-feely moments like this were way out of my comfort zone.

She needs you, I told myself. *Quit being Mr. Groff for once. She needs David right now. The man who loves her.*

I held her for as long as she needed, allowing her to decide when to let go. When she did, she looked into my eyes.

"Thank you for telling me how you feel, David. I know that kind of thing isn't easy for you."

I nodded grimly. Of all the times I could have told her— over a candlelit dinner, after a Broadway show, or after we'd made love—*anything* would have been more romantic than sitting in a hospital room.

"I'm sorry I'm such a mess about stuff like this."

"I'm guessing your family didn't say 'I love you' much, huh?"

I laughed bitterly. "Indeed. I'll never forget the one time—"

I shook my head, as if to shake off the bad memory. There was no reason to trouble Susannah with my sob stories, especially when she was so weak.

"What?"

"Never mind. It's stupid."

"David, please tell me."

Her voice was so gentle and her eyes so full of concern that I couldn't help but unburden myself. For once, I looked into her eyes instead of looking away.

"My family never said 'I love you.' Never. My parents never said it to each other, and they sure as hell never said it to me or my brother or sisters. Even as a kid, I knew it was weird. I'd heard my friends' parents say it, and you know they say it on TV all the time. It's just ... I mean, you're *supposed* to say it to your kids, right?"

"Yes! Of course," Susannah said, her eyes still full of worry.

"I wanted to hear my mom say it. Just once, you know? So one day I said 'I love you' to her just to hear her say it back." I swallowed hard. "She laughed."

Susannah gasped in horror. I hated pity, but it made me feel a little better that she was so shocked. It was reassuring to know I wasn't crazy to still feel devastated after all these years.

"My mother laughed and looked at me like I was nuts. Then she told me to go do my homework."

Susannah stroked my cheek gently. "My God, David. That's horrible. I don't even know what to say."

"I do ... I do love you, Susannah. I've wanted to tell you for a long time. I told myself I was just waiting for the right time, but that's not entirely the truth. I was just ... I just ..." Christ, how I hated being so screwed up. I hated that this was difficult, and I despised feeling so exposed, but it was time to be brutally honest with her. I blurted out the rest as quickly as I could. "I wanted to tell you I loved you, but there was a part of me that was afraid you would laugh at me too."

"David," Susannah spoke in a shaky voice, her eyes filled with tears. "I would never, *ever*—"

"I know that, baby. Intellectually I know that. It's just ... I hadn't thought my mom would laugh, either."

I shook my head a bit and sat up straighter. I really didn't want to talk about my past anymore.

"I'm so glad they aren't keeping me here overnight," she said, and I loved her dearly for it. It was a simple statement, but it was her way of telling me that she understood that I didn't want to talk about my family anymore. She was incredibly intuitive that way. She waited patiently and always gave me time to say what I needed to say, but she never pushed me harder than was comfortable for me.

"Me too. I just want to get you home so I can take care of you."

Susannah nodded and lay back in the bed. She looked pale and fragile. It was scary.

"Are you all right?" I asked.

"I'm tired," she said weakly. "I'm so tired."

"I know you are. You have to stop pushing yourself so hard. You're making yourself crazy, and you're ruining your health."

"I know." She looked so sad that I could hardly bear it.

I leaned forward and gently stroked her cheek. "It was hard on you, wasn't it? Seeing Rosemary up there onstage."

She looked shocked at my words. At first she didn't speak, but then her eyes filled with tears. Finally, she nodded and whispered, "I'm a terrible person."

The tears spilled down her cheeks, and this time it wasn't hard for me to draw her back into my arms. It was a reflex— a primal urge to comfort and protect her.

"Baby, baby, baby," I said as I stroked her back. "You're not a terrible person."

"B—b—but why can't I be happy for her? She's my best friend."

I rubbed her back for a moment longer, then I pulled back and gazed into her eyes. "Think about it. I mean *really* think about it. Are you happy for her?"

Susannah contemplated it for a moment. Her eyes softened a bit. I thought about Rosemary's face when she told us she had gotten a part on Broadway. Tears of joy running down her face. It was a beautiful sight to see, watching somebody you care about realize their dream. I wondered if Susannah was thinking the same thing.

"Yes," she answered at last. "I really am happy for Rosemary."

"You can be happy for her and sad for you at the same time. It's not a crime. It's a normal human reaction."

Susannah nodded and smiled gratefully. "You're probably right."

"I know things have been rough for you lately, but I'm sure Rosemary probably went through the same things you're dealing with. You should talk to her about it."

"I guess."

I got the feeling Susannah wouldn't confide in Rosemary any time soon, though I wished she would. It could really help her. At least now she knew she could confide in me.

"I know how much you want to succeed with your performing. You have to remember, as a singer and a dancer your body is your instrument. You need to take care of it."

Susannah nodded, then gently kissed my lips. "I will. Thank you for being so understanding."

I wrapped my arms around her and held her close.

Maybe I wasn't so terrible at this relationship stuff after all.

CHAPTER 21

I felt much better on the limo ride back to David's house. I stretched out across the seat with my head resting in his lap. He stroked my hair, and I felt calmer and more at peace than I had in a long time. I was so lucky to have David in my life. He took such good care of me. He never treated me like I was crazy, even though I knew I was acting crazy.

Joey had been especially sweet to me when he picked us up at the hospital, and Kate and Dina were waiting for us at the door when we got home.

"Are you all right?" Kate asked, giving me a worried, motherly look. David must have told her what had happened to me.

"I'm fine, really. Don't worry," I said. I was touched at the genuine concern I received from all of David's staff members. I didn't see them as employees anymore. They were more like family.

"She'll be okay. She just needs to *rest*," David said sternly, looking at me.

"Yes, Mr. Groff," I teased.

Kate chuckled, then asked, "Can I get you anything?"

"A glass of wine would be lovely," I said.

"Alcohol will only dry you out more," David said. "When the doctor said drink plenty of fluids, I don't think he meant Prosecco. Remember what you always tell your kids. *Hydrate.*"

"I know," I said. "Kate, would you please bring some iced water, too?"

"Absolutely. Scotch?" she asked David.

"Please."

"Are you hungry?" Dina asked, looking as worried as Kate. "Can I get you two anything to eat?"

David looked at me.

"I'm a little hungry," I said. "I don't want a whole lot, though."

"Okay," Dina said. "How about a cheese plate to go with the wine?"

"Oh, that sounds perfect. I am so spoiled with you guys around. Thank you so much," I said to both women, who smiled warmly at me.

"Bring it to our bedroom," David said gruffly. Then added, "*Please.*"

I exchanged another smile with Dina and Kate. David put his hand on my back and led me to his bedroom. Or, as he had just put it, *our* bedroom.

Within a few minutes, Kate knocked on our door. She wheeled in a room service-type cart with a bottle of wine, a pitcher of ice water, David's scotch, and a delicious-looking tray of cheese and fruit. It was still hard to wrap my mind around this incredible, luxurious life I was living with David these days. It was crazy. And wonderful.

After a few sips of wine I felt a bit calmer and more relaxed. Still, a knot of anxiety tightened in my stomach every time I thought about the audition I had coming up on

Monday. It was a dance audition, and I really needed my routine to be perfect. I was nowhere near ready. I could always do my go-to "Buenos Aires" routine, but I really wanted to try the dance routine from *Chicago* that I'd been working hard on. The one I kept screwing up before I collapsed.

"Try to relax, baby," David said, watching my face intently. He could tell I was stressing myself out again. "You really need to take it easy this weekend."

"I know. I'm trying," I told him, taking another sip of wine as I relaxed in one of the super comfy chairs in his bedroom. The few bites of cheese I took were enough to ease the edge of my hunger. I drew in a few deep breaths and willed myself to chill out.

David sat at the small table on the other side of me. After eating some of the cheese and fruit, and draining his scotch, he stood and walked over to me. I gazed up at him from my seat. He looked especially huge to me when I was sitting down. As always he looked incredible, clad in a navy-blue suit.

"I'm going to help you relax, baby," he said in a deep, sensual voice that sent shivers of delight down my spine.

"Is that so?" I asked, setting down my wineglass.

David bent to kiss me, and I put my arms around his neck. I ran my fingers through his hair as our kisses grew more intense and passionate. His lips traveled down my neck while his hands rubbed my breasts outside of my clothes. The wetness of desire pooled between my legs. I expected him to take my hands and pull me to the bed, but I soon discovered he had other ideas.

David knelt before me. He pushed my skirt up, then gripped my panties with both hands and slowly slid them off me. He grasped my right ankle and placed it on the chair next to me, then took my left and rested it on the chair on my other side. My legs completely spread-eagled before him, I watched, breathless, as he looked between my legs at my most intimate spot.

It was probably the most erotic moment of my life, and he was only getting started.

David lifted his head and met my gaze. The raw desire in his eyes made my breath catch in my chest. Then he lowered his head and began stroking my inner thigh with his tongue. He slowly, tortuously made his way toward my most sensitive spot. He started stroking my clit with his tongue, and I felt like I would lose my mind.

I threw back my head and closed my eyes, letting out a low moan of desire.

"Oh, David," I croaked. "Oh God ..."

He stroked his tongue up and down on my clit, sending ripples of bliss throughout my body. I kept my eyes closed for a while as David pleasured me, lost in sheer ecstasy. The sharp, sweet sensations of pleasure grew stronger by the second, and I knew it wouldn't be long before I came. I realized I wanted to watch David give me an orgasm, so I opened my eyes.

David looked up at me while he tongued me, those dark brown eyes filled with power and control. I was completely at his mercy, and he knew it.

"David," I gasped.

He moaned deep in this throat, and the vibration sent another thrill through my body.

I gripped the arms of the chair as I felt my orgasm starting to build. "D—David ... David ..." His eyes never left mine as he stroked faster, and faster, and faster. My breath came in harsh gasps as my climax took hold.

I let out a long, high-pitched cry of passion when I finally came.

Kate and everyone else in the penthouse probably knew

exactly what David was doing to relax me, and I found couldn't care less.

I lay back on the chair, panting, recovering from my intense climax. I was relaxed all right.

David pulled down my skirt and offered me that cocky, half-grin of his. "Feel better?"

"Yes," I said, letting out a deep breath. I reached for him and pulled him into my arms. He felt heavy on top of me in the chair, but I didn't care. I was reveling in post-orgasm bliss, and I was filled with warmth and affection for my sweet David.

"Your turn," I said, tugging on his trouser pants.

"No, baby. Tonight is just for you."

"But I want to be with you," I said, continuing to undress him. I looked up at him and said, "You told me you loved me tonight. Now show me."

David nodded, then took me by the hand and led me to the bed. I knew he had an easier time expressing himself through lovemaking than he did with words.

We made love, and it was tender and perfect. David was so aroused by going down on me and watching me climax that it didn't take him long to finish, but that was fine by me. As long as I was close to him, I was happy.

Afterward, we brushed our teeth and snuggled together in bed, exhausted but content. I lay on my side, gazing into those gentle brown eyes of his.

"I love you, David."

"You too, baby," he replied.

He reminded me of Patrick Swayze's character in the movie *Ghost*, who always said "ditto" instead of saying "I love you" when his girlfriend said it. If I hadn't collapsed and wound up in the hospital, maybe David never would have said it at all.

"This bed is so comfortable," I said, luxuriating in the feel of the silk sheets. I slept a lot better here than I did in my noisy apartment building, that was for sure.

"I've been thinking," David began cautiously. Empathy welled up in me as I could see it was hard for him to say whatever was on his mind. I smiled softly, trying to encourage him to speak freely. "Have you ever considered … I mean … do you think you might want to move in with me?"

I gently ran my fingers through his hair. "Well, I have thought about it. I'm not sure yet."

"Oh. Okay."

"Hey," I said gently, gazing into his eyes. "I'm totally sure about *you*, David. I love you, and you make me incredibly happy. Still, it would feel weird to be a so-called struggling actress and be living in the lap of luxury. Does that make sense?"

"Yes, actually. It's the same reason Rosemary still takes the subway."

"Exactly," I said, thrilled that he understood. Though it would be weird to live in New York like some wealthy heiress while busting my tail, trying to find work in theater, I'd love to live with David. To sleep beside him all night and wake up in the morning right next to him. Would that make me a sellout? Not a real New Yorker theater wannabe, but some spoiled princess? There was so much to think about.

"Don't stress, okay? Try to get some rest," David said, looking worried. He always knew when I was stressing out and overthinking things.

"I'll try," I promised, closing my eyes and cuddling closer to him.

I lay there for a while, trying to focus on how lucky I was. I knew I needed to concentrate on what I did have as opposed to what was missing in my professional life. I had an amazing, handsome man who loved me. He was *rich* and had actual servants. I was currently resting comfortably in a soft bed with silk sheets and had 24/7 room service available.

The luxury of David's lifestyle was incredible, but I knew I would trade it all in a heartbeat if I could only reach my dream of making it to Broadway. I would gladly live in a noisy, roach-infested apartment in Brooklyn if it meant I could be onstage every night, doing what I loved.

I was exhausted, but it still took me a long time to fall asleep.

CHAPTER 22

*S*usannah woke up way earlier than I did, even though we went to bed at the same time. I had no idea how she got by on so little rest. I needed my sleep. Otherwise, I was even more unpleasant than my usual not-so-jovial nature. I found her in the kitchen having coffee with Kate. I loved that Susannah got along so well with my staff, and I hadn't given up hope that she might eventually move in with me.

"Coffee, Mr. Groff?" Kate asked.

"Yes, please," I said, and Susannah smiled. I felt a bit whipped sometimes that Susannah had convinced me to be more polite, but it made her happy, so I kept it up. I gratefully accepted the cup of fragrant coffee from Kate and took a few sips to help clear my tired head. "So, what do you want to do today?"

"Well, we can go out tonight if you want," Susannah said. "But today, I have to get back to the foundation and work on my new dance routine."

"Are you serious?" Now she wanted to work on the weekends? She was supposed to be resting, not working more hours.

"Yeah, why not?"

"Because you're overworked and exhausted." I glanced at the cup of coffee in front of Susannah. Coffee, like alcohol, could dehydrate a body. "Kate, get her some ice water. She should be drinking lots of water."

"Yes, sir," Kate said, hurrying off. She put a glass in front of Susannah, then touched her shoulder gently and smiled. Kate was like a mother hen, and I was pleased to see she was concerned about my girlfriend's health.

"Thanks," Susannah said to Kate, then obliged us both by drinking some water.

"You're going to stay home today, Susannah," I said sternly, realizing too late that it was the wrong tactic to use with her. Unlike other women, Susannah Peters did not take orders from me.

"I'm not staying home today, David. I have a really important audition on Monday. You saw how messed up my routine was yesterday. I'm nowhere near ready."

"Then maybe you can save the new routine for when you feel better. Give yourself more time to prepare. Use your old routine for the audition. Your "Buenos Aires" one. You do that one quite well."

She smiled sadly. "Not well enough, obviously. Hasn't gotten me anywhere so far."

"You just have to give it time, baby." God, I hated the idea of her rehearsing all day. What if she collapsed again? "Maybe you can wait to audition again until you're feeling better."

"You think I should skip my audition on Monday? Why would you say that?" Susannah demanded, her voice rising.

Kate discreetly slipped out of the room to give us some privacy.

"You don't have to get angry. I'm just worried about you. You have to rest. You need to at least take the weekend off to recover. You were just in the hospital for God's sake."

"I was just a little dehydrated. It was no big deal."

The image of her lying unconscious on the stage flashed through my mind, and a shudder went through me. I had thought she was dead; it was a very big deal.

"Susannah, you have to take it easy."

"You don't understand," she said, sounding angry and frustrated. "Everything is easy for you."

"What is that supposed to mean?"

"You don't *have* to work. You just choose to. Your family pays for everything you have."

It was a low blow, and it hurt. I may not be the most emotional person in the world, but I still had feelings. Why was she suddenly being so cruel?

"Well you don't *have* to be a performer, either. Look, I understand that it's important to you—"

"No," Susannah said, eyes flashing. "You *don't* understand. I do have to do it. It's who I am."

"I know that, baby. I get it. I don't have to design clothing either, but it's important to me. I do understand that—"

"It's not the same thing, David. Designing doesn't mean as much to you as performing does to me."

"How the hell would you know? You have no idea what's going on with my design business or how I feel about it, because you never ask. You're too wrapped up in your own career!" I yelled.

I knew she was upset and I felt bad for yelling at her, but she just made me so damned mad. I felt like all I did anymore was carefully dance around her mood swings, trying to meet her needs while ignoring my own. Most of the time she refused to talk to me about what was bothering her, and I was out of ideas of what to do to help.

209

"How can you say that?" Susannah screamed, jumping out of her seat at the kitchen table. "All I'm asking for is a little bit of understanding from you. Is that too much to ask?"

Furious, I took a step toward her and got right near her face. "I have always been there for you, and how *dare* you suggest otherwise. I have listened to you, supported you, and comforted you even when you're acting completely crazy. All I ever do is take care of you. *What more do you want from me?*" I yelled.

She flinched and took a step back. I drew in a deep breath and tried to calm myself. I was still mad as hell, but I was a lot bigger and stronger than her, and I certainly hadn't meant to frighten her. All I wanted was to be heard.

"Baby," I said in a quieter voice. "I just don't understand why you have to make yourself so crazy over this."

"No," Susannah said, her eyes filling with tears. "You don't understand. You don't understand what it feels like to want something so much it hurts. To feel like you don't know how you'll ever be able to survive if you don't make it. To feel like you'll never be good enough. You don't understand me at all."

She grabbed her purse. "I have to go rehearse."

A renewed sense of fury raged within me. Maybe she was right. Maybe I didn't understand her. She may as well have been speaking a foreign language, because I couldn't make any sense out of her sudden anger at me. I had done every-thing I could think of to take care of her, and it still wasn't enough. Maybe one had to be an arty, touchy-feely performer to understand this insanity.

"Fine! Go hang out with Luke. I'm sure he understands you better than I ever could."

Susannah looked at me like I had completely lost my mind and then stormed out of the penthouse.

* * *

I HADN'T SPOKEN to Susannah in over a week, and I felt like I was losing my mind. I felt terrible for yelling at her, but I was still angry with her. She was being totally unreasonable.

Wasn't she?

I wasn't sure what to think. Part of me felt like I should apologize, but wasn't she the one who was wrong? I didn't know what to do. All I knew for sure was that I missed her terribly, and I felt horrible every time I pictured her with tears running down her face. God, I hadn't meant to make her cry. I knew she was hurting. She felt like she wasn't good enough to succeed at the thing she wanted most—the dream she had pursued her whole life. I knew she was in pain. I wanted to fix this mess, but I also wanted her to understand my point of view. I cared so deeply about her hopes and dreams. Didn't she care about mine?

I met up with Johnny at our usual steak joint. Times like this I really wished I was better at talking about my feelings. Johnny was a good friend, and he would understand. Sometimes I envied women and the way they could easily discuss their troubles over a bottle of wine.

"You all right?" Johnny asked, and I was grateful to him for giving me the perfect opening to talk.

"Not really. Susannah and I had a fairly big falling out."

"Ohhhh," Johnny said, nodding. "So that's what's wrong with her. She's been upset all week, but she just tells me she's fine whenever I ask about it."

"Is she okay?" I asked.

"I guess so. She seems pretty sad, though."

I nodded. Johnny looked at me, waiting for me to elaborate on the situation between Susannah and me. I took a bite of steak and a healthy swig of scotch before answering.

"She's ... well, she's been going through a hard time lately, and ... Look. I'm going to level with you. Susannah loves

211

Rosemary like a sister, and she's happy that Rosemary found success on Broadway, but ..."

Johnny nodded, his eyes full of sudden understanding. And compassion. "But it's been hard for her to see Rosemary succeed when she's struggling. That makes sense."

"Yes," I said, feeling relieved. I didn't want Johnny to be annoyed with Susannah for begrudging his girlfriend's success. "Exactly. She doesn't want to feel that way, but she can't help it."

"So that's why she's been pushing herself so hard. I know she's stayed late after teaching her classes at night, but I'm pretty sure she's been coming in early before I get there, too. No wonder she collapsed. Christ, that was scary."

"Tell me about it." My chest clenched just thinking about it. "I know she's stressed and she's overwhelmed. She's frustrated about how her auditions are going, and it breaks her heart that she hasn't gotten a part in anything since she's gotten to New York."

"And I bet it breaks yours, too," Johnny said.

I never would have been able to say that out loud, but I was thankful Johnny said it for me. I nodded.

"I have no idea what to do to help her. I've done everything I can think of to be kind and sensitive. You know, all the things I'm *not*."

Johnny chuckled. "Yeah, dude. Kind and sensitive are not words I would have ever used to describe you. But that was before you met Susannah." He popped a french fry in his mouth. "Hell, I was a total asshole before I met Rosemary."

"You're still an asshole, Johnny."

He chuckled. "True. But not to Rosemary."

Johnny really wasn't an asshole anymore. Not to Rosemary or anybody else. Having Rosemary's love and working with underprivileged kids had humbled him considerably.

"In the beginning, Susannah was really supportive of me

and my design business. Lately, she's been too distracted to pay much attention to me or anything I'm interested in. I know she's going through a rough time, and I've done every damned thing I can think of to support her. I've tried to cater to her every need, and then she accused me of not being there for her. She yelled at me and told me I didn't understand what she was going through. She was pissed because I didn't want her to spend all day on a Saturday rehearsing when she just got out of the hospital. I'm driving myself nuts trying to figure out if I'm crazy and this is somehow my fault, or if she's just being emotional and unreasonable."

"Sounds to me like she's being unreasonable, David."

"I'm terrible at all this relationship stuff, but I'm doing the best I can. I guess it's just not enough. It can be tough being in love with a diva theater artist, you know what I mean?"

Johnny grinned, and I realized too late what I had admitted. "You really in love with her?"

I let out a short, annoyed breath through my nose, then grudgingly nodded.

"That's cool, man. Really," he said, giving up the perfect opportunity to bust my balls. "I get what you're saying. But I'm pretty sure I'm the diva in my relationship."

"No doubt."

"I hear ya though. Rosemary's gone through stuff like that before."

"Really?"

"Sure. I mean, maybe not quite as bad as Susannah, and she's never really taken it out on me, but she gets upset from time to time. She questions her talent and wondered if she would ever get another part. Everybody in that line of work goes through that stuff."

I felt slightly better. God, if only Susannah would quit being stubborn and go talk to Rosemary. It might make her feel better. Susannah was incredibly talented. Her voice, her dancing, her presence, and that passion and life that she brought to the stage. I would give anything in the world to see her smile again. To see that sheer joy that emanated from her the day she first set foot in The Creel Foundation.

Yes. I would give anything to help her. Which gave me an idea.

"Maybe," I said, thinking out loud. "Maybe I could grease the wheels for her somehow. You know, with these casting agents. There must be some kind of donation I could make. To the actors' union maybe. Something I could do to get the ball rolling for her."

Johnny's expression suddenly turned serious. "I know what you mean. You see the woman you love in pain and you would do anything in your power to stop it. Her dream is right there. It's so close, she can almost touch it. And you know all you have to do is donate to the right person, and you can make her every dream come true."

I nodded slowly, taking in Johnny's words. Perhaps it wasn't just luck that had gotten Rosemary into NYU. And onto a Broadway stage.

"Johnny," I began, "did you help Rosemary like that?"

He stared into my eyes for a moment and then said, "No. I was tempted like you wouldn't believe. Rosemary would have been heartbroken if she didn't get into NYU. God, every time she checked her email to see if she'd gotten anything from the admissions office, I wondered if I'd done the right thing by not interfering. Thank God she made it in on her own. I thought about it a lot afterward, and I knew it was a good thing I hadn't paid anybody off. First of all, you don't want to lie to your girl. These things have a way of coming to light eventually."

"I guess so," I said, not wanting to give up on the idea of using my wealth to help Susannah. I thought about how happy she'd be if she got the phone call she'd been waiting for, telling her she had landed a role.

"You can't do it, David," Johnny warned. "Think about it. If you did and she found out, that would be the end of you and her. Not only that, but then she would never believe in herself again. Can you imagine if she got all excited about getting a part and then found out she didn't earn it?"

"God, she'd be devastated."

Johnny nodded, then smiled softly. "Do you remember when Rosemary came in and told us she got a part? She was so happy, she cried."

"You cried like a baby too, as I recall."

He laughed. "Yeah, I sure did. She was so happy. It was the moment she'd waited for her whole life. Performers like her and Susie, they *have* to earn it. It's just what they have to do, and we can't take that away from them. No matter how much it hurts to watch them suffer."

I let out a deep sigh of regret. "You're right. I hate it, but you're right."

"It's a rough patch, David. It will pass. She'll get her confidence back. You just gotta do whatever you can to be patient with her."

I nodded.

"It's not all bad dating theater performers," Johnny said with a grin. "I don't know about you, but seeing Rosemary up on that stage gets me so hot."

"I know what you mean. Good God, that day at the foundation when she did the dance from *Evita*? I'd never been so turned on before in my life. Every time I see her perform, I just want to take her right there on the stage."

"I know what you mean." Johnny's eyes sparkled with mischief. "It'll get better, dude. I promise. Just hang in there."

CHAPTER 23

*I*t had been more than a week since I'd seen David, and I was utterly miserable without him. I knew there was only one person I could turn to with my troubles, so I scheduled a long-overdue lunch with Rosemary. I hadn't talked to her in a while, both because she was busy with her Broadway schedule and because I had been avoiding her. I was horrible friend to her, and a horrible girlfriend to David. I really needed to pull myself together before I lost everyone I loved.

We met for lunch on a Friday afternoon in a small café in Brooklyn. Between my day job at The Creel Foundation and Rosemary's show that night, lunchtime was the only time we could meet. I sat at a table and saw Rosemary walk in and scan the room. Her pretty, green eyes lit up when she saw me.

Rosemary looked so happy, and it warmed my heart to see her.

She greeted me with a hug and then took a seat across from me.

"I feel like it's been forever since I've seen you," Rosemary said.

"I know. Things have been crazy lately. We have to be better at getting together."

"Agreed."

We chatted casually for a bit. I wanted to wait until we'd placed our order before I got into the heavier stuff I needed to get off my chest. Our server took our order, and when she walked away I looked over at Rosemary.

"So, how's everything going?"

"Great," she said with a smile. "Busy. The schedule is crazy, but it's great. How are things with you?"

"Well," I said slowly, hardly knowing where to begin.

"You okay?" I was touched by her look of concern, and I realized I should have confided in her a long time ago.

"I think I really messed up with David."

"Oh," she said in a sweet, gentle voice. "What happened?"

I drew in a deep breath, knowing I had to admit the truth. "I guess I have to explain a few things first. Look Rosemary, I hope you know how happy I am that you landed a role on Broadway. You've worked so hard for so long, and nobody deserves this more than you. But ... but ..." Tears formed in my eyes, and I looked away in shame. I didn't want to look at her when I said the rest. "It's been hard for me to see your success when I'm getting nowhere with my own career. I feel awful. You're my best friend, and I'm supposed to be happy, but it hurts. I know it shouldn't, but it does."

"Susie," Rosemary said. When I didn't look up, she spoke more firmly. "*Susie.*"

I looked up at her, and her gentle look of compassion made me want to cry harder. "You have nothing to feel bad about. That's a perfectly normal reaction. I'm sure I would feel the same way."

"I doubt that, Rosemary." She was so sweet and wonderful.

"Susie. Think about how you feel when you see the cast list for a show. Whether it was high school, or community theater, or what have you. You see the cast list, and you see your friend's name as the lead instead of yours. If you're anything like me, two thoughts run through your head: good for her, and you *bitch.*"

I laughed, wiping my eyes with a napkin. "That's true."

"I understand, Susie. It hurts when you see somebody else get a part instead of you. It hurts every time. You don't want it to. You feel like you should be a bigger person, develop a thicker skin, and all those clichés you're told. But you can't stop it from hurting. It means you care, Susie. You're passionate about performing. It's your dream, and it's really hard to see somebody's else's dream come true when yours hasn't yet. Even if it's your best friend."

I reached across the table and squeezed her hand. "Thank you for understanding."

"I wish you had told me sooner. This is why you've been pushing yourself so hard. Johnny's been worried sick about you, and that was even before you collapsed. He knew something was wrong, but he didn't know what."

"Yeah. That's why I've been so nuts lately. I'm just frustrated that I can't seem to get a part in anything, no matter how hard I try. The day after I collapsed, David didn't want me to go rehearse because he was worried about me. I completely flipped out and yelled at him, and accused him of not being there for me. And the thing is, it's not true at all. He's *always* been there for me. He's been kind and patient, even though I've been acting like a spoiled brat. I'm the one who hasn't been there for him. He's really uncomfortable showing any affection for me because of his horrible childhood, but he does it anyway. David's always so sweet with me, and he tries so hard." I drew in a deep breath and said in a shaky voice, "We haven't spoken since the fight. I don't know what to do."

Rosemary opened her mouth to respond, but our food arrived. We both smiled and politely thanked the server, waiting until she left to continue our conversation.

"You just have to apologize to him, that's all. Tell him you're sorry for getting so upset, and thank him for supporting you. He loves you so much, Susie. He'll understand."

"Do you think so?"

"Yes."

"How can you be so sure?" I took a bite of my salad, though I didn't have much of an appetite.

"Well, he talked to Johnny a little bit."

I put down my fork. "He did? What did he say?"

"Johnny didn't tell me much. Just that David was upset that you two had a fight, and that he wished he knew what to do to make you feel better."

"Oh, that poor man. All he ever does is try to make me feel better. Did he say anything else?"

Rosemary hesitated, and my stomach clenched with fear. What if David had decided I was too high-maintenance and not worth the trouble? Who could blame him?

"You can tell me," I said.

"I just … well, I'm not trying to make you feel worse, Susie. But David said he was kinda hurt that you didn't take more of an interest in what he was doing. You know, his design business and all that."

"He's right. He's absolutely right. Not only have I not taken an interest, but I actually told him it wasn't as important as what I was doing." I let out a sharp breath. "You know who I sounded liked? Carl. Carl, who always told me that being a doctor was so much more important than my theater stuff. How could I say the same thing to David? What the hell is wrong with me?"

"Nothing is wrong with you. You made a mistake. You said things you didn't mean because you were upset. Not to mention exhausted and not feeling well," Rosemary said kindly. "We've all done it. I'm telling you, it's not too late to fix it. Go see David and tell him you're sorry, and then you can make more of an effort to be involved in his life. His interests. David loves you. He's not gonna give up on you because of one fight."

"I hope you're right."

"It'll be all right, Susie. I promise," Rosemary said.

"When he was mad, David said something about how I should just go hang out with Luke because he would probably understand me better. I guess it bothers David that we work together."

Rosemary put her hand over her heart. "Good God, is Luke gorgeous or what?"

"Right? He could be an underwear model or something," I said. We both giggled, and it felt like old times. "Luke's a great guy and we have fun working together, but he's just a good friend and a good scene partner."

"I know it bothers Johnny sometimes when I'm making out with some hot guy in a show, but he's learned to deal with it. Remember how jealous he was of Ryan?"

I threw back my head and laughed. "Oh, that's right! I had forgotten about that."

Johnny had been fiercely jealous of Rosemary's close relationship with Ryan until he found out Ryan was gay.

"Oh, by the way, Ryan's coming for a visit soon. I'm planning an amazing surprise for him, and I'd love your help with it."

"Of course. Anything I can do. I miss him so much," I said.

"Me too."

Rosemary smiled at me. "Feeling a little better?"

"Yes. But enough about me. Tell me what it's like to be on Broadway."

"You really want to know?" she asked gently.

"Of course I do," I said with a smile.

"It's amazing, Susie. Really. Every night onstage, it's like I still can't believe where I am. And the energy of the crowd is like nothing I've ever experienced. I've never performed before such a big audience, and it's like you feed off their energy, ya know?"

I nodded, feeling the tension in my stomach relax. I loved seeing Rosemary so excited, and I understood exactly what she was talking about. Every performer knew the delicious excitement of doing a show for a crowd who was really into it. It was a high like no other.

"And *Hairspray* is such a high energy, fun show. I'm usually so keyed up that it's impossible to sleep much." She laughed and added, "Seriously, I just woke up like an hour ago."

"That sounds so exciting, Rosemary."

"It is. It really is. You should know, even though I made it into a Broadway show, I still have doubts about myself like you do. I don't think that feeling ever really goes away."

"Really?"

"Oh, yeah. I mean, it's wonderful, but sometimes I can't help but think, what if this is it? What if this was a one-shot deal, and when the show closes or my contract is up, I never make it back? I mean, I try my best to live in the moment and enjoy it, but you can't help having those doubts."

It was such a relief to talk to Rosemary about the struggles of being a performer. "Can I ask you something? Did you ever get turned away at an audition before you even got in the door?"

Rosemary's eyes opened wide as she sipped her Diet Coke. "Are you kidding? Of course. That happened to me for my first three auditions. I remember going home and crying to Johnny about it. I can't even get in the door. How I am ever going to get a part if I can't even get in the door? What do I have to do, get there at 3am?"

I laughed. "I know, right? I was afraid it was just me."

"Susie, there were so many times I wanted to give you advice about auditioning, but I didn't want to sound like a know-it-all. I have so much I can tell you, and not just because I got in a show. It's mostly because I've spent the last two years knocking around New York, and I've made about every mistake in the book."

I leaned forward at the table, suddenly hungry for any advice she could give me. "How often did the casting directors ask for more from you? You know, other than the first sixteen bars you sang?"

She smiled. "They asked for more from me at the first audition that I finally made it in the door. After I sang my second set, they thanked me and showed me the door. On my way out, I heard one of the casting directors mutter that I sounded better in that video."

"Ouch," I said. Though I was relieved that I wasn't the only one who got rejected, it brought me no comfort to think of Rosemary being insulted like that.

Rosemary let out a short sigh. "Yeah. That goddamned video. I can't tell you how often I still get recognized for it. And then people see me as the girlfriend of the famous Johnny Creel."

"That sucks."

"Yeah. I mean, at the time, I had no idea I was being recorded by somebody's cell phone, and I'm glad I sounded good when I sang. But the thing is, I wasn't acting. I was still hurt and angry. So when I sang back to him, there were tons of emotions running through me. All of that was *real*, so it's not a compliment to tell me I'm a good actress based on that slice of real life."

"I see what you mean."

"So anyway, it did take me lots of auditions to land a role. When I finally got in a show, it made it a bit easier to get another. Then my agent saw me perform."

I nodded, taking mental notes of everything she said.

"And that's how I got my agent. She saw me doing an off-Broadway show. But she didn't talk about the show when she first approached me."

"She talked about the video."

"You got it," Rosemary said ruefully. "Part of me will always wonder. Did I get this part because I'm well-known from some viral video?"

"Of course not," I said, but Rosemary looked doubtful. "Well, look at it this way. Maybe you were given a *shot* because your fame preceded you. Maybe it helped you get an agent or whatever, but they wouldn't have *cast* you in a show if you weren't genuinely talented."

"That's what Johnny said. Oh, it is so good to finally get a chance to catch up with you. Feels good to finally talk about this stuff."

"Yeah, it really does." I felt as if a huge weight had been lifted. Hearing Rosemary talk about the wonders of Broadway was kind of cool. And it felt really good to confide my insecurities to her. "I'm sorry I've been so scarce lately. I wanna go back to the way things used to be with us. We've always supported each other through this crazy journey. We need to keep that up."

"Agreed," Rosemary said, toasting me with her Diet Coke.

I was thrilled that things were good between Rosemary

and me again. I just hoped I could soon say the same about my relationship with David.

True friend that she was, Rosemary picked up on my emotions immediately. "It's gonna be fine, Susie. Tell him you're sorry. Tell him you love him. And everything will be good again."

I nodded. "God, I hope so."

CHAPTER 24

J was so nervous, I felt like I was going to be sick.

The doorman at David's penthouse let me in because he knew me by name and knew I was David Groff's girlfriend. Well, at least I hoped I still was. The elevator ride to the top was excruciating, and I hoped to God that David was home. I needed to see him right away.

I knocked on the door, and Kate answered. She looked surprised but pleased to see me.

"Susie," was all she said. It seemed like she wanted to say more, but she didn't want to overstep any professional boundaries.

"Hi, Kate. Is he here?"

"Yes. Come in, come in," she said, opening the door wider and motioning for me to step inside. "He's in his office." Kate paused for a moment, then quietly added, "He's been miserable without you."

"He's been a real treat to work with, too, I'll tell you that," came Dina's voice from the kitchen doorway. She smiled at me. "Nice to see you, Susie."

"You too," I said, then muttered, "Wish me luck."

I swallowed hard, then headed to David's office. I tentatively knocked on the door and waited for him to answer. He opened it, probably expecting to see Kate. I drew in a deep breath. He looked so handsome in his dark gray suit.

"Susannah," he said, eyes wide. His expression softened. "It's so good to see you. Baby, I'm sor—"

I pressed my finger against his lips. "That fight was completely and utterly my fault. Oh David, I'm so sorry."

David gazed at me with that tender look I loved so much. "Are you all right?"

"That depends. Do you still love me?"

"Baby," he said with a gentle laugh. "Of course I do."

He reached out and pulled me into his arms. It was rare for him to initiate physical contact with me. He must have really missed me. As he held me, I could feel his tenderness. His love. Maybe he wasn't great at saying "I love you" out loud, but he had other sweet ways of showing it.

After we held each other for a moment, I took his hand and led him over to the leather couch by the window so we could talk.

I faced him as we sat close together. "I'm so sorry I yelled at you."

"I'm sorry I yelled too, Susannah."

"You have nothing to be sorry for. You yelled at me because I was being completely unreasonable." I couldn't help smiling. "I've never seen you that mad before. I didn't think you were capable of losing your temper."

David gave me that half-grin of his. "You're the only one capable of making me that crazy, Susannah."

I took his hand in mine and squeezed it. "You've been so sweet and so patient with me. You were right when you said all you ever do is take care of me."

"I worry about you, baby. I just wanted you to rest for a

little while. Susannah, when you collapsed … For a moment I thought I'd lost you. I really thought you were …"

David's voice caught with emotion, and it broke my heart. For the first time, I imagined myself in his shoes. How would I feel if he'd been the one to suddenly fall unconscious right in front of me? Of course I would have wanted to protect him from further harm in any way I could.

"I'm sorry. I didn't mean to scare you. And I do appreciate everything you do to take care of me."

"I like taking care of you, baby." He looked at me with affection, and I could see that it was true.

"I like taking care of you too, David, even though I've done a terrible job of it lately. I'm sorry I haven't been there for you. I promise I'll be better."

He nodded.

"And David, you know there's nothing between me and Luke besides friendship, right?"

David laughed, looking slightly embarrassed. "I know, I know. I shouldn't have said that. That was way out of line. I guess I just worry that only another actor can really understand what you're going through."

I tenderly stroked his cheek. "You understand me better than anybody else ever has. I'm so sorry I was mean to you."

"It's all right, Susannah. I forgive you."

I let out a deep breath, relieved to hear those words. He had forgiven me. He still loved me.

"David, I want you to know how proud I am of you. I've done a lousy job of showing it lately, but I am. You're so creative, and your designs are so beautiful. I want your every dream to come true. Tell me everything you've been up to. What have you designed lately? Did you choose a corporate logo? What about the office space you rented?"

"There's so much I want to tell you, baby," he said with a

tender smile. "Lots of things I want to share with you, but not right now. We'll talk about it later."

"Okay, if that's what you really want. I want to make it up to you somehow. I'll do anything, David." Then I added seductively, "*Anything.*"

"Hmm," David said, tracing my chin with his finger. "Believe me, Susannah, I am very much looking forward to having make-up sex with you. But right now, I have something else in mind. Will you do something for me?"

"Of course. Anything," I told him.

He nodded, then stood up. He walked over to the intercom.

"Kate, could you call Joey and tell him we need him please?"

"Sure thing, Mr. Groff," came Kate's reply.

I wondered where we were going, but I didn't ask. It really didn't matter, as long as we were together.

It felt good to be cuddled up close with David in the limo after being apart for so long. I was only half paying attention, but it soon became clear that we were driving the familiar route to The Creel Foundation. I wondered what David had in mind.

We pulled up to the curb outside of the building. David pressed the button, and Joey quickly opened the door and took my hand to help me out.

"Thanks, Joey."

"My pleasure, Susie," he said with a warm smile.

David and I stood at the door of The Creel Foundation for a moment. It was closed, as it was late on a Friday night. I looked at David expectantly.

"I don't know the code," he said.

"Oh. Right." I punched in the code to let us into the building.

Once inside, I flipped on some lights and awaited further

instructions. He took my hand and led me down the hall and into the big auditorium. It was the place where I always rehearsed, and where I had collapsed. David took me up to the front, and we sat together on the stage.

David turned to me. He had that gentle, affectionate look on his face. The one that made me feel cherished and adored.

"Remember when you first came to the foundation?"

I thought for a moment. Yes, I did remember that day. I was so excited to see Rosemary, and I was overwhelmed by the place, with its many classrooms, the stage, and the dance studio. It was funny to think I hardly noticed David's presence at the time.

"Yes," I answered simply.

"I'll never forget that day I first met you. You were so beautiful when you got up on this stage and sang to Johnny."

"Oh, that's right," I said with a laugh, recalling how I had serenaded him with "Johnny One Note."

"You were a natural up here, and I couldn't believe how lovely you were. Your voice was powerful, beautiful, and strong. Just like you."

"Oh, David," I responded, not knowing what else to say.

"Do you remember when you first saw the dance studio here?" I nodded, and he went on. "You cried. Do you know why you cried? Because you were overwhelmed with the sheer joy of it all. The joy you have in your heart for singing and for dancing. Susannah, you need to find a way to rediscover that joy."

Tears glistened in my eyes. How could I ever have accused David of not understanding me? It was like he could see right into my heart. I had never loved anyone, or anything, more than I loved him in this beautiful moment.

"Now, here's what I want you to do," he said. "I want you to perform something on this stage right now. I want you to pick a song, any song you want, and sing it with all you've got. Dance if you want to. Let yourself be free." David tenderly took my hand in his. "You'll always be a star to me, but that doesn't matter half as much as how you see yourself. Get up there and find your passion again. Don't do it as practice for an audition or because I'm here. Do it for the sheer joy of it, baby."

"Yes," I whispered. I closed my eyes for a moment, taking a few deep, cleansing breaths as I thought about what I wanted to sing. I opened my eyes. "I know the perfect song. It's from the movie *La La Land*. It's funny; I wasn't all that crazy about the movie, but there was this one scene ... Oh, David, it's so perfect. The main character performed it for an audition. It's called "The Fools Who Dream." It even comes at a part of the movie where she's been on one disastrous audition after another and feels like giving up."

David nodded, and I squeezed his hand. "That song always really spoke to me. The way it talks about how much it hurts to try to make it as an actress, but something deep inside keeps you going anyway. I even choreographed my own dance to go with it. Know why I did that?"

He shook his head, and I smiled.

"For the sheer joy of it. I don't use it for auditions or anything. I just ... love it."

"Perfect," David said. He took my hand and helped me up. Then he left me onstage and took a seat in the front row. "Remember, I can't wait to see it, but you're not doing this for me."

I nodded. I took a deep breath to center myself. I did a few brief vocal warm-ups, and then I began to sing. And dance.

It wasn't long before I felt my tension ease and my euphoria begin to build. Oh, how I loved to sing and move my body in rhythm with the music. This was such a powerful song, and it expressed the deep emotions of being a performer so eloquently. The beauty, the heartache, the joy, and the pain. I looked directly at David when I sang the line about the mess we make as artists, and he cracked that sexy half-smile of his.

I wasn't sure when, during the song, I began to cry, but eventually I became aware of tears dripping down my face.

Tears of joy.

It didn't matter if I was performing for one person, for an auditorium full of students and parents, or on a Broadway stage before thousands of people. I was a performer. It was who I was. It was what made me feel alive.

I felt free as I sang and danced. Despite all my doubts and insecurities, I knew deep in my heart that I was good at this. I wasn't perfect, but I was genuinely good at my art. Yes, I was *good.* The realization helped heal my broken heart.

Through my tears, I proudly sang on about being a rebellious artist, one among all the crazy and wonderful painters and poets and dreamers. Oh yes, I was a fool who dreamed. And I would never, ever stop dreaming.

I ended my song with a flourish, my breath hitching a bit from crying. Emma Stone had teared up during that number in the movie, and I began to wonder if her tears were as real as mine.

David stood up and applauded. He walked up to me, and we sat down on the stage again.

"And you were so impressed with that Ben guy from *Dear Evan Hansen* because he could sing and cry at the same time. Turns out you can do it too," David said, tenderly wiping my tears as he spoke.

I laughed softly. "I guess so. Thank you, David. I didn't realize how much I needed to get back to the basics of performing and remember why I do this in the first place. I'm so sorry for putting you through all this. I'm such an idiot."

"You're not an idiot, baby. You're a diva."

I laughed at that. He was right on the money.

"It's true, but that's not bad," David said kindly. "I mean, you kind of have to be a diva, don't you? To get up in front of so many people all the time and do what you do. You *are* a diva. You're fiery and passionate and a little crazy sometimes, and I wouldn't change one damned thing about you."

I pulled him close and we held each other for a moment. I felt at peace for the first time in quite a while.

David let go slightly so he could look at me. "Face it, Susie."

My eyes opened wide. He'd never called me that before.

"We're a couple of spoiled brats who get to do what we love for a living, and that's more than most people ever get to do. It's easy to forget how good we have it. I know Johnny will always remember how tough it was when he had to work a day job he hated. You and me, we don't have to work in a cubicle all day. Instead, we get to run around New York pursuing our dreams, and when things aren't going great, we still have each other."

"You're right. I am a spoiled brat."

"Well, you're in good company with me around." David laughed. "I remember one time, not long before I met you, I had a bad meeting with some investors. I'd had high hopes for that meeting, but they said my designs were amateur and derivative."

"Oh, David." My heart ached to think of how that must have hurt.

"So I was sitting in my living room, brooding. And then Kate came in and asked me if I needed anything. I almost laughed out loud at the absurdity of it all. I was sitting there, feeling sorry for myself, and my *butler* came in to attend to my every need. I thought, what the hell is wrong with me?"

I rubbed his shoulder. "Still, you had every right to be upset."

"Yes, but it's important to keep it all in perspective. We need to keep each other grounded. Agreed?"

"Agreed. You call me out when I'm being a diva, and I'll call you out when you're being a snob."

David laughed. "You always do. And Susannah ..." He looked a bit uncomfortable but went on anyway. "I know I don't say 'I love you' nearly as much as I should, but ... I do, you know."

"I know," I said softly. "You tell me you love me all the time, David, just not with words. You say it every time you call me to see how an audition went, or when you text me in the middle of the day just to check on me. Or when you take me by the hand or put your hand on my back when you lead me into a room. You may not say 'I love you' out loud, but I hear you loud and clear, David."

"Good," he said, looking relieved.

Although he wasn't grandly romantic like Johnny was, David loved me in his own sweet David Groff way, and that was more than enough. Besides, bringing me here to the foundation and showing me how well he understood me was a pretty romantic gesture.

"David?"

"Yes?"

"I wanna come live with you."

"Really?" His face lit up, but he seemed cautious, like he was afraid to believe me.

"Yes. I still feel kinda weird about living a luxurious life while being a struggling artist, but it's stupid to make things any harder than they are. I mean, I'm still not gonna take a limo to auditions, but other than that, it will be wonderful. But most importantly, I've realized that weekends aren't enough for me anymore. I want to be with you every night and every morning."

David smiled. I mean, *really* smiled. It was adorable, like he couldn't contain himself. "That's wonderful, baby. I'm so glad."

He put his arm around me and asked, "Are you tired?"

"Very."

"What do you feel like doing now?"

"I know exactly what I want to do now. I want to pick up some Louie's pizza and bring it back to our place and eat it in our bed while we watch trashy TV. Then I want to hang out with you and be lazy all weekend. Then on Monday I'll be ready to take on the world again."

David smiled again, looking pleased to hear that I was planning to finally get some rest. "I can't think of anything more wonderful."

CHAPTER 25

I loved my new office space. It was located in the city, not too far from the garment district, so working there made me feel like a real designer. I couldn't wait for Susannah to see the place.

Susannah had been true to her word; she had actually rested over the weekend. We took it easy and just enjoyed spending time together. I'd told her all about what was going on with my design business, and she took great interest in it, like she had when we first met.

It was around 5pm on Monday night, and the rest of the staff was getting ready to leave for the day. Susannah was teaching at the foundation tonight, so I figured I might as well stay late and get some work done. Just as my administrative assistant, Erin, was gathering her things to leave, the door swung open.

"Susannah!" Erin said with a warm smile.

Susannah smiled as she looked at me, and then turned to Erin with a quizzical look on her face. They had never met before. Erin reached out her hand, and Susannah shook it.

"Mr. Groff has a picture of you in his office," Erin explained. "That, and he talks about you constantly."

Susannah's warm blue eyes softened at Erin's words. It was true. I was forever bragging about my beautiful, talented girlfriend.

I walked over to Susannah, struggling to suppress a goofy grin. I was so excited to see her here. "I thought you had to work."

"I did, but I asked Luke to cover the class tonight. I wanted to come and surprise you." She glanced around and turned to look back at the glass doors she'd just come through. Both the door and the wall in the reception area displayed my new David Groff logo. "David, the logo is beautiful. I love it!"

"Really?" I felt giddy to see Susannah proud of me.

"Oh, I really do," she said, walking over to the wall and touching the 3D logo with reverence. "It's lovely, David. Perfect. Soon we're gonna be seeing this logo all over New York City. Not to mention Paris and London."

"That's what I keep telling him," Erin said with a smile. She was in her mid-twenties and had brown hair and brown eyes. She was sweet, and quite competent as an administrative assistant. "I'm glad I got in on the ground floor with him before he hit it big."

"Yes, well, we'll see. I certainly have a great staff here. We work well together."

Erin nodded. "I was just about to head out. Unless there's anything else, Mr. Groff?"

"Nope. You go on, and have a good night."

"So nice to meet you, Susannah," she said.

"She *insists* that you call her Ms. Peters," I said to Erin.

"Oh, shut *up*," Susannah said, punching me in the shoulder and making me laugh. "Call me Susie. Please."

"Sure thing, Susie," Erin said. "Oh, me and some of the

guys want to come see your *School of Rock* show at the foundation, if that's okay with you. Opens in a few weeks, right?"

"Yes. Are you kidding? I would love it if you all came."

Susannah smiled at me. I think we both loved the idea of our worlds intermingling a bit.

"Cool. Okay, see you guys later."

"Have a great night," Susannah told her. Erin waved as she sailed out the door.

I gazed at Susannah, hardly believing she was here. "Baby, I'm so glad you came to see my new place."

She wrapped her arms around me and kissed me. "Better late than never. So, give me the grand tour!"

"There's not that much to see, but I'll show you the rest."

I took her hand and led her down the hallway. "Everybody else has left for the day, but I have a few other employees. I have a bookkeeper and an assistant designer so far. I might hire more employees in the future, but I've got all I need for the moment."

I showed her the break room, which had a full-sized refrigerator, a microwave, and a toaster oven. It also had a state-of-the art coffee machine.

"Wow, you sure treat your employees right."

I shrugged modestly. "Well, I try to. They're good people."

I also took her to the room where we put the clothes together. It had sewing machines and scraps of cloth spread out over three different tables. There was a long rack of ties and several mannequins in various states of dress.

"You guys are already super busy, aren't you?"

"Yes," was all I said, but my emotions were running wild. I felt like I was living my dream, and I was incredibly excited. "And in here is my office."

I reached across Susannah, opened the door, and then gestured for her to go inside first. I shut the door behind us.

She drew in a deep breath. It was a bit like my home

office in that it was filled with expensive furniture. I had a huge wooden desk with a fancy black leather chair, and lovely wooden bookshelves attached to the walls with lots of old-fashioned books. Off to the side, there was a big wooden table with six chairs, suitable for meetings.

I watched Susannah carefully as she took in her surroundings. Maybe I was imagining things, but she seemed, well, *turned on* by what she saw.

"David, this place is amazing," she said, her eyes wide. She put her arm around me and looked up into my eyes. "I think it is so damned sexy that you're the boss around here, David."

Okay, so perhaps I wasn't imagining things. She *was* aroused.

I dipped my head to kiss her. Our kisses were passionate and sensual, and within seconds I was rock hard.

It had always been my fantasy to have sex in my office. I wondered if Susannah would be willing to go for it.

Over the weekend, we'd had tender, loving make-up sex. It was nice, but now I was in the mood for something a tad hotter.

"Oh, Mr. Groff," Susannah whispered seductively into my ear.

I chucked softly, but her words really turned me on. I never considered myself the type to role play in the bedroom, but I found the idea of pretending that I was Susannah's boss rather exciting. I was dying to go for it, but I didn't want to look stupid if Susannah had only been joking.

She let go of me for a moment, then walked over to my desk and sat on the edge of it. She opened her legs slightly. "Looks to me like this desk is big enough for two. Are you up for a little after-hours fun, Mr. Groff?"

Her words were teasing, but her tone was serious. She looked at me hungrily.

I wanted to rush over to her, spread her legs and take her

immediately, but I forced myself to take my time. I strolled to the other side of the room, and then slowly and methodically began removing items from the desk to make room for us. I supposed in these situations, one should simply swipe all the items dramatically onto the floor, but that simply wasn't my way.

Susannah drew in a sharp breath of anticipation, and I realized my method was better.

Take your time. Make her wait for it.

Once the surface of the desk was clear, I slowly walked over to her. She bit her lip and looked at me expectantly. Susannah was handing total control over to me, and I found that notion thrilling.

I began unbuttoning her blouse and then pulled it off. Next, I slipped off her bra, baring her breasts. She drew in a breath, which jutted her breasts forward.

"You want this, don't you? You need this very badly, don't you?"

"Yes, Mr. Groff," she said in a whisper. Her words should have sounded silly, but they didn't. They sounded *hot*. She was a terrific actress, after all. She played the part of the horny secretary, hot for her boss, to perfection. What really turned me on was her genuine arousal. Her hard nipples betrayed her real attraction, and I would bet she was soaking wet for me.

"Take off your skirt," I commanded.

"Yes, Mr. Groff."

Susannah slid down from the desk in one smooth motion, then obeyed.

"Take off your panties."

"Yes, Mr. Groff."

I fought the urge to moan. I was determined to stay in control of the situation, but Susannah was so goddamned sexy that it wouldn't be easy.

Susannah was completely naked, and I was fully clothed. And that was exactly how I wanted it. I always felt more powerful when I wore a suit, and the idea of having sex with a beautiful woman while wearing one aroused me like nothing else.

"Turn around. Put your hands on the desk. Hold on. *Tight.*"

Susannah gasped, then said, "Yes, Mr. Groff."

Then she did as she was told.

Once she had her back turned, I bit my lip and looked her up and down. Her hands gripping the desk, legs open, and ready for me, Susannah was a vision. Keeping control was going to be quite the challenge, but I knew I was up for it. I unzipped my pants, pulling them down just far enough to gain access to my cock. I waited, letting her anticipation build.

Then, with no warning, I rammed my cock into her. She cried out, and for a moment I feared I had hurt her. She gripped the desk tighter and said, "Mr. Groff ... oh God, Mr. Groff ... that's so ... good ..."

Her breath came in sharp gasps, and I found myself wondering how much of this was acting and how much was genuine ecstasy.

I was determined to stay silent, but it was quite a challenge. I'd never been so turned on in my life. Being in my office, my name and logo on the walls, wearing a five-thousand-dollar suit while fucking a completely naked, gorgeous woman against my desk was more than enough to shove me over the edge. Susannah made me feel *powerful*, and I loved her for it.

Susannah's cries grew louder, and I realized I wasn't the only one losing control.

"Oh ... Oh ... Oh ..." she cried. I knew that *Oh*. That was Susannah's *I'm about to come, Oh*. I wasn't ready for this incredible sexual adventure to end, and I wanted to torture her a bit before I satisfied her.

With no warning, I pulled out of her. I pulled up my pants, but couldn't zip them. I was too hard.

"No!" she cried.

"You'll come when I say you can come," I told her, hoping I wasn't pushing the whole boss bit too far. Susannah turned around to look at me. She looked frustrated and a tad annoyed. I couldn't blame her.

"I'll take care of you, baby. You know I will."

She nodded, her expression softening a bit. I always satisfied her. *Always.* I decided to test my luck and see if she was still willing to follow my orders.

"Lie down on the desk and spread your legs."

"Yes, Mr. Groff."

Susannah lay down on the desk and looked at me, fierce desire in her eyes. She was desperate at this point, and would do anything I said, as long as I made her come. But she was the woman I loved, and I didn't want her doing anything that made her uncomfortable. And yet, I did have one more idea.

I walked over to the two mannequins I had dressed up in my own custom designs. I took a necktie and walked over to Susannah. I pulled the tie taut between my hands. She drew in a sharp breath, and I looked into her eyes to make sure she was okay with what I was going to do. Her eyes twinkled, and she nodded almost imperceptibly. She wanted to give her consent without breaking the mood of our role playing.

I took Susannah's left wrist and tied her to one of the knobs at the end of my wooden desk. Then I walked over to the other mannequin, removed its necktie, and then tied Susannah's right wrist. I climbed up on the desk, towering over her. I took in her incredible naked form. I felt powerful, in command over this stunningly beautiful woman, bound with my custom-designed ties. Susannah was sex personified, her beautiful breasts pushed up because her hands were tied, and her legs open and ready for me.

"My God, you are one beautiful woman, Susannah."

"Thank you, Mr. Groff."

I growled in my throat. I couldn't help it. I forced myself to wait. Wait until she asked for it. Begged for it.

"Please, Mr. Groff," she said at last. "Please, I need it. I need *you*."

I nodded. "That's a good girl."

I gazed into her eyes and plunged into her. Susannah cried out with pleasure, her wrists pulling against her necktie restraints.

"Oh, Mr. Groff … oh, Mr. Groff …" Lost in her ecstasy, she began crying out my first name. "David, David! Don't stop this time. Please, please," she begged. "I mean it, please don't stop!"

I kept hitting that special spot of hers, and oh, God how I loved to hear her beg me to satisfy her. She had more than earned her release.

"I won't stop, baby," I assured her as I slammed harder and harder into her.

"Oh …Oh …" she cried, as she tugged harder at her restraints. I watched her lovely face when she finally came. Eyes closed, she threw her head back and screamed my name one final time as I brought her to sweet release.

I couldn't give her time to recover from her climax; I was past the point of no return. Gripping the corners of the desk for traction, I pounded her until I came. I didn't even try to suppress my harsh grunt of pure pleasure and relief.

We both panted for quite some time afterward, before we caught our breath. I let out a deep breath of sheer content-ment. This was probably the happiest moment of my entire life, being here in my office after having fantastic sex with the woman I loved. It just couldn't get better than this.

"Oh, David," Susannah said in a sultry voice. "That was the best sex of my life."

"Me too," I said. And it was. By far. "I don't see how I'll ever be able to concentrate on work in here again. All I'll be able to think of is my gorgeous girlfriend, tied up naked to my desk."

"You look so sexy in your suits, David. But someday, *some day*, I will get you to wear good old-fashioned jeans."

"Don't count on it, my darling."

Susannah giggled softly, then tugged on her restraints. "I can't put my arms around you."

I kissed her tenderly, then pulled out of her. I stood up, zipped up my pants, and went to work untying her. I could feel her eyes on me as I undid the ties. She looked at me with adoration and love. I still felt powerful and in control. I knew I would never forget the way this incredible woman had made me feel tonight. I could only hope that I made her feel as loved and cherished as she was. I hoped she knew just how much I loved her, even though I rarely said it out loud.

I lay back down with her, and she cuddled up next to me. She shivered a bit as she was still completely naked. I let go of her for a moment so I could take off my suit jacket. I gently covered her with it to keep her warm.

Susannah glanced at the jacket that I had tenderly placed over her. She smiled. "I love you too, David."

I smiled and nodded.

Yes. She knew.

CHAPTER 26

I had just finished up with my class at the foundation. It was a special night as Ryan had finally arrived for a visit, and Rosemary had a wonderful surprise in store for him. She had a rare day off from *Hairspray*, and I was glad she was here.

"The show looks great," Ryan said, as he took a seat on the edge of the stage. He had watched our full-dress rehearsal. *School of Rock* was coming along well, and my kids were really excited. Seeing their smiling faces filled me with warmth, and I was so proud of them. Maybe it wasn't as exciting as being on a Broadway stage, but it felt good to be working on a show again. It felt right, and Luke and I were having lots of fun playing against each other as the adult leads of the show.

"Thanks," I said, taking a seat next to him. I threw my arm around him and he rested his head on my shoulder. "I've missed you so much."

"You too, sweetie," he said. I wished Ryan would move to New York, but he didn't share my theater ambitions. He enjoyed doing community theater back in D.C. as a hobby but never considered it as a career option. Besides, once he and his fiancé, Jack, got married, they would live wherever Jack was stationed.

"How've you been?" I asked.

"Doing okay, I guess. I'm going crazy without Jack."

I bit my lip. "How much longer now?"

"A couple of months," Ryan said with a sad sigh. "The last few months are the hardest to wait, ya know?"

"I'm sure," I said, stroking his hair.

Rosemary came into the auditorium and walked over to us, giggling.

"What?" I asked.

"Have you seen David yet today?" she asked.

"Not really. I mean, he was asleep when I left for work. Why?"

Rosemary giggled again. "You'll see."

The door to the auditorium swung open, and David walked in. I gasped.

He was wearing jeans.

Jeans and a tight black button-down shirt to be exact.

I rushed over to him. I couldn't help but laugh. I walked all around him to get a good look. He just looked so different. "David, you look amazing!"

"I feel naked," he grumbled. "I did this for you. Don't get used to it."

I threw my arms around him and murmured in his ear, "Those jeans really show off that tight ass of yours, baby."

"Fabulous," he said gruffly, but I could see he was pleased with the compliment.

The door opened once again, and Johnny came in. He locked eyes with Rosemary and nodded. That was the signal that Ryan's surprise was ready.

"Hey, Ryan. Do me a favor, would ya? Would you run

lines with me for a few? It's just a short scene I need to get ready for class," Rosemary said.

"Sure," Ryan said, putting his arm around Rosemary. He kissed her cheek. "I can't believe you're still doing classes when you're in a big Broadway show."

"Well, I cut way down on my classes for now. Might take me a while, but I'm still determined to get my degree. Okay, here's the scene," Rosemary said, handing Ryan the pages.

Ryan scanned over the lines. He laughed. "This is cute. I get to be your husband."

"Yeah," Rosemary said with a smile.

They ran through the scene a couple of times while Johnny, Luke, David, and I watched. It was a fun scene with a married couple bickering. It started out with Ryan saying, "If she's not home in the next thirty seconds, I'm gonna—" and then Rosemary comes sailing onto the stage saying, "Honey, I'm home!"

Little did Ryan know, the third time through the scene it wouldn't be Rosemary who stepped onto the stage.

My stomach tingled with excitement as I watched from my seat in the auditorium. David held up his cell phone camera, ready to record the big moment.

"If she's not home in thirty seconds, I'm gonna—"

"Honey, I'm home!" boomed a deep, male voice.

Ryan's eyes opened wide as Jack, looking resplendent in his military fatigues, stepped onto the stage. The pages slipped from Ryan's hands and fluttered to the floor.

Jack, who was the tall, dark, and handsome type, opened his arms. Ryan stared at him for a moment, processing what he was seeing. Then, on shaky legs, Ryan walked over to him.

"Jack, oh my God," Ryan said, looking him up and down as if trying to figure out if this was really happening. He wrapped his arms around his beloved fiancé's neck and held him tight.

We all stood up from our seats and applauded loudly. Rosemary, still up onstage, was crying as she watched the beautiful reunion.

Jack and Ryan held each other close for a long time before finally letting go. A lump formed in my throat as I watched them together. I could not begin to imagine the agony of having someone you loved being so far away for so long, not to mention having your loved one in harm's way every day. I was overjoyed for Ryan. For them both.

Rosemary walked over to them, and Ryan grabbed her and hugged her.

"I might have known you would do something like this," Ryan said as he held her.

Johnny and I laughed. We both knew Rosemary could watch those military reunion videos for hours and just sit there and cry.

Johnny walked up onto the stage and Ryan hugged him as well. "Thanks, man. Thank you so much."

"Well you know this was mostly Rosemary's doing," he said with a smile. "Listen, why don't you guys go into the dressing room here so you can catch up a little in private. Then you can come out here and catch up with your friends for a bit. After that, I've arranged for you to stay at a five-star hotel in midtown Manhattan for a few days, so you can *really* catch up with each other." Johnny grinned, and Jack and Ryan laughed.

"That's amazing, Johnny. I don't even know what to say," Ryan said.

"It's my pleasure, really," Johnny responded. He gestured toward the dressing room, and Ryan put his hand on Jack's back and led the way.

I had helped Rosemary get the dressing room ready earlier. We chilled some champagne and put up a sign that read, *Welcome home, Jack.* There would be even more surprises in store for them once they got back to their hotel. Johnny had left a $500 gift card in their room for a restaurant near their hotel, and David had provided two custom-designed suits as a pre-wedding present. Rosemary had called their respective mothers for their measurements, and I couldn't wait to see pictures of them sporting David's beautifully-designed clothes.

Rosemary sat down in the middle of the stage and let out a sigh of relief. "Oh, I'm so glad we were able to pull that off. Thank you so much for your help, everybody."

Johnny sat next to her, and I sat on her other side. "This was so much fun. I'm so glad I could be here for it," I said.

David looked at us uncertainly for a moment. He was not exactly the sit-on-the-floor type. "Aw, come on. It's not like you're wearing a suit."

"Don't remind me," he said. I smiled and patted the floorboards next to me. He grumbled, but sat down beside me on the stage.

Luke sat down across from us. "They certainly make a good-looking couple."

"That's the truth," Rosemary said with a smile, still wiping tears.

Johnny gazed at Rosemary with amusement and affection. "You're gonna be a mess at their wedding."

Rosemary nodded. "You're not kidding."

We sat and chatted for a little while, and eventually Jack and Ryan came back out to join us. Their eyes were red from crying, and both of them sported red blotches around their mouths where their five o'clock shadows had scratched each other while kissing. They looked *adorable*. Johnny jumped up when he saw them. The rest of us stood as well.

"Thanks so much for the champagne, Johnny," Jack said.

"There's more where that came from," Johnny said.

"We were going to have a little party in the conference

room," Rosemary said, looking around at all of us standing on the stage. "But somehow, I think staying here onstage is more fitting, don't you think?"

Johnny smiled at her and nodded. "Agreed. Let's keep the party in here. Hang tight, we'll be right back."

While we waited, I introduced Jack to Luke and then to David.

"Jack, this is David Groff."

"Great to meet ya, David," Jack said, shaking his hand firmly.

"Likewise," David said. "Welcome home."

"Thanks. It's good to be home," Jack said with a soft smile. He glanced over at Ryan as if to say that home was wherever Ryan was. Jack turned back and looked David up and down. "Love those designer jeans, but a good lookin' guy like you ought to be wearin' a suit."

David shot me a wry look.

Jack laughed. "I'm just messin' with ya, man. Susie told me to say that."

David chuckled good-naturedly. "I might have known."

A few moments later, Johnny and Rosemary came back with a cooler containing champagne and some cheese and other munchies. We all sat back down, forming a lovely circle of friendship on the stage. After the glasses of champagne were handed out we made a toast.

"To Jack's safe return," Rosemary said, eyes glistening with tears again.

"I'll drink to that," Ryan said, pure relief in his eyes. We toasted Jack, and Ryan kissed him tenderly.

We sat and talked for a while, and it felt wonderful to be among such good friends.

"So, how's theater life in New York, Susie?" Ryan asked. "How goes the auditioning?"

Rosemary shot me a sympathetic look, and David reached

over and squeezed my hand. Ryan meant well, but it was a sore subject.

"Well, there was a part I auditioned for recently that I want so bad. It's a new off-Broadway show that's getting a lot of good buzz lately. Lots of dancing in it. It's been a while since I auditioned for it, but I haven't heard anything back. So, I guess it's not looking good."

"That's too bad," Jack said. I didn't know Jack well, but I already liked him. He was the love of Ryan's life and he treated him like a prince, and that was all I needed to know.

"It's okay," I said. "On to the next, I suppose."

"Susannah," David said. "There's something I wanted to give you. I was going to wait until later, but this feels like the right time. Okay baby, you're either going to love this or get really mad at me."

"Hmm, I'm intrigued," I said. "And a bit worried."

David reached into his back pocket and pulled out a small velvet pouch. He took out a sparkling necklace.

It had the word "DIVA" spelled out in diamonds.

I laughed happily. "Oh, David. I love it. I love it!" I held it up and explained since some of my friends weren't sitting close enough to read it. "It says 'diva.' And it's perfect for me."

Rosemary smiled, absently fingering the necklace around her own neck. A present from Johnny, it was the comedy and tragedy masks made of emeralds to match her eyes. It, too, was a gift to show support for her theater dreams.

David fastened the necklace around my neck, then gazed into my eyes. "I'm so proud of you, Susannah. You're working so hard, and you never give up, no matter how hard it is."

He looked nervous for a moment, but I wasn't sure why. He took a deep breath.

And then he began to sing.

The song was "You'll Never Walk Alone." He'd heard me

practice the song with my kids a few times, but he must have gone out of his way to actually learn the words. It was the perfect song, with a message I really needed to hear right now.

David gazed deeply into my eyes, and through the song, told me to walk on through the wind and the rain, even when my dreams were tossed and blown. Tears dripped down my face as I listened to David serenade me. He wasn't kidding when he said he couldn't sing, but that was what made his gesture all the more touching. He stumbled a few times, knowing he was hitting the wrong note. He gently laughed at his own mistakes but forged on. He was willing to make a fool of himself in front of my friends just to show how much he cared.

And yet, I didn't think any of my friends thought David was foolish. They sat and listened with quiet reverence as he sang the whole first verse telling me to walk on with hope in my heart, because I would never be alone.

He stopped singing after the first verse, and just looked into my eyes.

"Oh, David," was all I could manage to say as I wiped my eyes.

We sat in silence for just a moment.

Then, in a deep, booming voice, Johnny began to loudly sing the next verse. We all laughed, and quickly joined in singing the rest of the song. Johnny put his arm around Rosemary, and they started swaying back and forth as they sang. David and I began to do the same, as did Jack and Ryan. Jack was the only one who didn't know the words, but he smiled and swayed happily with Ryan. Yes, Jack was already a part of our close-knit group. Luke, the only stag member of our impromptu singalong, put his hands dramatically in the air like he was at a religious revival as he sang.

I fought back more tears, feeling utterly overwhelmed at

the friendship and love I felt in the room. Ryan and Jack were reunited and were so much in love. Johnny loved Rosemary, and they both loved and supported me. Luke was single at the moment, but I hoped he knew how glad we were to have him in our circle of friendship. And David, my soul mate and best friend, loved and understood me in ways I could never have dreamed.

I looked out at my friends as we sang a beautiful song about hope and never giving up. I was living in New York City, pursuing my dream, surrounded by people who loved me. I would never stop following my dream, even when it felt impossibly out of reach. Maybe it would come true someday and maybe it wouldn't.

One thing was for sure; I would never have to walk the journey alone.

BELOVED READER,

I want to let you know that if you sign up for my email list, you will receive a FREE steamy sports novella that is EXCLUSIVE to my email list subscribers! It's the prequel to the baseball romance series, The Boys of Baltimore.

Thanks so much for sharing in David and Susie's love story.

Now...are you ready for the jolt of humor, rock-and-roll energy, and insanity that is Luke Rannells?

Luke's got the heart of a theater artist, but his day job is working as head of maintenance in a Manhattan high-rise. There, he's got his eye on icy senior executive, Elyse Pippen. She's gorgeous but cold and businesslike.

Or so Luke thinks.

He's surprised to find Elyse is a completely different person outside of work. She's sweet, sensual, and even enjoys clowning around on stage with him.

Elyse keeps her personal and professional lives strictly separate. She must keep her love affair with Luke a secret at work, at least until she lands her dream promotion.

What happens if they get caught in the act...at work?

I hope you'll join us in NYC as the theater friendship circle expands in LOSING HER INHIBITIONS.

WAIT! BEFORE YOU GO!

Don't forget to join the email list if you want a FREE, steamy sports romance novella!

Sign up today, and I will send you a **FREE** novella entitled Starting From Zero. The novella is available **exclusively** to Author Linda Fausnet email list subscribers, and it is the prequel to my steamy sports romance series, The Boys of Baltimore Series.

Join the email list so you will always know when I've got a new book out.

I promise not to cram your inbox with too many emails – pinky swear!

You can also keep in touch by:

Following me on Amazon
Following me on Bookbub
Following me on Instagram
Joining my Author Reader's Group on Facebook.

Why Leave a Book Review? I'll give you 3 good reasons.

You can do it in <u>less than a minute</u>! Just choose a star rating from 1 to 5 stars and add a sentence or two on how you felt about the book.

1. Most readers choose the books they read based on the reviews, but <u>only a few readers </u>are kind enough to leave a review.
2. Most readers are not aware of this, but authors live and die by reviews. We really do.
3. It only takes a minute to leave a review, but the impact lasts for the lifetime of the book.

Thank you so very much.

ATTENTION ROMANCE NOVEL FANS!

I hope you'll join my romance novel fan club, Romance Novel Addicts Anonymous, on Facebook, Instagram, Twitter, and Pinterest. Join the email list, and you'll receive WHAT'S YOUR PLEASURE? RNAA'S OFFICIAL GUIDE TO FINDING YOUR NEXT GREAT ROMANCE READ.

ACKNOWLEDGMENTS

There is a lot of Susannah Peters in me, as my family members can attest. The life of any artist is filled with ups and downs, and you never do know quite what to expect. You can be riding high after a good day of writing, only to be suddenly crushed by a vicious one-star review. Artists put so much of themselves into their art, and it can be painful to keep moving forward in the face of rejection, but that's what we do. That's who we are.

Heartfelt thanks to all the wonderful people in my life who put up with the madness. My husband, my kids, parents, sister, and friends.

Thank you all.

Thanks to my terrific editor, Linda Hill and my fabulous beta reader, Joanna Hughes.

To all the fools who dream - *keep dreaming.*

www.ingramcontent.com/pod-product-compliance
Lightning Source LLC
Chambersburg PA
CBHW070907180626
46817CB00003B/958